FERRYMAN, TAKE HIM ACROSS!

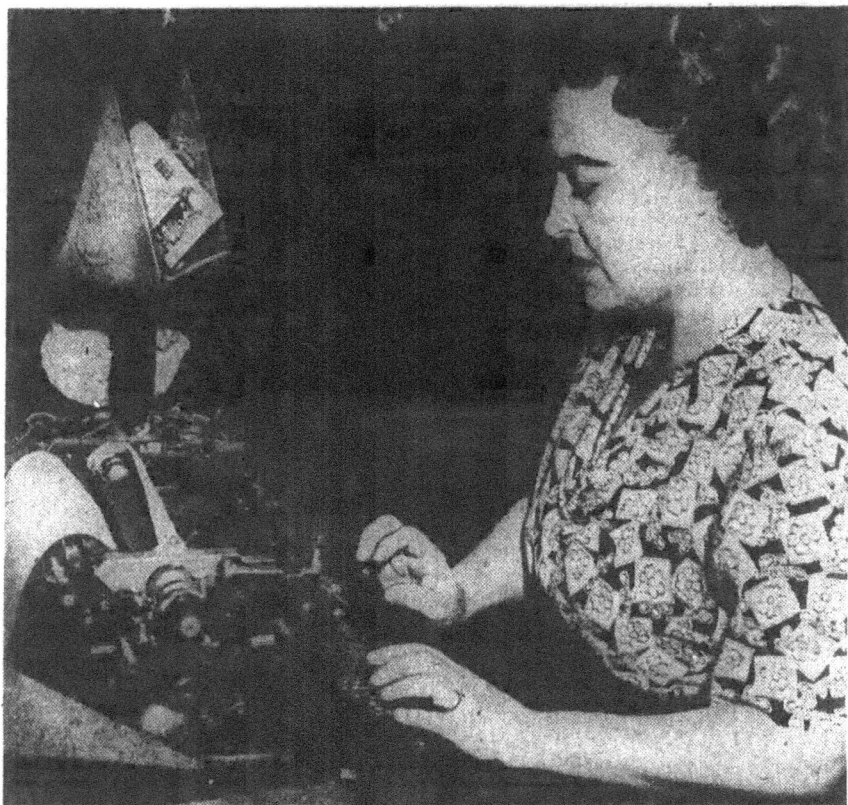

VIRGINIA RATH

FERRYMAN, TAKE HIM ACROSS!

VIRGINIA RATH

20·00

COACHWHIP PUBLICATIONS
Greenville, Ohio

Ferryman, Take Him Across!, by Virginia Rath
© 2019 Coachwhip Publications

Published 1936
No claims made on public domain material.
Cover image: Dancing feet © Mirko Macari

CoachwhipBooks.com

ISBN 1-61646-472-0
ISBN-13 978-1-61646-472-1

FERRYMAN, TAKE HIM ACROSS!

To Helen
My Favorite "Audience"

CHAPTER ONE
REGARDING GRAY HAIRS

Rocky thumbed through a sheaf of typewritten pages and tried to look as if their contents were of great importance, but it was no use. Eleanor slid from the arm of the chair onto his knee and put her red head under his chin so he couldn't read.

"We are going, aren't we?" she repeated.

Rocky tossed aside the last report of the grand jury and prepared to deal with the subject at hand.

"When you take that honey-sweet tone we are always going to do just what you want to. But I never could understand," he observed, "why women are so crazy about dressin' up in a few yards of loud colors and a lot of beads and think no one will ever rec'gnize them in that getup."

"We aren't to wear masks, and I'm not going to wear a lot of beads."

"Another costume you ain't going to wear is a little girl's," Rocky said mildly. "Why any grown woman wants to run aroun' in a panty-dress and a big hair bow— Oh, your legs are all right. I don't mean that."

Eleanor giggled. "It's usually the women who'll never see one hundred and fifty pounds again that come dressed as little girls. Though I had a friend who always wore panty-dresses to costume parties because she had dimples in her knees. But she made her husband dress to match her, and he had scrawny legs and knobby knees. Now, your legs—"

"Never you mind them," Rocky said modestly. "They'll be covered. I reckon no female can ever understand how it takes away a man's confidence to appear in public without his pants. I had to act in *Julius Caesar* in high school once— What is this rig you're dyin' to wear?"

"My mother's wedding dress. It's swell. She was married in 1907. Nancy has one that was made in 1908, but she hasn't long hair so she won't have a pompadour to go with it. I suppose you won't go in costume?"

"I wasn't figurin' on it. Did you have somethin' in mind for me?"

Eleanor looked at the bearskin rug on the floor. "Tarzan," she suggested. She did not move quite fast enough. "That stung," she complained. "You have a very heavy hand. Do you really mind going, Rocky?"

Rocky grinned. "No, I was just assertin' myself a little. Aren't you going to Merton in the afternoon anyway?"

"I said I would. Mrs. Kline—the principal's wife—is giving a bridge party and asked me to come. But I won't stay for the dance unless you go with me."

Rocky picked the Merton *Chronicle* off the table. "Well, it says right here that 'this elab'rate an' colorful masque will be the event of the season and is for a very worthy cause.' What worthy cause?"

"To feed and clothe the shiftless of Merton this winter. That's why the dance is in the high-school gym: because most of the proceeds go to charity."

"I don't like dances in that gym. You have to go outside ever' time you want to smoke. Does it bein' held there have anything to do with them banning masks?"

"Everything. You've never met Mr. Kline, but he's an awful old fuss-budget. Nancy says he doesn't think anything is done right unless he does it himself. He even takes a turn at the lawn mower to be certain the janitor is running it the right way. He's heard about the rough and tough Merton dances, though of course he's never been to one downtown. I heard he said very seriously that he believed the wearing of masks encouraged 'license and boisterousness' and he'd prefer that they be dispensed with."

"He's goin' to be busy as a dog with fleas if he figures on eliminatin' boisterousness among all those present—an' in a building the size of that high school."

"He will probably want your help. You know Dud Williams always gets drunker than the drunkest."

"Most usually," Rocky agreed, of Merton township's constable. "Dud prob'ly won't be there at all. He'd feel out of place. Well, we can go up tomorrow mornin'. After breathin' the refined air of Brookdale for a spell I kind of like to spend a few hours in Merton. Anyway, I want to have a look aroun' the jungle. There's a fellow we're keepin' our eyes peeled for—"

"It isn't that Negro who killed Mr. Burns, is it?"

"No; not him. That n—'s in some other state by now," Rocky lied cheerfully.

There was no use worrying Eleanor by letting her know that the Negro who had killed Burns, railroad special agent, was supposed to be working his way up the canyon. The Negro, known as Buck Harvey, was labeled dangerous. He suffered from delusions of persecution and carried a razor-sharp knife in his belt. Poor Burns had never had a chance after the man jumped on him down in Oroville Yard. . . . But Eleanor was saying:

"I hope he remains in some other state. I suppose we can stay all night at the cabin?"

"I don't see why not. No use comin' back here at 3 a.m. when we got a place to stay. An' if we fly we'll have to stay there till mornin'."

They had bought a four-room log cabin six months ago when they had first returned to Merton and supposed they would spend at least half of every year there. Houses were difficult to find in Merton, and they knew they could always rent this one whenever they chose to go back to Texas to spend some time with Rocky's father.

But Jake Thompson, who for twenty years had been the mountain county's sheriff, said abruptly that he was "used to my asthma, but this rheum'tism's gettin' me down. I'm goin' to drink the water at Richardson Springs a few weeks if it kills me—even 'at spring 'at smells like rotten eggs. Then me an' the wife'll spend the winter with my boy in San Diego."

To Rocky he said, "I'm leavin' you in full charge, son, an' don't let that dumb D.A. bother you any. I intend you shall be the next sheriff in this county. I ain't runnin' again if I don't quit before 'lection, so you might as well be learnin' your job. You can lick most any man in the county, an'

after the way you figured out that day-of-judg-
ment business over at Coon Hollow, I don't know
what more anyone could ask for."

Jake's calm pronouncement regarding his suc-
cessor in office was received by Brookdale citizens with some resentment, but no one seriously
considered disputing his wishes. Jake was, in a
small and rather benevolent way, a political boss.
Brookdale contented itself with remarking acid-
ly that Allan was a fool for luck, and that since
Merton produced most of the crime in the county
perhaps it was fitting that a Merton man should
deal with it.

Certainly it was no hard task to enforce law
and order in Brookdale. The Thompsons departed
late in September and left Rocky and Eleanor in
possession of their old white house with its prim
garden and vine-covered porch.

"This place is dead on its feet," Rocky said.
"But Eleanor don't mind it. It's a prettier town
than Merton to live in. When we've been here
twenty-five years all the best fam'lies may speak
to us." As a matter of fact, after discovering that
Eleanor's grandfather had been a forty-niner, the
town's most solid matrons decided to waive the
usual period of probation.

"Nancy wants to go to the dance with us," Eleanor said now. "She's— Wait a minute, and I'll read

you her letter. You couldn't make head or tail of her writing," she added, sitting on the floor in front of the fire and putting her head back against Rocky's knee. "Let's see. . . .

> "Dear Eleanor:
> "It's too bad there isn't something be-
> sides men to marry or go to dances
> with. Why are men's business engage-
> ments always so damned important? I
> suppose playing for a Hallowe'en dance
> comes under that heading. Anyway, the
> Merton Melodians are playing for the
> grand event Saturday and find them-
> selves shy a saxophone player because
> a grocery clerk got fired. So 'our' Mr.
> Heath is going to fill in, which leaves
> 'our' Miss Towers in the position of
> humbly asking if you and Rocky would
> mind my tagging along with you. It's
> tough to be an old-maid schoolma'am."

Eleanor stopped to say, "Nancy's all of twenty-five," and read on:

> "Oh, I could go with my feminine col-
> leagues, but I do get sick and tired of
> going everywhere with them. 'Here

come the teachers with a bang, bang!' We get awfully bored with each other anyway, and after an afternoon spent playing bridge together an entire evening in the same company is too much. So I'll count on you, please.

"I suppose you're still coming to Mamma Kline's party? Saturday is the damnedest day to have it, but Papa Kline doesn't like her to have parties on school nights very often because it impairs the efficiency of his teaching staff the next day. At least having to play bridge does keep us from being forced to help decorate the gym with several hundred pounds of black and orange paper.

"I hear Clarice Selby is going to make an eighth at bridge. Mrs. Dr. Jordan is out of town again. I don't think Mamma Kline listens to gossip, do you? She probably thinks she's being nice to 'that nice Miss Selby.' If you show this letter to Rocky—which you will—and he says anything about that having all the earmarks of a dirty dig, tell him I know I'm a cat.

"Nancy"

Rocky laughed. "She's a funny little thing. But the Melodians are Jazz Mitchell's outfit. If Heath is goin' to play with them tomorrow night I'm afraid there'll be a discord or two in the music."

"Were Gerald Mitchell and Mr. Heath at outs last year? Nancy's only been teaching in Merton since August—"

"Nancy? I wasn't thinking about her. Do you mean she an' Jazz—"

"He's wild about her," Eleanor said with a smile that pitied masculine stupidity. "And Mr. Heath gives a very good imitation of being a heavy suitor."

"You do hear things, don't you?"

"And I tell them to you, but sometimes you only listen with one ear because you think it's just feminine gossip and therefore unimportant. Anyway, I supposed you'd talked to Jazz—"

"I haven't hardly seen him for the last two months. But I do know he's always hated Heath's guts. You know Jazz used to run aroun' with Clarice Selby quite a lot?"

"And Mr. Heath cut him out? I heard that when we first came back to Merton last spring."

"Well, I think it was pretty near all over between Jazz an' Clarice before that, from what Jazz said. Even so, he probably resented Heath cuttin' in since he took one of these quick dislikes to him. I don't like the fellow myself. Will you tell me what his fatal fascination for women is?"

"I wouldn't know from personal experience. He's too conceited for my taste. But he looks like a gentleman adventurer and makes everything he says to you sound just like a secret too thrilling to be shared with anyone else. Jazz," Eleanor said judicially, "has the appeal of the eternal bad boy. Sort of James Cagneyish. He acts so tough sometimes and has such perfectly extravagant lashes and that funny, crooked smile— I like Jazz."

"So do I. He's a good kid, but he's too hotheaded. He's one of the best operators on the road, but he's always collectin' brownies for talkin' out of turn to the dispatcher or fighting with some other op."

"I love to hear him sing."

"It's almost too bad he was born in a railroad fam'ly. He's a swell drummer. I reckon he never was any place he didn't get up some kind of orchestra. Heath played with them awhile last year and tried to run things, so he and Jazz locked horns about that. Nancy's letter is int'resting for the things it don't say."

"It is, though I didn't expect you to see that. She doesn't even mention Jazz, so she must be angrier with him than with Heath."

"Jazz always plays for dances, so she'd ought to expect he would for this one. Judgin' from her remark about Clarice Selby, she's been hearin' some town gossip even if Mrs. Kline hasn't."

"Marvelous, Sherlock! Of course Clarice does play the piano in the orchestra, so she can't very well be ignored. She couldn't anyway: she's too spectacularly good-looking. Do you think her reputation is deserved?"

"As you just remarked, I wouldn't know from experience. She's not been secretary at the hospital for much more 'n a year. Most small-town reputations are pretty well exaggerated. Does Dr. Jordan's wife usually play bridge with this bunch?"

Eleanor laughed. "Yes, she does. I guess you missed that one. Of course Mrs. Jordan never spends any more time than she has to in Merton, but getting Clarice to fill her place *is* rather funny. People say she has filled Mrs. Jordan's place in more ways than one. That was what Nancy meant us to think she meant—not that she has anything personally against Clarice."

"I'd like to see Jazz get married," Rocky said thoughtfully. "It'd settle him down a lot."

"As it has you?"

"Hasn't it? Look at my gray hairs. . . ."

"I don't see any gray hairs," Eleanor said, looking up at the sun-browned yellow head bent down for her inspection. "It looks lighter on the temples because you've just had your hair cut. I'd like to see Nancy married too, before she gets that stamp on her that teaching so often does seem to put on people. But she'd better not marry a sheriff or she'll be the one to get gray hairs. . . ."

"Yours still seems just carroty red to me—" Rocky looked at her closely; said, "Aw honey! Come on up here," and lifted her into his arms. "Now; what is it you're worryin' about?"

"That damned Negro! You don't fool me one bit, Rocky. I know you don't think he's in some other state. And even if you did hide that circular from me, I g-guess I could read all about him in the p-post office. It would be just like you, if you got word he was down in one of the jungles, to go charging d-down all by yourself. Six-Gun Allan! Or maybe you wouldn't even take a gun with you!"

"Oh, I don't think I'm that kind of damn fool," Rocky said soothingly. "Even if I can't take a n— so seriously, bein' brought up where they're trained to get off the sidewalk for white folks. Listen, sugar—no one's really seen the n—. There's been rumors he's been seen here an' there, but that's all. I don't expect to find him in Merton tomorrow or any time. I don't see how he'd dare hit for one of the larger places where there's more people to keep an eye out for him."

"It sounds very sensible, and of course I'm acting like a silly little goop—"

"Well, you don't very often. Anyway, I'll take Dud Williams with me, an' you know even if Dud does look kind of like an ape he's tough as one in a fight. O.K.?"

"O.K. I don't expect you to stop to collect a posse every time you have to make an arrest, but you're the only husband I've ever had and I'd hate to have to break in a new one."

"Sure you would. Here—take my han'kerchief, an' I'll pretend to think you've just got a little cold in your nose. . . ."

CHAPTER TWO
"OUR" MR. HEATH

"Having a good time, girlies?" Mrs. Kline said. Eleanor managed to produce some vaguely agreeable mumble, and Mrs. Kline smiled her way on to the other card table.

"She always makes me feel eight years old with my front teeth missing," Nancy whispered. "Questions like that kill all the conversation I ever thought of possessing. What time is it?"

"Three-thirty."

"At least another hour before refreshments appear. I hope you didn't eat much lunch?" Nancy said, still in a cautious undertone. "Everything comes with whipped cream on it here, as you may have guessed."

Eleanor looked at an immense plate of fudge, divinity and panocha, in the center of the table. "What I'd like is a cigarette."

"Not a chance, sister. We don't— Do you think there will be a large crowd at the dance tonight?"

"The Hallowe'en dances have always been very well attended," Eleanor said, mimicking Nancy's prim tone. "I'm sure this, one will be. I suppose you are going, Miss Newman?"

Florence Newman settled herself opposite Nancy and folded her hands on the table's edge. "Oh yes, since it's being given for charity and at the high school. I have never attended the town dances."

It wasn't really necessary for her to tell you that, Eleanor thought. You knew just by looking at Miss Newman that she would spend Saturday evenings with a good book, a bit of mending or perhaps ironing a white collar-and-cuff set like the one she wore today with her navy-blue silk.

Eleanor had never seen her wear any other type of dress or anything but sensible, Cuban-heeled oxfords. Her clothes and her glossy black hair were always exquisitely neat; she had a clear, smooth complexion and large, dark-brown eyes. Her voice was low and very clear: you felt that fifteen years of gently but firmly disciplining little Johnnies and Marys was responsible for that and for a certain rigidity to the corners of her mouth.

Nancy always spoke of Miss Newman as "the English teacher personified," but Nancy was credited with having said "Damn it to hell!" when she tripped over a chair in her classroom. Nancy was forever trying to live down the fact that she was really a very efficient commercial teacher. She succeeded fairly well, her appearance being very much in her favor.

She had a pale, pointed face, golden-brown hair and eyes, a generous and expressive mouth. Rocky had once remarked that the size of Nancy's mouth and a certain squareness to the line of her jaw kept her from being "just a pretty little baby doll."

"I wish," Miss Newman said gently, "that Miriam would hurry. We're going to keep the other table waiting."

"You know it takes Miriam fifteen minutes to powder her nose," Nancy said. "Fifteen when there are no men present and half an hour when there are."

"Nancy—dear!"

"I would just love to hear you make one catty remark sometime, Florence."

Miss Newman smiled tolerantly. "Perhaps I did when I was your age. But you know we are so often dependent on one another for companionship, and there *are* little happenings that may easily lead to friction, so it's wiser not to— It's your deal, Miriam."

"Is it?" Miriam Atkins sat down, shuffled the cards languidly and dealt. "I guess I made a mistake. You'd better all count your cards. Well, you take one of mine, Nancy, if you're one short. I don't like bridge very much, do you, Mrs. Allan?"

"That's probably because you don't play bridge, honey," Nancy said. "What are you doing?"

"Oh, is it my bid? Oh—I pass." Miriam inspected her shining vermilion nails. "I didn't want to come to this party anyway. I was going to Reno to buy some clothes."

"You've got more clothes now than you can wear out in two years," Nancy said. "One spade."

"Well, I suppose I have, and goodness knows they're wasted on this town, but it does make me feel better to buy them."

"Miriam is a gilded plutocrat. She has a car, and she's really only teaching for the experience. Sort of slumming, as it were."

"Don't look at her that way, Mrs. Allan," Miriam said serenely. "Nancy knows I never get mad. And of course I wouldn't be teaching if my grandfather weren't a self-made man. I mean, he wanted me to earn my own living for at least two years, and he's got so much money I have to humor him."

"I pass," Miss Newman said with quiet force. "Mrs. Allan?"

"Nancy can have it. I haven't held any cards all afternoon."

"I'll play it fast," Nancy promised, glancing toward the other table. "We'll catch up, Florence. They're very slow over there."

With Miriam as a partner it didn't matter very much how you played your hand. She would never return your lead or notice that you'd already taken a trick when she had a spare trump in her hand. But at least she never knew when her partner had made a bad mistake. Nancy said the words "beautiful but dumb" must have been put together with Miriam in mind.

This was her second year in Merton, and Eleanor remembered having heard that Mr. Kline had not wanted to keep her on but that she owed her job to the local trustee, who said, "Miss Atkins tries hard, and she'll learn, and she does sing lovely." She did have a well-trained soprano voice and was a fair pianist. With these two assets and a melting smile she managed to get through her work.

At the end of the four hands Eleanor and Miriam moved to the other table and paired off with Mrs. Kline and Clarice Selby. Clarice greeted Eleanor effusively, though they had not met more than half a dozen times. Clarice seemed to feel

that her being secretary at the railroad hospital
and Eleanor's having once been a nurse there gave
them "a good deal in common." Perhaps the effu-
siveness was also due to the fact that she was not
very often invited to parties of this sort.

Clarice had the same sort of easy good temper
as Miriam Atkins but none of her almost bovine
serenity. Her hair was so dark a red that it looked
black in some lights, and she wore it in small, perfect curls that glistened as if each one had been
carefully lacquered. She wore no rouge but was
generous with lipstick on a full, sensuously curved
mouth. This afternoon her dress was a black satin that would have been entirely unremarkable
on Miss Newman but managed, on Clarice, to be
both an invitation and a promise.

Mrs. Kline, flat and dowdy in brown silk, kept
glancing nervously at the clock between hands
but without ceasing to smile. Eleanor understood
why Nancy complained of that smile, but the poor
woman probably couldn't help it. No, certainly
she couldn't. She was telling them about the death
of her sister's youngest child and how grieved she
had been to hear of it—but she went on smiling.

Miriam helped the game to go on by putting
a card on the table when it was her turn to play
and eyed Clarice thoughtfully. When she finally
smiled and looked away Eleanor hastily turned a

laugh into a cough, bringing Mrs. Kline's solicitude and prescriptions down upon her. She was certain Miriam had finally decided that she was definitely better-looking than Clarice and that she preferred her own very expensive dark-red dress to Clarice's. . . .

"I heard you come in," Clarice was saying. "Any time a plane circles over town and then lands everyone says, 'Sheriff's in town.'"

"Sheriff? Oh," Miriam said, "is that good-looking deputy sheriff your husband? I didn't know that. I like blond men because I'm so dark myself."

"Rocky certainly is good-looking," Clarice agreed, "but he's also very much married, Miss Atkins."

Eleanor laughed: there was nothing at all malicious in Clarice's remark—at least, the malice was not for her. Miriam said placidly:

"Oh, I never fall for married men. It's a waste of time and very inconvenient. Didn't he used to be a railroad man?"

"Fireman," Eleanor said briefly. "One no-trump."

"Well, it certainly must be exciting, flying around in an airplane," Mrs. Kline said. "Won't you have some more candy, Miss Selby? Well, maybe it would spoil your appetite for what's coming. I think you're very brave, Mrs. Allan—"

"Brave? Oh, you mean to fly with my husband? Do I get it for one no-trump? He's a good pilot and a careful one, though he hasn't had his license very long. You can't do night flying up here because most of the landing fields—except in Reno, of course—are makeshifts and aren't lighted. But even so, you can get places so much more quickly by plane. It's your play, Miss Atkins."

As Eleanor raked in the last trick and reached for the score pad Mrs. Kline said, "Now, if you'll just add up all the scores—will you do that, Miss Selby?—maybe there will be something nice for the one with high score. And I'll just see about the refreshments. Oh, and if one of you will just put down that extra card table over there. I knew our men-folks would be all tired out from decorating the gymnasium, so I told Mr. Kline to bring them back here to get something to eat. Now, if you'll just excuse me . . ."

"Leonard will love this," Mrs. Fulton said, moving over to stand before the stove. "He always has a great deal to say about the messes women eat at bridge parties, and he knows this means he won't get any dinner It's a load off my mind. I hate to cook when I'm not hungry—or any other time. Mrs. Kline should have told Mr. Allan to come in."

"You couldn't drag him into what he calls a hen party," Eleanor said, watching Clarice add scores. "He will take ham and eggs and like them."

Mrs. Kline came back into the room with a tray of dishes, set it down and attacked the fire. "Oh yes, I must make it up. I'm sure you're cold, Gertrude. It *is* getting so much colder these last two weeks."

"It seems to me I'm always cold in this daarned town," Gertrude Fulton said. "Last winter was simply awful. I really almost hoped Mr. Kline would fire Leonard—"

"Oh, my dear!" Mrs. Kline was smilingly shocked. "Of course you don't mean that. Mr. Fulton is such a good coach, and the boys in the shop turn out such lovely work. That bookcase over there— Mr. Kline depends on him so much."

Mrs. Fulton looked unenthusiastically at a wobbly bookcase loaded with small vases, candlesticks and pictures. She said, "No, of course I didn't mean it. A job's a job these days, and I get tired of packing up and moving more than once every two years."

She shivered and stood close to the stove again, spreading her long white hands to its warmth. Another good-looking woman, Eleanor thought. It was really remarkable that there should be so many gathered together in one room. Mrs. Fulton was an ash blonde, tall and graceful—too slender, perhaps, her face too thin. Her mouth was petulant and discontented; her voice matched it.

Mrs. Kline went back to the kitchen: reappeared staggering under the weight of a loaded tray. "Oh no, I can manage all right. Not heavy at all— Oh, thank you, Louise. If you'd just put them around on the tables. I do hope you aren't going to be critical because you're such a good domestic-science teacher. I'm just a good, plain cook, you know. Now I'll see about the coffee . . ."

Nancy came over and sat down beside Eleanor and looked morosely at a confection composed of half a large orange filled with orange jello and decorated with whipped cream and sliced licorice gumdrops.

"God help us if she ever goes fancy on us," she muttered.

Louise Whyte looked at Nancy and grinned. She put a plate down before her, leaned over and whispered, "My child, being nice to the principal's wife is one of the fundamentals of successful schoolteaching. The sooner you learn that, the better."

"I guess there aren't any jobs where you don't have to be nice to the boss's wife," Clarice said. "But I think Mrs. Kline is real sweet."

"Oh—very," Nancy said. Clarice flushed resentfully. Nancy had made it evident she considered Clarice's commendation of Mrs. Kline sheer impertinence. It was probably just as well that Nancy and Clarice had not had to play at the same table. . . . "Let me help you, Lou."

"Sit still. There's nothing to do." Louise went on to the other tables. Even in that crowded room she walked with a long, free stride that went well with her tall figure, lean to the point of angularity.

"She looks a little bit like Katherine Hepburn, doesn't she?" Clarice said. "Only not dark. Sort of attractive-homely. I like that kind of haircut. I'd like to wear mine cut short and straight, but I'm just not the type."

"It's very becoming to Miss Whyte," Eleanor said hastily, because Nancy was getting ready to snub Clarice again. And Clarice certainly had no idea of being impertinent: she was perennially interested not only in her own appearance but that of other people. "Is the orchestra going to be in costume tonight, Miss Selby?"

"I wanted us to be, but the men wouldn't hear to it. They never want to dress up fancy. Last time we played for a masquerade they wore cowboy outfits, and Jazz said no more chaps for him. He nearly roasted to death in the things."

Nancy got up to help Mrs. Kline put cups of very weak coffee on the table. "We can begin in a few minutes now. I see our menfolks coming down the street from the high school."

Clarice giggled and leaned closer to Eleanor. "'Our' Mr. Heath is good," she whispered. "I wonder who he should be assigned to." She looked at Nancy, at Miriam and Mrs. Fulton, and shrugged expressively. "Oh, I'm no lady, Mrs. Allan. And I do know when people put the freeze on me. Right now I'd say Miss Towers was high—"

"Me? I didn't have any score at all."

"We weren't talking about card scores," Clarice said. "I think Miss Whyte wins that prize, and I hope *it's* a good one."

"Well, ladies! All through playing, I see. And who won the prize? I suppose the conversation was more interesting than the game. . . ."

Mr. Kline's social manner was one of heavy joviality, which never succeeded in its object of putting people at ease. "Come right in, boys. I think the three of us can handle these women. . . ."

The "boys" came in: Paul Heath with a faintly mocking smile, Leonard Fulton with a look of stolid resignation on his square, ruddy face. Mrs. Kline hovered about them solicitously. Were they warm enough? Where would they like to sit? Of course they were hungry, and she had made coffee just for them; and was Hamilton sure he hadn't got overheated and caught cold?

Mr. Kline said that he had let the "young fellows" do all the work, and took off a heavy overcoat and knitted muffler. "Now; where shall I sit?

Over here? Miss Whyte, you'll keep me company? And Miss Newman? Sit down, boys, sit down! Don't be bashful."

"I'll sit here," Leonard Fulton said abruptly; brushed past Paul Heath and took the last vacant seat at the table where his wife was sitting. Heath raised his eyebrows and sat down opposite Eleanor, with Nancy on one side and Clarice on the other.

"So much the better for me," he said. "I draw the three prettiest women in the room."

Clarice smiled; Nancy jabbed a fork viciously into a slice of gumdrop, and Eleanor said, "Will you have cream and sugar?"

"Thank you. Will you be at the dance tonight, Mrs. Allan? We must make conversation, you know."

Heath's calm effrontery was rather amusing. He should have a small black mustache, Eleanor decided. It would go well with his thin face and make him look more than ever like an English army officer just home from India.

"The weather is always convenient," she said.

"Oh yes, the weather. Well, the weather is—"

"Darn cold," Clarice said. "I've got to get out my electric pad. I simply can't sleep without my windows wide open, though Ma Jenkins—where I room—is always saying it isn't healthy and it isn't safe to have windows open right down to the ground. Is the gym decorated?"

"The gym is a symphony in orange and black—just like this salad. Is it salad?" Heath murmured. "Thank you; I always like to know what I'm eating. But I see there is a lettuce leaf under it. Cross, Nancy?"

"No," Nancy said ungraciously. "Why should I be? Can you see what Lou's prize is, Eleanor?"

Mr. Kline was heard saying, "Very pretty; very pretty, indeed. What is it?"

Miss Newman laughed dutifully. "It's a guest towel, Mr. Kline."

"Oh yes; the kind you must not wipe your hands on. Leonard and I know all about that, don't we, Leonard?"

Fulton seemed to have his teeth entangled in a gumdrop. He nodded, drank his coffee and unconsciously made a face over it. Miriam complained that her costume wasn't "a bit what I really wanted." Miss Newman and Mr. Kline began to talk about the limited opportunities afforded by the town for healthful juvenile recreation. Mrs. Fulton stopped pretending to eat, and Mrs. Kline brought out orange sherbet trimmed with whipped cream and large slabs of chocolate cake with orange icing. Nancy muttered:

"I will die from this! Oh yes, Mrs. Kline, Louise is looking after us very well—"

"And everything is perfectly lovely," Eleanor said, heroically consuming cake. "No; no more coffee, thank you."

"Are you having supper with me tonight, Nancy?" Heath said abruptly.

"No, I'm not."

Clarice laughed. "'Miss Otis regrets . . .'" She was amused at Heath's quickly hidden chagrin. "You *would* try to improve matters by talking out of turn, Paul."

"I don't know what you mean."

"Oh yes, you do. And so does Miss Towers."

Nancy picked her cake to pieces with her fork, her usually pale face flushed. "I think we all have very bad manners. I'm sure Eleanor isn't interested in this."

"Maybe not. I've got some work to clear up before supper," Clarice said, rising. "I can't stay any longer. I—I really didn't mean to be nasty."

"That's all right," Nancy said uncertainly. "Can't we go too, Eleanor?"

CHAPTER THREE
"THERE'S NONE LIKE NANCY LEE"

"You'll have to breathe in again, honey," Rocky said. "I could cinch you into this thing by main force, but I'd prob'ly tear half the hooks and eyes off."

"I can't hold my breath forever," Eleanor complained. "Haven't you fastened most of them?"

"All but about six in the middle. I begin to apprec'ate those old-time jokes about men sweatin' over hooking up their wife's dress. How'd your mother get into this thing?"

"She wore a cast-iron corset and tied the corset strings to a bedpost and backed away to get them good and tight. All right; I'll hold my breath once more—"

"That does it. And there's someone at the front door."

"Probably Nancy. She said she'd walk over if she got ready before we came for her. You let her in: I'm not quite finished."

"I was all dressed, and I got tired of sitting around," Nancy said. "Rocky, I'm dying from strangulation of the middle."

"After just hookin' Eleanor into that dress of hers I can b'lieve you must be. Your mothers must've been some smaller in the waist than you are."

"My aunt Jenny, to whom this dress belonged, boasted an eighteen-inch waist," Nancy said sadly. She surveyed her gown of yellowed and much shirred white silk, ran her finger around the inside of the high neck and tilted an absurd picture hat over one eye. "You look so damnably comfortable, Rocky. And all dressed up. I don't think I ever saw you in your best bib and tucker before."

"If I wasn't wore out from being lady's maid I'd get up and strut for you. Eleanor seems to think this suit is worth the money I gave the tailor for makin' it. Cigarette?"

"Thanks. Did Eleanor tell you about all that terrible sweet stuff we had to eat this afternoon? And what a perfectly beastly party it was?"

"She didn't say exactly that, though I did gather that you might've had a more hilarious time of it an' still been right well behaved."

Nancy sighed. "Well, it's mean to make fun of Mamma Kline. She does the best she can. Have you ever seen one of those plays where a group of British families is isolated in some outpost of empire?"

"Yeah. They talk a lot, an' the wrong husbands and wives fall in love with each other, and they dress for dinner and keep havin' parties and get very tired of seeing each other."

"That's us. We see too much of each other, and we're a community in a community. No one in the town takes us to their hearts."

"Merton people in gen'ral never pay much attention to the school," Rocky admitted. "They're nicer to the teachers in Brookdale."

"Well, even when they are we're still just transients. So we do have to stick together, and we don't have much town gossip to talk about so we talk about school problems—and each other. Of course we're always very welcome to do good works in the town—"

Eleanor came out of the bedroom, struck an attitude and sang:

> *"She don't have to wear rats in her hair,*
> *Or a straight front X-Y-Z . . .*

"Gosh, Mother was a better woman than I am. Let's have a drink before we leave. Nancy can chew a clove afterward."

"I'd better. Some principals are broad-minded but not our Mr. Kline."

"He always reminds me of a minister I knew once," Rocky said. "Same kind of stooped shoulders and big, high forehead. And gray hair. He's not a bad-looking old fellow."

"Florence Newman thinks he has a very intellectual 'brow.' He's only in his late forties, I think. He's a good principal, but he fusses so about little details. He and Florence consider teaching a mission in life instead of a job. Though they do look down on the town people except as parents and aren't a bit interested in interesting scandal."

"What about the rest of you?" Rocky said, handing Nancy a tall, frosted glass.

"Oh, Lou thinks, as I do, that you should try to do any kind of job well. Miriam's hopeless. I don't know about Leonard Fulton. He's a good athletic coach, but he's the brawn-without-brains type. Beefy, you know."

"I've met him. He's got kind of a unimpressive upper lip. Maybe that's why he wears that toothbrush mustache. And Heath?"

"I don't know about him. He's a good teacher: sarcastic as the devil, so the kids are all afraid of him. I think he'd quit it in a minute if he found anything that paid better." Eleanor had gone back

into the bedroom; Nancy said, "Rocky, do you
know Clarice Selby?"

"To talk to," Rocky said with slight but unmis-
takable emphasis.

"I get it. Well, do you know— No, you wouldn't
tell me. Most men are funny that way. And some of
them are just—low! There's no other word for it!"

Rocky wondered if she were referring to Heath
or Jazz—or to both. But Eleanor came back before Nancy could go on and began transferring
handkerchief, compact and comb from purse to
evening bag.

"Do you need any money, Rocky? The parent-teachers are serving supper and will probably
charge three prices for it."

"I know. For a thin little san'wich and a piece
of cake. I'd rather go to the Greek's or the H. M.
an' J."

"What's H. M. and J. stand for?" Nancy said.

"Horse, Mule and Jackass. Healy, Morse and
Jarvis. It used to be the biggest speakeasy in town,
but since Repeal they had to put in a soda foun-
tain to make any money. What're you frownin'
about, sugar?"

"Oh, I lost my good-luck piece. That old nickel
your father gave me. I polished it up and carried
it around until I began to feel rather superstitious

about it. But the clasp on my purse needs fixing. It's always opening, and everything spills out."

"You should come up to the high school and solve the case of our many thefts, Rocky," Nancy said. "Things are always disappearing from our desks—they don't lock—and from the girls' lockers whenever they leave them open."

"Money?"

"Sometimes. They very seldom have any money to lose. But one girl did have two dollars taken from her locker. The next week Lily Rose McGee blossomed out with one of these dollar ninety-five permanents, which circumstance was felt to be slightly suspicious."

Rocky chuckled. The McGees were one of those shiftless families who would be supported during the winter by the proceeds of tonight's dance.

"They're the kind that gets permanents an' Woolworth jew'lry when they can't buy grub. You'll catch someone sooner or later. Did you have the same trouble last year?"

"Well, there's always a certain amount of petty stealing in any high school, but I don't think it happened so often last year. None of the teachers have ever lost anything valuable: a cheap string of beads, a little ivory elephant and a paperweight—things like that. Are we ready to go?"

The Merton High School was the last building on a street that ran north and south the length of the town, slowly ascending a sloping hill until, when you stood in front of the high school, you could see all the town below you. In back of the building was the beginning of the forests that climbed the peaks surrounding the town on three sides.

So far no houses had been built on the half-cleared spaces to left and right of the high school. A path across one led to the grammar school, set atop the highest elevation in town. A makeshift road had been broken across the other, winding around trees and rocks until it reached Mariposa Street.

The front steps of the high school were already crowded with men who had come outside to smoke. Inside, a few people were wandering about the corridors, looking curiously into classrooms. Four of these were off a corridor that ran at right angles from the main hallway. On the other side was a large study hall; then you went up half a dozen steps and found yourself in a wider hall.

The domestic-science rooms were to the right here—before the hall widened into a square with lockers built around three sides of it. You went down several steps to reach the double doors into the gymnasium, though there was a more impressive outside entrance in its east wall. Balconies had been built on that side, and a stage faced them on the other.

"They must've borrowed all the orange an' black paper that ever was used at Merton dances," Rocky said. "Some of it looks like old friends to me. The lanterns made out of punkins are new, but I'll swear they borrowed the battered-looking paper ones from the Oddfellows. They never put enough wax on this floor."

"The basketball boys and girls would be falling on their little fannies all the time if they did. Is it just lack of wax that's wrong? We never jiggle when we dance—"

"But we are now." Rocky drew her closer; lengthened his stride. "It's the music, as you might guess if you'd take a look at Jazz."

They were dancing past the stage, and they both glanced toward Jazz Mitchell, who was scowling savagely as he looked out over the crowded dance floor. Jazz was slight and wiry; he had slim, strong hands—nervously expressive hands with long, tapering fingers. All his movements, though controlled and graceful, carried a hint of nervous tensity.

At one time he had been given to talking sinisterly from the corner of his mouth. He had discarded that mannerism but still kept the crooked smile Eleanor had spoken of. That smile and the black eyes that were too large for his short face were the reasons why women called him good-looking when he was not.

"He doesn't look happy," Eleanor said. "Trying to locate Nancy—"

"So am I," Rocky said as the music stopped. "Where did she go to? Oh sure, go right ahead. . . ."

He watched Eleanor dance away with young Dr. Miller and, not seeing Nancy, backed off the floor to the edge of the stage. He said:

"You'd ought to play 'The Man on the Flyin' Trapeze,' Jazz."

Jazz went on drumming without bothering to look at his music. "It'd be damned appropriate," he said finally. "His Highness, up there, thinks he's on a trapeze. He can't leave the tempo alone: he jerks it up and he jerks it down; and that lousy trumpet player don't know what tempo is. He just follows whoever plays loudest."

He pounded out four thunderously distinct beats on the bass drum. "And Clarice has an idea she wants to play fancydoodles. This stage is hell to play from anyway. All the sound goes straight up instead of out to the floor."

"I thought she was a pretty good piano player."

"She is—for a woman. She can stand up under the grind, and she's a good sport—usually. Why don't you dance? Getting old?"

"I'd be obliged if you'd give me time to locate somebody I know between dances."

"We will when this one's ended. Clarice is signaling she wants to powder her nose. That's what she calls it."

Rocky grinned as he saw Mrs. Vane, who was fifty and a grandmother, prance by in stiffly starched short skirts and half-socks. It must be a complex of some kind: there was another big, hefty dame in rompers. Mr. Kline was tapping some high-school boy on the shoulder with a little-less-noise-please expression. Rocky hoped Kline wouldn't call on him to do police duty. Everybody was having a good time, and no one seemed to be drunk—yet.

Jazz struck his cymbals with unnecessary force, nodded to Clarice and, when she had left the platform, leaned forward and tapped Paul Heath on the shoulder with one of his drumsticks.

"Listen here, St Vitus, we're playing for people to dance, not for a bunch of epileptics to throw a fit to. I'll set the tempo for this orchestra, and you let it ride that way. People came here to dance, not to listen to you play a sax solo."

Heath rested his saxophone on his knees and raised one eyebrow. "So what? If you don't like the way I play a saxophone, what are you going to do about it?"

Jazz smiled dangerously. "I do know what you can do with that sax of yours," he said, and without raising his voice proceeded to tell Heath just exactly what to do with the saxophone. Heath's air of bored superiority vanished abruptly.

"You know I can't take you up on that here—"

"I'll be around," Jazz promised. "I'll remind you of it if your memory fails. And till this dance is over I'm running this orchestra." He turned to Clarice as she came back to the piano. "You cut out the arpeggios and keep time so these guys can hear you. You're not getting paid to be Paderewski."

"Gosh, the old maestro has got a grouch," Clarice said cheerfully. "I'll sacrifice my art for your sake." But she looked over Jazz's head until she caught Rocky's eye and then made a quick little gesture that said, "Don't let those two fight."

Rocky nodded. He didn't intend that they should fight, anywhere close to the gymnasium. Naturally, if they were determined to have it out, he couldn't ride herd on them all over town. He slid from the edge of the stage, tried to locate Nancy or Eleanor, and somehow found himself dancing with one of the nurses from the hospital.

It was nearly midnight when he suddenly came face to face with Nancy and took her away from some stranger in blackface. "He said just to call him Al Jolson. His makeup is running over his collar, and I've got some of it on me. What have you been doing?" Nancy said.

"Lookin' for you and Eleanor. Have you seen her?"

"Oh, she's been galloping around with Dr. Miller and that newspaper editor—"

"Tom Wright? He's a nice guy. I was interrupted once. Your Papa Kline came after me to put out a guy he thought wasn't fit for this s'lect company."

"Was he?"

"Well—no. It was Milt Glover, and Milt always gets cockeyed at dances, an' at a certain stage he wants to fight anyone that's handy. So I was glad enough to park him out in his car to sleep awhile. But I drew the line there. I'm not goin' to police the classrooms to see that none of the little girls an' boys are neckin' in them."

Nancy giggled. "Papa Kline was afraid of that when he decided to leave the rooms unlocked, but he thought the parents might want to see where their offspring get edicated."

The orchestra was playing a medley of old-time songs, and Jazz began to sing in a careless and entirely charming voice:

"Of all the wives as e'er you know—
Yeo ho! lads! ho, yeo ho! yeo ho!
There's none like Nancy Lee, I trow . . ."

"Damn him!" Nancy whispered suddenly. "Oh—damn him!"

Rocky waited a minute before saying anything. Then: "Do you think he's takin' an unfair advantage of you?" he asked.

Nancy said, "They believe in variety, don't they," as Jazz sang:

"Casey Jones, mounted to the cabin,
Casey Jones, with his orders in his hand . . ."

"You're kind of hard to please. There's nothing sentimental about that. . . . He's gettin' Bill Shaw to sit in for him so's he can dance."

"Dance? Rocky, I don't want to—"

Jazz said, "Mind if I cut in?" and hardly waited for Rocky's answering nod and certainly paid no attention to Nancy's mutinous frown.

"What," he said when they were halfway around the floor, "is the big idea of the run-around?"

"I don't know what you're talking about."

"I told you I wanted you to have supper with me—"

"And I said I wasn't interested."

"Not at first. You said it was all right. Then you said Heath had asked you to come to the dance with him—"

"And then, I suppose, you went and got him to play with you so I couldn't come with him."

"You've got a pretty damn good opinion of yourself. I liked having to let Heath play with us just like I'd like to take poison. You notice he didn't refuse to play—"

"May I ask what that has to do with the original subject of conversation?"

"Don't take that schoolteacher tone with me! Did Heath say—something to you about me?"

"What do you suppose he might have said?"

Jazz bit his lip. "A lot of things, and a lot of them could be true. But I wouldn't listen to any woman who tried to wise me up to any little lapses you might have made."

Nancy flushed guiltily. "He pretended he'd just let it slip without meaning to. I didn't like him for it—telling tales, I mean. I wouldn't have come with him tonight. But that doesn't alter things—"

"Between you and me? Does it matter—what he said? I'm—I'm crazy about you, Nancy."

"I imagine you'll get over it. You have before, haven't you? The dance," Nancy said sweetly, "seems to have ended. Thank you; I've enjoyed it too. Will you take me over to Eleanor and Rocky? They seem finally to have been reunited."

"Mad enough to bite nails," Rocky murmured as Jazz stalked back toward the stage. "They're going to play a grand march an' see who gets prizes. You two Floradora girls had better get in line. You'll probably win a box of stale candy from one of the pool halls. When that's over we'd better make a break for the cookin' room to see if we can't get fed ahead of the crowd."

It was nearly one o'clock before all those who ate supper at the high school were served. Dancing had begun again, but Mr. Kline reminded the orchestra that they were to play "Home, Sweet Home" "promptly at two o'clock."

"Suits me," Jazz said, looking at the back of Heath's head. "We'll stop, Mr. Kline, though the crowd isn't going to like it."

"We will run two hours into Sunday as it is," Kline said stiffly. "I want to clear this place as rapidly as possible after the last dance. There is no need for anyone to loiter about the premises." He turned to Rocky, who was leaning against the stage. "Will you help me see to that, Mr. Allan?"

Rocky hesitated, looking doubtfully at Jazz, then said, "Sure; I'll see that ever'body gets out of here right away."

He intended to be in the gymnasium when the last dance was played but at five minutes of two he was forced to go out and pry apart two unsteady pugilists who were trying to fight each other before the front steps of the high school. The cold night air was considerably warmed by their language before Rocky separated them, only to have them fall on each other's shoulders and tearfully vow eternal friendship. He heard the strains of "Home, Sweet Home" before he could start back to the gymnasium and, once there, found it deserted except for Jazz and Clarice.

"Oh, act your age!" Clarice was saying in a clear, carrying voice. "He said he'd donate his ten bucks to charity. Maybe he did know you had an extra reason for wanting to see him, but don't scowl at me. I'm not to blame for living, though you act like I was. He said he'd settle outside the school grounds—"

"Here's your money," Jazz said, and began to put the canvas covers on his drums. "I guess leave these here and get them later. Art Finley's already gone with his car. 'Night."

"I'm sorry, Jazz. I can't help it—"

"Well, we don't need to discuss it again." Jazz saw Rocky, said, "Eleanor and Nancy are waiting for you in the cooking room."

"We'll be startin' home in a minute or two—"

"We don't go in the same direction. I'm going home, and I think I'll get cockeyed. I'm laying off for three days, and that ought to be time enough."

Clarice frowned, watching Jazz walk away from them. "Do you think—"

"He said he was goin' home, and if he wants to get soused on his own time that's none of our business."

"Yes, if he only goes home. I wonder if it would do any good if— No, I guess I'd better not. Well, I'm going home too. No, I won't wait for you. I don't live on your street. Art Finley would have waited for me but I— Here comes old man Kline to lock up. Good night."

"I believe everyone has gone," Mr. Kline said. "I will go down and look through the shower rooms to be certain."

"Has Paul Heath gone home yet?"

"Mr. Heath? Oh yes; five minutes ago. Mr. Mitchell just asked me if he had. I'm afraid those two young men do not get along very well together. Thank you for your help, Mr. Allan. You don't need to stay. I'll look over the building and see that it is locked."

Rocky waited until he had locked the front door of their own house before he asked:

"Do you happen to know what Heath was doin' the last dance they played?"

"'Home, Sweet Home'? He wasn't there at all," Eleanor said promptly. "He got some high-school boy to sit in for him the dance before—"

"An' danced with Nancy?"

"That must have been his intention, but Nancy said she had this dance, thank you. So then he danced with Mrs. Fulton. And Mr. Fulton didn't like that."

"She's the tall, pale blonde, ain't she? I saw Miss Newman in that nun's outfit. It suited her. And you pointed out Miss Whyte when we were eatin'. I don't b'lieve I ever saw Miss Atkins to know who she was."

"The dark girl in a very elaborate Louis XV dress? She took a prize—"

"Oh, that one. I noticed her all right. That dress was cut so low in front it made me uneasy. Then Heath didn't dance the last dance?"

"No. It was a very short one, and we'd already gone into the domestic-science room to wait for you, and I saw him in the corridor outside just a few minutes before Jazz went by. Was he running away from Jazz?"

Rocky sat down on the bed and kicked off his shoes. They were new and beautifully polished and tight as the devil. "I wouldn't want to say he's afraid of Jazz, though if they ever do have a fight Jazz will beat hell out of him."

"Mr. Heath's quite a bit taller than Jazz."

"He's not very heavy, and he looks flabby to me. Jazz can lick 'most anyone his own weight. It does look like Heath was clearin' out in a hurry, but he's in the right of it. They oughtn't to have a row anywheres near the school as long as he's a teacher. . . . What's the matter?"

"I've been putting off breaking the sad news to you, but I simply can't unfasten all these hooks and eyes by myself."

Rocky groaned and got up. "I'd like to have met your dad. After this, we'd have had somethin' in common."

CHAPTER FOUR
"SHE SAID CLARICE WAS DEAD"

Someone was tapping loudly and persistently on the window: a callboy, of course, come to tell him he'd been called out. Rocky hunched the covers over his shoulders. Lord, it was going to be cold going down the canyon. An hour to get up and get something to eat and beat it down to the round-house. He mumbled sleepily:

"Who's the engineer?" and then sat up in bed. It was the callboy outside the window, all right, but he wasn't saying anything like "Extra west for three-thirty." The kid's teeth were chattering; the hand on his flashlight shook, and he said:

"You're wanted over at Ma Jenkins' right away. Somebody got killed!"

"Somebody? Don't you know who?" Rocky was already out of bed and reaching for his clothes.

"I know who." The boy's voice sounded as if he had been or was just going to be very sick. "It's Clarice Selby. I saw her—"

"All right; skip it for a while. Did anyone send for a doctor?"

"S-she don't need any doctor. But Ma said she'd call up the hospital. She sent me over here because you haven't any phone. But she thought you'd be here. D-do I have to go back with you?"

"Better walk a ways," Rocky said, struggling with his high-laced boots. Eleanor sat up, her red hair hanging loose over her shoulders.

"I hung your leather jacket in the closet," she said. "Is there anything else—"

"I don't think so." Rocky stooped to kiss her. "Go back to sleep."

"No. Put the light on when you go out. I'll probably get up and build a fire. You'll come back for breakfast?"

"Try to. You can keep some coffee hot. All right, Danny," Rocky said outside. "What time is it?"

"It's five-ten. I was giving Wilkins a six-o'clock call, and he always wants at least an hour. So it was about four-fifty when I got to Ma Jenkins'. You know she always leaves the front door open because so many fellows on the road board there. I went in and gave him his call—he's got a room on the second floor. Well, Ma heard me, and I guess she decided to get up and get him some coffee. You know she's goodhearted that way. Just as I got to the front door I heard her give this awful screech, and I went running and she was st-stand-ing at Clarice's d-door—"

"How'd she happen to go in there?" Rocky said to give the boy time to steady his voice.

"I never thought to ask her. The hall light's right there, so we could see plain. There was a lot of blood. Ma went in. I didn't," Danny admitted shamefacedly. "But she said Clarice was dead and for me to come after you."

"I reckon that about ends your part of the story? You didn't see anyone on the streets, did you?"

"Not a soul up around here. I've got some more calls to give—"

"All right; you can't be late with those. I'll let you know if I want to talk to you again."

Rocky went on alone: along Sierra, past Pine and Marin to Wilson. Merton's streets were named in a haphazard fashion, but to most of the towns-people Wilson was simply "the street Ma Jenkins' boardinghouse is on."

Jazz lived on the same street in one of the two-room cabins that were usually occupied by young, unmarried railroad men. The house, set far back from the street, was dark and quiet, but in Ma Jenkins' big, two-story house on the next corner there were lights in half a dozen windows.

A car was parked in front of the house, and the front door was open. Rocky walked in and met

Ma in the hall. "Doctor's already here," she said. "Didn't know he could move that fast. It's this bedroom back here."

Philip Miller, the younger of the two railroad physicians, looked up as Rocky came into the bedroom. "Have a look," he invited cheerfully, but his round face had lost a good deal of its usual high color. "Not that there's much to see."

Rocky looked, turned away and walked to the open window. "Were the covers off her that way when you found her?" he said.

"Just like that. And of course she wouldn't lie there that way in a chiffon nightgown that's nothing at all," Ma Jenkins said. "If it matters any. But there was a pillow over her face: the extra one. That was what struck me queer before I saw—the rest."

"How'd you come to look in here at all?"

"I wasn't sleeping good, and when I heard the callboy go upstairs I decided to get up and make some coffee for whoever was called out. I thought it was Wilkins and I'd have my own breakfast too. Had to pass this door to get to the kitchen. Well, it was a little bit ajar and I didn't want Clarice to get waked up, though goodness knows she slept sound enough. I didn't want the door open anyway and Wilkins maybe peeking in at her. I try to keep this house respectable, and she was always careless about closing doors. This one swings real loose, and it kind of swung out of my hand and I got a look in."

"Thanks. What about that pillow, Doc?"

"We-ell, I'd say it was held down over her mouth in case she screamed."

"That's what I thought. She'd be all covered up, and you couldn't stab anyone through those covers. She was stabbed, wasn't she?"

"Very much so. There's no weapon. I can give you some idea what kind it was after a more thorough examination. Looks to me like it was just an ordinary knife of some kind."

"You say she slept sound, Ma? Then she'd hardly be awake before she was killed. Pillow down over her mouth, pull the covers away with the hand that held the knife—" He looked down at the ground below the window. "Did she always keep these windows open at night?"

"Always. No matter what kind of weather it was. I used to scold her about it. For one thing, the windows on this side of the house are awful low to the ground because the house is built on a slope—"

"I was noticin' that," Rocky said. "See here, Miller—these smudges of dirt on the sill? And a scratch or two here—fresh ones."

"Looks like someone got in the room that way. Easy enough to do," the doctor said. "The windows are almost on the ground. But you leave your front door unlocked, don't you, Mrs. Jenkins?"

"I have to with the boys getting in at all hours, or give out keys, and I've never done that. Never screened the windows either. I wish I had. Of course you'd run more chance of someone seeing you if you came in the front door; or of running into someone in the hall. Well, I'm going out to the kitchen. I'll be there when you want to talk to me, Rocky."

"O.K. Any idea what time she was killed?"

"Oh, I've some idea," Miller said cautiously. "Not very long ago. Not more than an hour and a half before I got here, and that was five-five. Say between three forty-five and four-thirty, and that's strictly unofficial. But the coroner—"

"Old Sloane ain't a doctor: he's an undertaker. You an' Jordan will have to tend to a post-mortem. There's no use callin' Sloane before seven, because he hates to be waked up and he won't start for her before he gets his breakfast. I'll call Frank Laval an' get him to bring his hearse down and take her up to his place. Of course we're supposed to wait for the cor'ner, but Lorenzo ain't particular. I'll have to look over her things, but I don't want to do it right now."

"Don't blame you. I suppose it wouldn't matter if—" Miller pulled the covers carefully up over the bed. "After all, I knew the girl and liked her— well enough," he said apologetically.

"I think most people liked her even while they talked about her a lot. Does Jordan know about this yet?"

Miller grimaced involuntarily. "No; I didn't think it necessary to stop to telephone him. I'm always on night duty—sleep at the hospital, you know. He doesn't like to be bothered. Of course this will bother him. He hired Clarice and kept her on— Well, I'm being professionally indiscreet. Forget it."

Rocky smiled. Miller was often a little indiscreet, but everyone liked the tubby young doctor. And everyone knew that Max Jordan resented that fact and that Miller didn't very greatly care for his chief.

"In this case you ain't doing any harm. Ever'-body knows Clarice could get away with murder so far's her work was concerned and Jordan wouldn't say anything. Do you know any reason why she should've been killed?"

"Well, you always thought of Clarice in con-nection with men. Heath and Jazz Mitchell—"

"And Jordan?"

"The town says so. I wasn't one of her boy friends," Miller said, reddening. "You can check up on that all right."

"I always heard you an' her didn't hit it off very well. I'm going to call up Laval and Dud Williams. I can keep an eye on this door from the phone so you might as well go on. But try to be up at the mortuary about eight-thirty."

"What about Jordan?"

"If he wants to assist we'll be glad to have him. You'll have to be there regardless. You can tell him about Clarice if you want to—and ask him not to spread it all over town."

It was more than a quarter past six before Rocky could talk to Ma Jenkins. Dud Williams had arrived within ten minutes of Rocky's telephone call, and Dud had a healthy curiosity and a great many questions he wanted answered. Also he would have liked to go out and arrest someone immediately.

"Who?" Rocky said. "And why?"

Dud scratched his round bald head. "I can think of two or three. Why? To be doin' something."

Rocky finally managed to persuade him to sit in the hall and see that no outsiders entered the house. Then Laval arrived, and when the sound of his hearse had died away down the street again Rocky left Dud walking militantly up and down the hall and went out to the kitchen.

"Sit down and have a cup of coffee," Ma said. "Your wife's waiting breakfast? Well, don't tell her you ate anything here. Is that no-'count constable out in the hall? I told what people there are in the house to stick to their rooms and not come nosing downstairs."

Rocky sat down, thinking for the hundredth time that you really had to see Ma to believe her, and then you weren't quite certain you were seeing straight. A stranger would have supposed her costume to be a very informal one, but Ma had on the clothes that she wore at all times except the Sundays when mass was celebrated in the small Catholic church.

She wore run-over bedroom slippers, green woolen stockings, a very short gray jersey skirt. Meeting this was an odd knitted garment that might have started life as a sleeveless sweater. It was cut to a sun back and held together there with black tape. Underneath this was a faded orange house dress patched beneath the arms with bright, unwashed orange. Large pearl earrings and a blue ribbon around her shock of yellow-white hair completed Ma's ensemble.

When she went to mass she put on a black silk gown with a dejected bustle and a jabot of lace that Eleanor said was "priceless." She also got into a pair of hourglass corsets that creaked loudly when she walked. If you had ever taken a look at the contents of her clothesline on washdays you knew she must wear long drawers trimmed with a yard of ruffled lace to each leg, as well as an embroidered corset cover with elbow sleeves, and a stiffly starched white petticoat.

It was Ma's boast that she had never "run any kind of house that wasn't genteel. I know human nature, and if you want to entertain company the parlor's there to do it in." The extreme respectability of her boardinghouse was a proven fact, and it was the only place of its kind in town where you could get clean beds and good food.

"How many boarders you got now?" Rocky asked.

"Full up, as usual. Clarice and Goldie Thomas were the only women. Goldie had to take the night shift on the telephone board, and she won't be home till eight. You know about Wilkins. He's a nice young fellow, and he's engaged to a girl in Oroville. That leaves four on the second floor. Well, three of the boys are out on trips, and Milt Glover came home about 2 a.m. so drunk I had to steer him up to his room."

"I know he was pretty cockeyed. I put him in his car to sleep it off, and he must've had sense enough to come home when he came to. Well, I was just askin'. I'm pretty certain whoever killed her came in by the window. But nobody that lives here had any reason to do it."

"No. Clarice never went around with any of the boys here. I told her she had to behave herself when I took her in. People are going to sleep alone and in their own beds in this house. I don't doubt some of the boys tried to make her. But she couldn't be bothered, and no one got insulted over it."

"Where do you sleep?"

"In the front downstairs bedroom. That's on the other side of the house from Clarice's."

"There's too much vacant space in this town," Rocky said, more to himself than to Ma Jenkins.

"That's the truth. I never bothered to fence the place in. There's a road back between what you might call my back yard and the one that faces it. What you might call an alley."

"I know. It's like that all over town. Usually lots of space between houses too. You said you were up at two o'clock . . ."

"I'd heard people in the street coming home from the dance for about half an hour. I don't sleep very good. I got Milt settled and went back to my room. Smoked a cigarette before I put the light out. I heard Clarice come in at two-thirty."

"That'd be about right. She left the high school just before we did. She evidently came straight home."

"That's what I thought. Oh, it may have been a little after two-thirty, but it was pretty close to that. It was already quiet enough on the street by that time. I guess everybody that wasn't ready to go home went on downtown. I heard some of the folks who live on this street come home, but they were all in by the time Clarice was."

"There'd be more people going home down Pine—the street the high school's on—than any other. Oh, it'd be quiet enough aroun' here by three or even earlier."

"And no light to speak of. I been after the supervisors to put another light on this street. There ought to be one right in front of this house. They don't seem to think it's their business, and there's no town authorities to do it. It's a disgrace—"

Rocky had heard Ma hold forth on this subject before. He said quickly, "I'll have to look over her things. Want to come along?"

"You won't find anything you're looking for," Ma predicted, following him into the bedroom. "Say, Dud— There's plenty of coffee in the kitchen. And some doughnuts— Might as well get him out of the way. I suppose he wants to go out and arrest Jazz Mitchell?"

"He didn't mention Jazz by name, but I b'lieve he had him in mind," Rocky admitted. "Is there any place you can hide anything in this closet?"

"No. I told you you wouldn't find anything. Clarice hadn't anything to hide that I know of. I cleaned her room for her, and I know pretty well what's here. There's just her clothes in there. Kind of interesting ones, she had. Well, I don't believe Jazz Mitchell did it. He's too softhearted where women are concerned, for all he likes to bluster around. But people are going to think he did it."

Rocky's lips tightened. "I reckon they are. But I don't just see why."

"I suppose because he's fallen for another girl. She's a cute little trick, but there's nothing to her. No figger, I mean. Clarice was always fussing about getting fat, but she had curves. Men still like 'em."

Rocky suppressed a grin. "Because Jazz likes Nancy Towers doesn't mean he had to kill Clarice, does it?"

"Not to me it doesn't. Clarice never acted to me like what you'd call a woman scorned."

"*I* wouldn't—"

"Well, the newspapers would. Heath came after Jazz anyway, and Clarice wasn't one to try to hang onto a man when he wanted to quit her. And when she was the one who was tired she always managed to kid him out of being sore at her. I'm not so certain how willing she was to see Heath go, but she certainly never acted like she minded. There'd always be plenty other fish in the sea for Clarice."

"Jordan?" Rocky suggested.

"He was kind of a permanent fixture. I always did think she lived here instead of up at the hospital because up there Jordan would have excuses for being around. Of course his wife's one of these women that thinks her soul's being stifled to death in this town."

"Han'kerchiefs, underwear an' doodads," Rocky murmured. "What about Pat Healy?"

"Pat? Well, he'd have laid down and let her walk on him, and he's made plenty of money on that pool hall. But she was no gold digger. She just liked a good time. Men didn't go stark mad about her like you read about in books: not so they'd rather kill her than do without her. I knew a girl in Reno once— Of course all the old hens in town are going to say she was bound to come to an end like this, but I can't see it."

"If you've got the right slant on her it don't seem reasonable to me either. But in the meantime all I can do is check up on all these fellows. You hardly expect them to have alibis for around 4 a.m. unless they're married. If they're not they quite likely don't care about havin' to prove one. And Jordan's wife is out of town. Clarice did keep a few letters."

"Nothing important, I'll bet. That's probably all she got in a year. She never bothered writing to anyone. She didn't have any folks nearer than cousins in Michigan. I'll see she gets a good mass said for her. She lived from one payday to the next and put all her money on her back."

Rocky hesitated, then: "Would she have gone in for blackmail?" he asked. "You've got to consider all angles in this business."

"Well, not exactly what you'd call blackmail. I don't think she'd ever have shaken down anyone who couldn't afford it, but if she'd known anyone with more money than he needed, I don't doubt she'd cheerfully have relieved him of a little of it if she could."

"Yeah, a gal's got to live," Rocky said dryly. "She sure as hell couldn't ever have gotten much money out of most of the fellows in this town. I'll take these letters with me to read when I get time. I'll take a look at the ground outside this window, but it's baked hard—"

"Rains are late this year," Ma said. "Probably going to be an open winter. If the ground's too hard to hold prints how come those smudges of dirt on the sill?"

"Shoes always get dirty on the soles. I suppose you mean those little pieces of dirt, though. Looks like someone must've stepped in a damp place. People water lawns and flowers and even wet down the road in front of their houses to settle the dust."

"You're a swell detective," Ma said ironically. "You ought to take that dirt and have it analyzed and tell right where it came from."

"I always thought all Merton dirt was pretty much the same. An' I'm not a detective. I'm a dep'ty sheriff, and a sheriff that's called on to solve crimes is gettin' to be about as obs'lete as a country doctor. Well, I can't spend any more time here right now. I've got to call the cor'ner right away. I s'pose you'll have to testify at the inquest, Ma."

The old woman sighed. "In that case I'd better start getting into my things. It's an awful chore to dress up. Will nine o'clock be early enough for me to get to the mortuary? I've got to get some breakfast for Milt and Goldie first."

"Take your time. Sloane prob'ly will be late, and he'll have to get him a jury first." Rocky put the letters in his pocket. "Lock this room in case people get an idea they want to take a look in it. I won't insult you by askin' you not to talk."

Dud Williams hovered at his elbow while he was talking to the coroner and when he had hung up, said, "What you want me to do now?"

"Oh—" What Rocky most wanted Dud to do was to go away and leave him alone, but he couldn't very well say so. "I was just thinkin' it would be a good idea if you checked up on all the bums in town. You never can tell but what some of them may've been wanderin' around here last night."

Dud caught at this idea eagerly. "You know, I was thinkin' about that. There's a lot of these here hom—hom'cidal maniacs wanderin' around. I'll go down to the jungle and see what I can find. And I was thinkin' about Pat Healy. I like Pat but—"

"You might tactfully ask him what-all he was doin' last night. And it might be a good idea for you to go aroun' to the morgue about nine. Sloane should be there by then, an' he may want some help."

"Ain't you goin' to be there?"

"If I can. I might be late," Rocky said discouragingly. "You tell old Lorenzo that."

CHAPTER FIVE
"I SAW JAZZ . . ."

Directly across the street the Leamans were holding an informal Sunday morning reception on their
discouraged front lawn. Jack Leaman wore dirty
black trousers and a red flannel undershirt; his
wife was in beach pajamas and bedroom slippers
with a bathrobe thrown over her shoulders against
the chill of the morning air—standard attire for
an early morning front- or back-fence chat.

Rocky looked at the group unfavorably. Jazz
lived only half a block down from the Leamans on
the opposite side of the street, and everyone there
would be able to see where he was going. But he
couldn't put off talking to Jazz, and in an hour or
two there might be still more people gathered on
this street.

A small boy ventured halfway across the road,
staring round-eyed at the tan boardinghouse. Dud
promptly let out a deep roar and charged across
to the Leamans' front gate. He was heard advising

everyone to "stay right where you are. No one's goin' across this street. There ain't nothing for you to see over there anyway. We can't have you clutterin' up the sidewalks. You'd better all go home peaceable. . . ."

Rocky left Dud to it, with Mrs. Leaman shrilly inviting him to "just dare to lay a finger on me! I just dare you to! This is a free country, and I know my rights. . . ."

He hoped that Dud and Mrs. Leaman would engage all the crowd's attention, but before he had gone a dozen steps Leaman's voice said behind him:

"Wait a minute, Rocky. I want to talk to you."

Rocky turned and eyed the man unenthusiastically. He was the worst gossip in Merton and the kind who liked to get something on some other brakeman and then turn him in to the superintendent. Rocky despised him, and Leaman knew it. He wouldn't be smiling so pleasantly right now if he didn't know Rocky wasn't going to like whatever it was he had to tell. . .

"I suppose you're in a hurry to get down to Jazz Mitchell's place. Maybe he's already skipped out," Leaman suggested. "But you better listen to me first. I saw Jazz come out of his place about three-thirty this morning—"

"What were you doing up at three-thirty?"

"Well, we'd been to the dance, and after that we'd just about got to sleep when the wife got the idea I'd forgot to turn off the ignition on the car. I did it once, and she's never let me forget it. We argued some, but finally I got up and went out to see."

"Out the back door, I suppose?"

"Yes, but the garage's a little to one side of the house. I can see that cabin Jazz lives in from the front of the garage. Take a look at it yourself if you don't believe me."

"Oh, I wouldn't think of doubtin' your word, Jack. You looked all the way across the street and halfway down the block an' saw Jazz come out of his place at three-thirty in the mornin'. Go on from there."

"I did see him—or someone. And he didn't come out—"

"You said he did."

"He must have come out if he was goin' back in," Leaman said sullenly. "I seen him going back along that walk that leads into his place."

"I reckon you saw him so clear an' distinct you can tell me just what the expression on his face was?"

"That street light's right near his place, and it looked to be about Jazz's height and build. I guess

I could see that even if it was dark. A man tries to do his duty as a citizen and gets no thanks—"

"Oh, I thank you, and no doubt Jazz will too when he learns about it. With a black eye like that one he gave you two years ago," Rocky drawled. "You was wide awake at three-thirty and all full of int'rest in what was goin' on. That's fine."

"You wait a minute! I heard Jazz and that girl talkin' in the gym after the dance 'd stopped—"

"So did I." Rocky lighted a cigarette without offering Leaman one. "I can't recall they said anything out of the way. I didn't see you."

"I was outside on the main steps waitin' for the wife to get done sayin' good night to some folks. I could hear her—Clarice Selby. The doors was swinging open a little. I heard her say he acted like she was to blame for living. And them quarreling about Heath. I couldn't hear what he said—"

"I didn't think you could, or you might've understood what she was talkin' about a little better."

"Oh, I know you're a friend of Mitchell's," Leaman said unpleasantly. "But I guess there's some others that'll be interested in what I heard—and saw."

"And I don't doubt you'll spread it all over town. Better get back to your audience, Leaman. You've done your duty as a citizen plenty for one day."

He knew, as he walked away and left Leaman scowling after him, that he'd probably regret having talked to the fellow like that. Leaman would have talked a good deal in any case, and now he wouldn't care what he said. He could probably invent a few facts when he got tired of telling what he really knew. . . . Rocky stumbled over a loose board in the long walk that ran from the street to Jazz's ramshackle dwelling. He knocked; then pushed tentatively at the door and, finding it unlocked, walked in.

Jazz had taken off his shirt and his shoes, but that was as far as he had gone toward undressing. He was sprawled face down on the bed, but he squirmed over on his side and looked up as Rocky said, "Good mornin'."

"Oh, is it morning? I kind of thought it might be, but I didn't care much."

Rocky glanced at the empty whisky bottle by the bed, then at the dark smudges under Jazz's eyes and said, "No, I don't imagine you do. Has anybody else been in here this mornin'?"

"Not that I know of. And I didn't get that pie-eyed," Jazz said with a haggard smile. "Why? It's not very late, is it? Don't tell me my relief didn't show up."

"I suppose he did. I haven't been down to the office, but they always send a man up when they say they will."

"Well then, why 'm I honored with such an early morning call?" Jazz sat up wincing and wrapped his fingers around his left wrist. "Damn! That thing's sore."

"Let me see." Rocky looked at the discolored wrist and frowned. "I should think it would be sore. How'd you do it?"

"Oh—after I'd finished off that pint I thought I'd go downtown and get some more. I was just drunk enough to. Also to trip over that loose board out there in the walk and fall flat. I threw one hand out to catch myself, I guess."

"You scratched your face a little."

"Did I? Well, what of it?" Jazz said irritably. "It sobered me up plenty, anyway. 'And the pig got up and slowly walked away.' I knew every place downtown would be closed, so I came back and went to bed. Where are you going?"

"Out to the kitchen. I'll be back."

In the small, disorderly kitchen Rocky started a fire in the stove, put water to heat and measured coffee into a battered granite pot. Apparently every other utensil in the place was in the sink, along with a tower of dirty dishes. Rocky jerked open a drawer in the kitchen table and found a can opener, a potato masher and one very dull butcher knife. He went back into the other room, swept a pile of clothes off a chair and sat down.

"I'm makin' some coffee. You look like you need if in any case. And I think it might be a good thing if you didn't see a doctor about that wrist, Jazz. Someone killed Clarice Selby last night."

Jazz went a shade whiter. He put one hand to his eyes and shook his head as if he were a little dizzy. Then: "I get it," he said. "The scratches and this bum wrist—and the general setup. . . ."

"Right now there isn't any case against you—or anyone. That's the trouble. No clues, so you've got to think about motive. What I think isn't as important as the fact that when people start thinkin' about that, the first thing they're going to say is, 'What about the men Clarice knew?' You're one of them. I came to you first because I wanted to get it over with."

Probably Jazz was thinking, as Rocky was, about the two or three fishing trips they'd taken together and the time Rocky had spent two months at a Godforsaken O.S. station out on the desert where Jazz was working. There was only two years difference between their ages, but Rocky had always made those two years seniority the excuse for an older-brother attitude. Even out there on the desert they had managed not to get on each other's nerves, and that meant something. . . .

Jazz smiled crookedly. "I can see you don't like it any better than I do. Well, I live conveniently close to where Clarice does—did."

"So does Heath. On Marin, but that's only a block and a half away. I'll get aroun' to Heath. Meanwhile that guy Leaman happened to see you comin' back in here this mornin'. He said it was about three-thirty."

"Maybe it was. I couldn't swear to it. Leaman, hunh? I'll spoil his pretty face for him," Jazz promised pleasantly. "She was—killed around three-thirty?"

"Probably not that early; maybe a little later. Did you come straight home, Jazz?"

"I did, but how can I prove it? I was late enough that I didn't meet anyone after I left the street the high school is on. One car came by just as I got to the bottom of the front steps to the high school—"

"That'd probably be the Leamans."

"Would it? Well, it seemed to be the last one to leave there. I suppose you're wondering if I tried to see Heath. He'd evidently gone on home, and I decided that could wait. It didn't seem such a good idea—to beat up on him—after I'd cooled off a little. Clarice—Clarice said everyone would know why I did it and that wouldn't be very pleasant for Nancy. . . ."

Unconsciously he gripped his wrist again. Rocky said, "Wait a minute," and went back to the kitchen. The water in the teakettle was boiling, and he

poured part of it on the coffee and the rest into a
tin washbasin.

"Have you got any rags?" he said, putting the
basin on a table in the front room.

"That white shirt over there's not any good.
What—how was she killed, Rocky?"

"Stabbed. We didn't find any knife." Rocky tore
the shirt into strips, soaked them in hot water and
wrung them out gingerly.

"Well, you'd better look over my kitchen cut-
lery. Of course I always carry a private stiletto
around in my hair— Damn it! Are you trying to
parboil me?"

"Let it stay there," Rocky said, wrapping the
bandage more tightly about Jazz's wrist. "It'll take
the swelling out. Do you know how close to the
ground the window in Clarice's room is?"

"Of course I do. So would anybody who'd ever
been by Ma Jenkins' place. As a matter of fact, I've
talked to Clarice through it, though I was always
damn careful not to let Ma catch me at it. You
mean someone crawled in through that window?
Well, that would be the best way," Jazz said impersonally. "There's just a vacant lot on one corner across from it. I suppose you could argue I—if
I did it—stumbled getting out the window—"

"If you were in a hurry it'd be easy enough to do,
I reckon. But the window's so low to the ground a

kid could climb in it easy. An' you're too light on your feet to be apt to do a thing like that."

"You'd think she'd have heard— But she always slept like the dead. Oh yes, I know that. That's one thing you wanted to ask me, isn't it? That bandage is cooling off, if you want to put another one on."

"The only thing I'm interested in about you an' Clarice is how much can be proved against you."

"If anyone wants to investigate in Reno they can prove plenty. We had sense enough to be careful here in town. So what? Am I supposed to have a habit of killing every woman I ever slept with?"

"It's that fool public pros'cutor I'm worried about. He hasn't had a chance at a murder trial since he's been in office. I can see just what he'd make out of what he'd call 'an illicit relationship.'"

"And no one will believe the truth, now she's dead. Which was that Clarice was one woman who could call a thing quits and not insist on a dozen farewell performances after that. Of course we stayed friends. She was a good sport. We weren't getting anywhere, and we decided it just wouldn't work out if we got married. That was as much as ten months ago. I won't say I wasn't a little sore when Heath started cutting in—"

"Then he didn't, right away after he came here?"

"No; when he first came here he went around with Miriam quite a bit when he wasn't with the Fultons. Clarice and I haven't so much as gone to a movie together since last April: not even in the summer when Heath was away. Does it seem reasonable that all of a sudden she'd start raising a row because I wanted to marry another girl?"

"It don't to me, especially with what you an' Ma Jenkins have told me about her. But anyone makin' a case against you—which I'm doing my best not to—would say she might not have minded breakin' of with you just so long as you didn't marry anyone else."

"No one but Nancy can prove I ever wanted to do that. I'll swear I never had any honorable intentions. She may not like that, but damn it! she's got to be kept out of it. It'll be a rotten, dirty mess if they start digging it out. As far as I'm concerned, it'll finish me."

"If Freddie Haynes wants that kind of diggin' done I can probably find plenty of dirt for him," Rocky said. "Jordan an' Pat Healy and Heath. . . . The first two have got some influence, and Freddie handles people like that with gloves. Lucky this is a poor county and there's no investigators attached to Freddie's office. Does that wrist feel better now?"

"Yes. It wouldn't have bothered me if I'd tended to it last night. It won't need to be bandaged."

"That's good. I don't want any more talk than necessary aroun' here. What were you and Clarice talkin' about last night when I came into the gym after you'd stopped playin'?"

"Did someone besides you hear that? Christ, they've got long ears in this place! Not that I cared—then. Heath had donated his ten bucks to the fund, so he wasn't there for the pay-off. I was saying what I thought about him—again—and Clarice told me to sign off. You heard that?"

"Yes. What did she mean when she said she was sorry but she couldn't help it? Help what?"

"I guess that was pretty ambiguous. She meant she was sorry Nancy had put the freeze on me because Heath had told her about Clarice and me."

"Heath told her!"

Jazz nodded. "Pretended he just let it slip, Nancy said. Well, everyone's got his own idea about what constitutes hitting below the belt. I don't know how Clarice knew he'd been talking, but she seemed pretty sure of it."

"You'd think he'd have been afraid to start that kind of talk."

"Maybe he guessed I wouldn't tell tales on him. And if it got him in bad with Nancy, it would me too. So far as he and Clarice are concerned he

generally," Jazz said carefully, "is given the bene-
fit of the doubt."

"And you wouldn't want to say anything more
than that? Just the same, I'm going to have a right
interestin' half-hour with Mr. Heath."

"But Clarice never tried to hold onto Heath either. Can you imagine her a schoolteacher's wife?
I kidded her about that once, and she said nothing like that for her."

"Bein' a teacher don't seem to have cramped
Heath's style any."

"I think Clarice got a kick out of it whenever
Nancy took Heath down a notch. She does sometimes. Clarice said Heath had something like
that coming to him sometime. She offered—last
night—to tell Nancy she didn't have any claim on
me. I didn't think that would help matters any,
and she said she didn't either."

"It's too bad somebody couldn't have heard
that. Wait a minute. I'm going to get that coffee.
It must be strong enough to float a brick by now."

"It is," Jazz said, making a face over the cup
that Rocky handed him. "You know, lots of guys
find it quite a relief to get blotto now and then,"
he added reflectively. "I guess I never had enough
practice. You can't drink and keep a telegraph job.
I was thinking about Clarice. She didn't have any
relatives that have seen her since she was twelve

years old. You can tell old Laval I'll be responsible for her—her funeral expenses."

"You don't have to worry about that."

"Someone will have to. I guess I owe her that much. Wouldn't you think so?"

"Yes. But Ma Jenkins already spoke about that, so you forget it. For more reasons than one. . . ."

"You mean on Nancy's account?"

"I'm afraid she wouldn't exactly understand how you an' Clarice could be all washed up and yet you'd feel you owed her something after she was dead. However, I wasn't thinking so much about that. Nancy's the kind of girl who's always sayin' proudly that she knows the facts of life. So she might just as well learn to accept them. But I don't want you to start any more talk aroun' town. I've got to go meet the cor'ner now. . . ."

"What makes you think I didn't do it?" Jazz said abruptly, putting his coffee cup on the floor.

"I've made it clear I don't, haven't I? Well, let it go at that. Heath boards at Mrs. Pratt's, doesn't he?"

"He's got that cabin of hers. She built it when the old man was still alive. She had all the money, you know. She said she 'couldn't be bothered,' but if he wanted to stick around and do the chores and sleep outside the house it was all right with her." They grinned over this bit of town history, then: "Sloane never takes long over his inquests, does he?" Jazz asked.

"No longer 'n he can help. Lorenzo don't aspire to be a detective. I hope to God Freddie Haynes didn't come with him. Will you do something for me, Jazz? Well, stick to the house—"

"Why? I don't like the idea of acting like I was afraid to come out in the open."

"You know if you go downtown and meet someone who makes a crack you don't like there's going to be trouble."

"I suppose you're right. It's a good thing I happened to lay off. Nancy had been wanting to go to Virginia City, and I was going to get a car— Oh well, I'll stay in. But what the hell you think I'm going to do with myself?"

Rocky looked around the room: at the overflowing ash trays, the table littered with magazines, sheet music, empty cigarette cartons; at the piled-up chairs and disordered bed.

"You might put in your time cleanin' house," he suggested. "I'll be back. . . ."

CHAPTER SIX
"I DIDN'T TALK TO HEATH"

Somewhat sulkily the coroner's jury brought in its verdict and ceased officially to exist. Its six individual parts suffered from unsatisfied curiosity and, according to Lorenzo Sloane, "delusions of grande'r. I haven't got all day to waste pryin' into things that aren't my job.

"All you've got to say is whether the deceased died a natural death, killed herself or was killed by someone. Since you've got eyes you can see she didn't die naturally. The evidence 's told you she didn't kill herself. So your verdict's ready and waiting for you. You aren't called on to solve this case for the sheriff this morning, and I've got to get back to Brookdale."

When the jury had filed out of the room in which the inquest had been held, Sloane snapped his watch shut and remarked, "Well, that was pretty good time. Anything else I can do for you, Rocky?"

"Not a thing. I kind of thought Haynes would keep you company."

The coroner tapped Rocky paternally on the shoulder. "That's where you get a break, son. Freddie went to the city over the week end and won't be back till Tuesday unless he gets word of this right away and thinks it's worth cutting his trip short for. Well, I've got a funeral to conduct this afternoon, and I don't like to leave it to my son. He's just learning the business, and he hasn't got the right manner yet."

Rocky grinned behind Sloane's back, following him out to the entrance hall. He had never been able to decide whether Sloane had decided to be an undertaker because he looked like one or had come to look like the popular conception of an undertaker because he was one.

He left Sloane talking shop to Laval, who had once remarked that he'd probably be coroner himself one day if he only managed to outlive old Lorenzo, and that he'd certainly deserve the office after being defeated by Sloane in every county election for twenty years. Miller was waiting on the front steps. He said:

"Was everything all right? I didn't tell anything more than Sloane said was necessary."

"I'm glad you didn't. What do you think about the weapon?"

"Any ordinary knife with a blade about three inches long and about an inch wide. There weren't any peculiarities about the wound."

"Did you happen to look under her fingernails?"

"Yes, I did. I wanted to do a thorough job of it. She evidently didn't struggle at all. Probably didn't really wake up before she was stabbed. Did you think she might have put up a fight and scratched the person who killed her?"

"I didn't think so, but it's a point I wanted to get cleared up right now. You'll keep in mind I asked you about it if the question's ever raised?"

"Of course. Dr. Jordan didn't care to be present," Miller said. "He told me to make all the necessary arrangements."

"How'd he take it?"

"Not with the degree of professional calm you would expect," Miller said rashly. "When the news had time to soak in, perhaps with just a shade of relief. However, you'd better consider that not said. I may be wrong."

"I'll remember you didn't say it. Do you still think she was killed between three forty-five and four-thirty?"

"Yes. Though without analyzing the contents of the stomach—"

"I don't think that's necessary. It don't look like narrowin' down the time of death to the exact

minute would help any as long as she was killed
sometime aroun' four in the mornin'. It's a bad
hour to try to check up on where people were. I'll
probably come up to the hospital this afternoon
and talk to Jordan. I'm goin' over to the town hall
now."

What Merton proudly called its town hall was a
square building of red brick with a stunted tower
in which the fire siren resided. A secondhand fire
engine was housed on one side of the building,
and there was a small anteroom on the other with
a larger room opening off it. This was Dud Williams' official abode, and here the local J.P. kept
erratic office hours or entertained friends who
liked to talk over town affairs and take a drink
from the bottle in the upper right-hand corner of
the desk. A cold and lousy jail jutted off the back
of the town hall, with one of its barred windows
commanding a view of the presses of the Merton
Chronicle next door.

Tom Wright, the editor of the weekly paper,
was waiting at the door of his office when Rocky
came by. "You're going to give me a break on this,
aren't you?" he said.

"How? I thought I saw you at the inquest."

"I learned a hell of a lot there, didn't I! What's
the real dope on the thing?"

"Let's see. I've been on it for about five hours. You tell me, Tom. Anyway, your paper doesn't come out till Tuesday, unless you're going to print an extra."

"I thought about that," Wright said wistfully. "But I decided it wouldn't pay me to do it."

"It wouldn't pay you to print what I know right now. An' by Tuesday ever'body in town will know as much as you do and be sayin' a lot of things you can't print. Of course they'll like to read about it, because seein' things in print seems to make them more official."

Wright's long equine face lengthened gloomily. "That's the hell of running a small-town newspaper. I'll never be anything but a small-town editor, and I do know you can't run this kind of paper like you would one in the city and keep your circulation—if you can call it that. So you needn't be afraid I'll print anything that can't be proved. But you know I'm correspondent for the Sacramento papers—"

"Well, don't play it up any more 'n you have to. I don't want a flock of bright young city reporters up here. Anyway, you know the town never gets in the papers unless they run a snow-sport special up here or someone goes on a jag an' shoots up his fellow citizens. No wonder Merton's got a bad name. You give me a break that way, and as soon as I know anything def'nite at all I'll let you in on it."

"O.K. Meanwhile," Wright said, lowering his voice, "I don't believe this boloney some people are talking about Jazz Mitchell. We go to press tomorrow, and there's not going to be any hints about him in my story."

"I'm glad to hear that. If you've had your ears open to public opinion—just what is it?"

"Pretty unsettled so far. But don't you think everybody is going off half cocked with the notion Jazz is the only logical killer. He's pretty popular around town—also pretty much otherwise with some people. But they're a minority. I wouldn't worry about that."

"I'm not going to arrest anybody just to make an impression on the public, if that's what you mean. If I don't see you before," Rocky said, "I'll be over in the town hall tomorrow mornin'."

Dud Williams was waiting for him next door. "I brought three bums in," he said happily. "Just on gen'ral principles. They was tryin' to get hand-outs up an' down Main Street. The jungle's pretty well cleaned out. I guess a lot of 'em hopped that freight 'at pulled out about six. I got nothin' against these fellows, but you might like to talk to them, and they might as well spend the night here."

"I'll look them over when I get time. Did you see Pat Healy?"

"Yeah. Pat felt real bad. He called up Laval and told him to order a white satin coffin and never mind the expense. Pat's in the clear. Him and a bunch of the boys was playing poker in the back room till five o'clock after they closed up the pool hall. Matter of fact, I should've remembered about that. I meant to be there myself, but somehow or other it just slipped my mind."

Rocky did not need to ask the reason for Dud's forgetfulness. He picked up the telephone and put a call through to Brookdale.

"You goin' to get some help in from up there?" Dud asked.

"From Brookdale? Hell no! Jake's old deputies may've been good men in their time, but most of them are so fat now they can't see any part of their anatomy below the chest without lookin' in a mirror. All they can do is set aroun' on their tails an'— Hello! Is that you, Cy? What's doin' down there?"

Rocky listened with increasing impatience to the voice in Brookdale, then: "Well, you trot over to Indian River and talk to the fellow," he said.

"You don't expect me to leave here just because someone passed a bad check at an auto camp, do you? What? Then send someone else. Let Al Sully go. There's nothin' wrong with his health, is there? Tell him to get a description of the fellow and send out a warning, though he's probably miles away by now. I'll try to get back to town for a few hours tomorrow, so don't bother me for anything short of another murder."

He slammed the telephone down on the desk. "That's a fair sample of what to expect. I told Cy to stay in the office while I was gone, an' he's havin' kittens because some guy's been passin' rubber checks over aroun' Indian River. Seems to think I ought to come back and light out after him."

"They're like that in Brookdale," Dud said. "What's it matter? Just a lot of Swiss-Eyetalians over around Indian River. Of course they got a vote." He opened the top desk drawer, looked inside and swore. "This is the last time I leave any of my liquor around here where that old bastard can get at it! That bottle was half full last night."

"You know old Bartley soaks it up like a sponge," Rocky said unsympathetically. "The only reason they ever 'lected him J.P. was because his wife's the nicest old lady in town. I wish there was a phone in that place of ours."

"I'll take a message around if you say so," Dud offered. "Whyn't you take my car?"

"Oh, I can get a car from the garage, but I don't want to take time to go aroun' home. You go over an' tell Eleanor I'll try to make it for lunch. I'm going up to talk to Heath now."

Eleanor said, "Thank you, Mr. Williams," closed the door and turned back to Nancy. "He won't be here until lunchtime, if he gets here then, so please sit down and compose yourself, my child."

"Oh, you're not as calm and cool as you'd like me to believe. I'll go home if you want me to."

"Certainly not," Eleanor said impatiently. "All that I said was it's no certain thing that Rocky will tell you anything you want to know when he does come."

"No, I don't suppose he will. He'll tell you."

"After all, I've had some experience in this kind of thing. Come back to the kitchen. I want to put my roast in the oven."

Nancy walked restlessly about the kitchen, stopped to study a last year's calendar that hung on the wall, picked up a paring knife, put it down again and, finally, seeing that Eleanor was looking at her, sat down abruptly.

"Did you go downtown this morning?" Nancy said.

"For groceries, you mean? No, I saw the delivery boy going by and sent an order down by him. It's a blessing stores stay open till noon on Sundays. He brought the things back with all the latest news. How did you happen to be downtown, Nancy?"

"Louise came by and asked if I didn't want to go to the post office. We didn't get down yesterday afternoon, and a trip to the post office is quite an event in our quiet lives. Everybody downtown was talking—naturally. We got all the—the gory details in the drugstore, and we could hear more on the streets. I left Lou and came over here. I didn't want to go home anyway. Paul Heath said he'd drop by and see me this morning."

"Mr. Heath is probably otherwise engaged right now," Eleanor said, closing the oven door. "Of course Rocky will want to talk to him."

"Well, I hope he does! He caused a lot of the trouble."

"Mr. Heath, you mean? How?"

"Talking to me about Jazz and Clarice."

"Why did you listen to him?"

"I didn't! You aren't listening to people when they just start talking and you don't know what they're driving at until all of a sudden they pretend they said something they didn't mean to at all. And then say, 'But I did suppose you knew all about that.' And rather than be considered just a dumb cluck you pretend you did know it all along."

"Well, didn't you?"

"Of course, I knew they were—friends. And people referred often enough to the time when 'Jazz and Clarice used to go around together.' I understood that was quite a while ago."

"It was. Several months before we ever came back to Merton, and that was last May. Just what did Mr. Heath say, Nancy?"

"That he supposed I knew Clarice had the best claim in the world on Jazz if she wanted to exercise it."

Eleanor thrust a stick of wood into the stove and banged the lid down with unnecessary vigor. "That's just plain foolish. The claim she had on him was no claim at all. She wasn't any young and innocent girl he'd seduced. She knew what she was about, and I'm sure she never hesitated to go out after a man she liked. She'd probably be the first person to admit that if she could. What on earth are you looking for in the way of a husband, Nancy?"

"Who said I was looking for a husband at all! And don't act like I was something left over from the age of innocence! But it's a little different when you have a girl as good-looking as Clarice Selby pointed out to you."

"Y-yes, I suppose it is. The women we've never seen don't bother us, but I can understand it might be disturbing to have one of them right under your eyes—"

"And still in the picture. How do I know," Nancy said, "that Jazz still didn't like her a lot? Even if he hadn't gone around with her for a long time. Paul said they'd gotten very discreet. . . . Oh yes, I know that was a lie. Neither one of them is— was—the discreet kind. But things like that sting just the same."

"When you're jealous," Eleanor said, smiling.

"All right—I am! Jealous as hell! I d-don't know if I love Jazz or just plain hate him, but I know the idea that Clarice Selby had—had him first made me f-furious!"

"And you let him know it?"

"I didn't say 'Choose between that woman and me!' I'm not quite that idiotic. But I did make him pretty mad. That's not a hard thing to do," Nancy said with a forlorn smile. "I wish I knew he didn't quarrel with Clarice about it. What good would it do him to—to kill her?"

"None at all that I can see. I'd like to tell your boy friend what I think of him."

"Paul? He's no friend of mine. I told him not to try to see me this morning, but I'm afraid he'll not pay any attention to that. I'll never speak to him again—except as one faculty member to another. I don't see," Nancy said, "why two men had to fall in love with me. Just one really nice one would have been plenty. And I don't think Paul really is, anyway. He thinks he is right now, but if I'd just start fluttering a little every time he approached he'd soon change his mind. But I admit I don't know anything about men. I thought they never gave each other away."

"I don't think they very often do. Jazz didn't ask you if you had made inquiries about Mr. Heath's relations with Clarice? I didn't think so."

"Paul has a funny sort of feminine streak in him. I've heard that men who understand women very well sometimes do. He can be just as malicious as any woman I ever knew. Eleanor, how much did that delivery boy tell you?"

"I didn't let him talk. Why?"

"Then you probably don't know they were saying downtown that Clarice was very likely killed by someone who entered her bedroom by her window. Don't you remember that she said yesterday afternoon—"

"She did say that her windows opened right down to the ground and that she always left them open. I suppose everyone at Mrs. Kline's heard her: she had a very clear and carrying voice. But anyone knows—that is, anyone in Merton knows—that without her telling them."

"Oh. I thought it might be important though goodness knows who among those present could have wanted to kill Clarice—unless Paul did. When you say everyone in Merton knows about those windows you mean everyone who's lived here a long time and knows that boardinghouse. I wouldn't have known it if I hadn't heard Clarice. I suppose no one but the boarders could get in by the front door?"

Eleanor frowned. "Ma Jenkins always leaves her front door unlocked. Everyone knows that too. She doesn't approve of latchkeys and she keeps a stern eye on the goings and comings of everyone who lives there."

"I've heard that. And that she used to run a house over in Reno."

"She did. She married an engineer from the Eastern division and made him an admirable wife. When he died she came over here and started her boardinghouse. It has been many, many years since anyone has spoken of it with anything but the greatest of respect." She put a bowl of apples in Nancy's lap. "Here; peel these. It will give you something to do."

An apple pie was cooling on the table and Eleanor had taken the roast from the oven before they heard Rocky coming around the house to the back door. Fatigue had erased the little lines of laughter from about his mouth and two parallel lines were etched between his eyebrows.

"It's hot in here," he said, taking off his heavy leather jacket. "Hello, Nancy. I didn't intend to stop to eat, but if it's all ready I might as well. That pie looks good."

"Oh, don't make polite conversation!" Nancy said. "Do you—do you want me to go? I'd just as leave."

Rocky grinned briefly. "No you wouldn't. I don't want you to anyway. When I come to think of it there's no tearing hurry about me getting out again. I might as well talk to you now."

"Oh, Mr. Sheriff—I ain't done nothin'! Consider my reputation as a schoolteacher. Our faculty will get a bad name with your interviewing Paul Heath and now me."

"I didn't talk to Heath," Rocky said.

"You didn't? I thought— But of course it's none of my business."

"I'm afraid it may be a little bit your business, Nancy. I didn't talk to Heath because I couldn't. Nobody can."

"You mean—he—"

"He was killed sometime this mornin'. Same way as Clarice." Rocky sat down, hands linked loosely between his knees. "Go on with dinner, honey. We've got to eat just the same."

"I'll—I'll help," Nancy said finally. "I don't want anything to eat, but let me help—"

"Everything is ready, so you don't need to," Eleanor said. "You'll at least drink some coffee. And don't ask any questions until we've finished."

"I won't. I haven't, have I? I think I'm behaving very nicely." Nancy sat down and drank black coffee and smoked, chain fashion, until Rocky pushed his plate aside and reached for a cigarette.

"Yes, you're behavin' very nicely," he said. "Did you care anything about that fellow, Nancy?"

"No—no! But after all, I did know him—and I want to know what—what happened."

"I suppose you both do. I went up to talk to him. He lived in a little house back of Mrs. Pratt's. I suppose you know that, but it's kind of important, because when he didn't show up for breakfast she didn't think anything about it. When he'd been out late the night before he usually turned up for an early lunch. I went aroun' to this place—it's just one room—without speakin' to Mrs. Pratt. The door wasn't locked. . . ."

Rocky looked at the table without seeing it, his eyes yellow as topazes. The door had been unlocked: he had discovered that when there was no answer to his knock. He thought Heath must be still asleep and even hoped, briefly, that he might have cleared out. He pushed the door open and went in.

Heath lay on his back perhaps ten feet from the door. Falling, he had struck the one large chair in the room. It lay on its side close to his head. The gray suit he had worn the night before was red-rusted with drying blood. . . .

"He was lying on his back," Rocky said carefully. "He'd been stabbed, and there wasn't any knife around. He hadn't had time to undress. As a matter of fact, it don't look to me like he had time to lock his door after he went in. The key was in his pocket like he'd stuck it there—"

"You mean he'd just unlocked the door and was going to lock it on the inside when someone he knew turned up? And he put his hand in his pocket with the key in it?" Eleanor said.

"That's it. Because if he'd already locked his door after he'd gone in and unlocked it again for someone, he'd not take the key out of the door. At least, most people do leave a key in the door when they've locked it. That's important mainly as showing he was killed almost as soon as he got home."

"Then—then the time he was killed was important?" Nancy said.

"It looks like it was goin' to be. I got the doctor there right away. Luckily Mrs. Pratt's hard as nails and didn't try to go hysterical on me when I went in to phone. Well, Miller can't swear to it yet, but he's pretty sure Heath was killed quite a while before Clarice was."

"Which changes the setup completely," Eleanor said.

"Offhand, I'd say it did. There's nothing to prove it yet, but if he was killed first it looks like there's a possibility Clarice was second on the list because she knew too much. That's only a guess."

Nancy brushed spilled sugar into small mounds, destroyed them, built them up again. "D-doesn't that help Jazz?"

"In a way it does. It may take Clarice's death out of the 'crime of passion' class. But I'm not certain it would even do that—for a lawyer. He could just argue that Jazz had a double motive. It looks worse for him than ever," Rocky said. "I can state the case like it's going to appear to other people. . . .

"Ever'body knows Jazz hated Heath. I suppose there's a lot of folks that didn't miss the fact that they quarreled last night. An' that Jazz told Heath he'd settle with him after the dance. Heath left about two o'clock—"

"Yes; we saw him go down the hall," Eleanor said. "That couldn't have been more than a minute or so after two, because he hadn't played for the last dance."

"I haven't checked on how long it would take him to walk home, but it shouldn't take more 'n five minutes if he walked right along. We don't know that he did. Jazz didn't leave till about two-ten. He stopped to ask Kline if Heath had gone home, and that won't make a very good impression."

"But Paul should have been home by a little after twofive," Nancy said. "If he was killed before he had a chance to lock his door on the inside—"

"We can't prove he was. He may've taken his time going home. He may not have locked his door the minute he got in. If Jazz followed him home an' walked fast he could've got there by two-fifteen. Someone should've seen Heath, but by the time Jazz left there wasn't anybody aroun' to see him after he'd left Pine Street. That's the one the high school's on."

"Mr. Kline was so set on clearing the place quickly that the crowd didn't linger at all," Eleanor said. "There was only a handful dancing to 'Home, Sweet Home.'"

"Well, Clarice started home after Jazz did. She'd go the same way he did, and it's easy enough to argue she might be just in time to meet Jazz comin' away from Heath's place or maybe to see him going into it—"

"I don't see how you can go on talking like that! It sounds like you—you . . ." Nancy's voice faltered under Eleanor's scornful glance. A shower of sparks flew onto the tablecloth as Rocky crushed out his cigarette in a saucer.

"Jazz is a friend of mine," he said evenly. "If I don't understand what the case against him is going to be I can't help him much."

"I'm—I'm sorry."

"That's all right. I don't think Jazz did it. I wouldn't think so anyway, but there's one funny thing about Heath's death. Someone had put an old coin in his mouth. . . ."

CHAPTER SEVEN
"TO PAY CHARON'S FARE"

"If it had been one of our own pennies or nickels I wouldn't think so much about it," Rocky went on. "Gangsters put money like that in a fellow's hand sometimes when they've taken him for a ride. I can't imagine anyone here doin' a thing like that, but they might possibly. But this was the kind of thing a coin collector might have."

"How old was it?" Eleanor asked. "I mean, when was it issued?"

Rocky hesitated; then shook his head. "Somethin' tells me not to let anyone know that. Just say it was an old coin—plenty old. I didn't even let Miller see it close enough to be able to describe it, though I let him see where I took it from. Heath's mouth was a little open, so I just happened to see the thing. And why put it there and not in his hand?"

Nancy twisted about in her chair and looked out the window, mechanically creasing the table-cloth with her fingers. She said finally, her small face paler than usual:

"I want to tell you something. If I seem to be making an awfully long story out of it, it's because you don't know— us. And perhaps you should. Last Tuesday night we were—all of the teachers— at the Fultons' house. . . ."

Mrs. Fulton was obviously sulky because some hint had been given her that it was her turn to entertain the faculty. At the beginning of the year Mr. Kline had suggested these "little get-togethers so that we can keep in touch with each other."

"We suffered from them last year," Paul Heath told Nancy, "at least once every six weeks. Good God! As if we needed to keep in touch with each other! What we need is to keep out of touch with each other after school hours."

But Mrs. Kline had already entertained, and it was now Mrs. Fulton's turn. They were not able to play bridge because there were nine of them. Mrs. Fulton offered to look on—tactlessly adding that she didn't "mind, anyway, since we can't play contract because Mr. and Mrs. Kline haven't learned how"—but Mr. Kline insisted on some game that they could "all play." He suggested Pit and showed them how to play it.

Fortunately Mr. Kline did not believe in keeping late hours on a school night. Ten-thirty was his invariable bedtime; he had remarked on this

fact so often that no one could possibly have forgotten it. So at ten o'clock Mrs. Fulton thankfully
served dubious pumpkin pie and excellent coffee,
with glasses of milk for Miss Newman and Mr.
Kline.

The former was murmuring to Nancy and Louise Whyte about "paying our social debts. Surely
one of our landladies will let us have the use of
a living room one night. I'll speak to Mrs. Werner—"

"You don't need to," Louise said. "If we really
have to do something like that, my Mrs. Barker is
a very obliging person. Since her husband is janitor she feels the high-school ladies really belong
to her. She admires to fix a nice bite to eat, and
she and Mr. Barker always sit in the kitchen anyway."

"Very convenient—if it's absolutely necessary,"
Nancy said. "Don't you think, Florence, that this
week's dizzy whirl of social activity will do us for
quite a while?"

Miss Newman smiled absently. "Oh, of course
we are not expected to do *very* much. But I do
think, as a nice little gesture toward Mr. and Mrs.
Kline—"

"I can think of a gesture or two," Nancy said
for Louise's ears only. "What are you going to do
to help us out, Miriam?"

"Me? I wasn't listening.—Oh, about another party? Do we have to give one? Well, I'll buy anything you want me to. I'm afraid there isn't much else I can do. I could sing—"

"You do, dear. We hear you half the day up at the high school," Nancy said ungratefully. "Well, wait until sometime around Thanksgiving, Florence, and I'll grit my teeth and try to bear it."

"We might make it a rule that anyone who mentions school problems shall be fined severely," Heath said. He had chosen to make a fifth at their table. He seemed never to have a great deal to say to his principal, and he and Leonard Fulton were barely on speaking terms. "We'd probably take in a nice sum during an evening if we did that. We could send it to the Home for Aged Crocodiles."

"I know I would be fined rather heavily," Miss Newman said stiffly.

Heath said carelessly, "Oh, you can't help it. Very admirable of you to worry so much over the little brats you teach, I'm sure."

"I try to forget them after 4 p.m.," Louise said quickly, "but sometimes I wake up in the middle of the night and think, 'What's to be done with Edwin Weaver?'"

"The thing to do with Ed," Nancy remarked, "is to tie a good, heavy weight to him and throw him over the bridge."

"No secrets, ladies!" Mr. Kline called from the other table. "Tell us what the joke is."

Heath whispered plaintively, "Am I one of the ladies?" as Nancy said hastily:

"You wouldn't call Edwin Weaver a joke, would you, Mr. Kline? But let's forget our little problem child while we can and think about the—the dance Saturday night."

"I hope they have a good attendance," Miss Newman said. "The children from two or three families need good warm clothing. Stockings—so many of the girls don't wear them at all—"

"They wouldn't wear them if they had them," Louise said. "There was talk of trying to get up some sort of entertainment. Has that been given up, Mr. Kline?"

"The parent-teachers suggested the high-school children might put on one or two acts. I didn't think it wise. Preparing for anything of that sort disorganizes our teaching schedule. I suggested that some of the town people get up a little skit, but no one seemed willing to perform."

"I told Hamilton some of you girls ought to be able to think up something," Mrs. Kline said. "But I suppose you're really too busy for that. I hear your costume's very pretty, Miss Atkins."

"What? Oh, I guess it will do. But it wasn't what I wanted. I had it sent up from the city. I couldn't think of any other kind than colonial—I guess that's what it is. Maybe it's French. I went to the Parilia once—the art ball in San Francisco, you know. They wore these real old costumes, all white and draped—"

"Greek," Miss Newman said patiently. "But you surely weren't thinking of *that* kind of costume, Miriam?"

Louise grinned. "If she followed the general style of the Parilia costumes she'd cause a sensation even in this town," she said to Nancy. "The majority of them are Gunga Din type. You're not the Greek type, Miriam."

"The Greek costume is very beautiful," Miss Newman said. "When I was a girl—I attended a school where the classics were stressed to an unusual degree—we gave a pageant in which we all took the parts of gods and goddesses. I remember that I was Athena—"

"That's the same as Minerva, isn't it?"

"Minerva is the Roman name, Nancy. The Roman names are most commonly used," Miss Newman said instructively. "And a good many people use both the Greek and Roman—"

Heath had a habit of interrupting people when he thought they were going to bore him. He said, "Well, why don't we go in a body as wanderers from Olympus? That would cause a sensation."

Mr. Kline frowned ponderously, but Heath went on: "Miriam could be Venus—"

Nancy giggled. "Arising from the wave?" she said cautiously. "Never mind, Miriam. You wouldn't know. I think Lou would make a good Diana."

"The huntress?" Louise said. "Make the arrows sharp, then. What are you reserving for yourself, Nancy?"

"Oh, I don't know. I could be Proserpina and spend the evening fleeing from Pluto."

"Pluto?" Miriam said with an accent of bewilderment that made Louise grin again.

"God of the underworld, my dear. Of course Mr. and Mrs. Kline would be Jupiter and Juno. They were the rulers of Olympus, weren't they?"

Mrs. Kline was gratified by this offered distinction, though when Nancy looked at Mr. Kline she thought at once of some quotation regarding "Jove's awful brow." Mr. Kline was obviously not amused, particularly when Heath said smoothly:

"You know all was not amity and sweet accord among the gods over whom Jupiter and Juno ruled. And they had their own domestic troubles. I seem to recall some dame named Io—'ox-eyed Io. . . .'"

"But isn't there some goddess for Gertrude to be?" Mrs. Kline said. "And Leonard?"

"Don't bother about me," Mrs. Fulton said nastily. "There will probably be something left over that will do. I suggest Mars for Leonard."

For an instant Leonard Fulton somewhat resembled the god of war. He growled, "Mars wasn't married, was he? Wise guy. Wasn't there a Mercury? Quicksilver—"

"God of chance and messenger of the gods— dangerously eloquent," Louise said. "Do you volunteer, Mr. Heath?"

"It might be very entertaining to carry messages from one god to another if that meant the privilege of reading them."

"Why not Achilles," Mrs. Fulton said languidly. "The famous vulnerable heel, you know."

She was looking sidewise at Nancy as she said it, and Heath reddened angrily. What had begun as the most trivial conversation was rapidly becoming the medium for more or less polite insult. Nancy had perversely done her part in forwarding the talk, but now she thought it time to stop. Mr. Kline was clearing his throat portentously, but Heath persisted:

"Fulton could wear armor, I suppose, but can't you pick out someone for me who wears a few clothes?"

"Not very many of them did, did they?" Miriam said. "I remember in all the pictures I ever saw—"

"There was Charon," Miss Newman said quickly. "He ferried the dead across the Styx. He is generally represented as a strong but stooped old man in a black robe."

"Paul isn't old or stooped. Ferried them across? I don't remember ever reading about that," Miriam said.

"Oh, you must have, in your high-school English. The ancients always put a coin in the mouths of the dead to pay Charon's fare. It was equivalent," Miss Newman said in her low, precise voice, "to saying, 'Ferryman, take him across.'"

Rocky said, "And that was all?"

"Except that then Mr. Kline squelched us with a heavy ha-ha and 'Very interesting; very interesting, indeed. But quite impracticable, of course. We have our professional dignity to consider.' Then he said it was time to go home, and we went home."

"Did the subject ever come up again?"

"Lou and I amused ourselves by picturing Mamma and Papa Kline all decked out in Grecian robes. And at faculty meeting the next afternoon—this Thursday—before Mr. Kline called us to order, Miriam asked Paul if he were going to come 'dressed like that old man Miss Newman was talking about.' Paul said he wasn't coming to the dance in costume. I wasn't speaking to him by then," Nancy added.

"It fits in like it was made to order," Rocky said. "That sort of sticks in your mind—'Ferryman, take him across.' But you see what you've

done, Nancy? You've suggested to me it was someone among the eight of you who are left that killed
Heath."

"I know. Well, I couldn't help it, could I? Professional loyalty is all very well, but there are—
other things. Besides, is the idea an entirely new
one to you? Somehow I don't think it is."

"No," Rocky admitted, "it isn't. I wanted something like you've just told me to go on. Even so,
who is there in town that hated Heath enough to
kill him—except Jazz? I know some people didn't
care an awful lot about Heath. But he didn't have
much to do with the town people. He knew the
others in the orchestra—Art Finley and Orin
Roberts—but except for them and the Jordans he
didn't have much more than speaking acquain-
tances aroun' town."

"The Jordans asked him to dinner now and
then. And he was at an evening bridge party Mrs.
Jordan gave. She asked him and Mr. Fulton along
with some other men."

"But town talk never connected him with Mrs.
Jordan in any way. She's away right now anyway.
Of course Jordan's here, and I'll have to talk to
him. His only motive for killin' Heath would be
because he couldn't stand him havin' the inside
track with Clarice."

"And why wait until now, when they'd broken
off, to do that? Why not have killed Jazz a year

ago if he felt that way about Clarice?" Eleanor said. "No; even when they bored him, Mr. Heath stuck to his colleagues."

"He didn't join organizations and work with them like Mr. Kline and Leonard Fulton do. He just couldn't be bothered," Nancy said. "He went away as often as he could. Women—women seemed to be about his only diversion here."

"Well, even if he'd had half a dozen known enemies in town, if they were the ord'nary run of what you can call the natives, they don't know any class'cal mythology. They don't have old coins to stick in people's mouths."

"How old is it? Nancy won't tell, and neither will I. You don't have to describe it to us."

"It ain't a Greek coin, if that's what you're thinkin', though it's dated way back. I could describe it, and you still couldn't tell me what it's called unless you're an expert."

"My father used to be interested in old coins. I think I have a book of his in those boxes we've never opened."

"Then we can look it up when we get to Brookdale again. I doubt if it's very important exactly what it's right name is. The important thing is that it was used the way it was an' that someone happened to have it to use. Did you ever see anyone have a pocket piece like that, Nancy? Or . . ." Rocky hesitated, then finished: "wear one around her neck? Because there's a little hole at the top of this big enough to put a thin chain through."

"I've never seen anyone I know have anything of that kind at all," Nancy said positively. "But they—we—would be more apt to have something like that than—than—"

"Jazz? I guess plenty of people could swear he'd never had anything like that in his possession, though there's always the possibility the thing's a fam'ly heirloom and might belong to the last person you'd expect. But while Jazz went through high school and I reckon was taught something about mythology—I know I suffered from a book on it—I don't imagine he remembers any more about it than I do."

"I certainly have never observed his conversation being studded with classical allusions, though once when I told him a composition we'd been listening to over the radio was Brahms—wanting to be smart—he calmly set me right. It was Bach. I'm pretty shaky myself on mythology, except for a few broad facts," Nancy said. "You forget an awful lot of the stuff that's poured into you in the name of education. It seemed almost a new story to Miriam. You know that Miss Newman knows the classics—and so does Mr. Kline. But no one needed to have known—of their own knowledge—after Wednesday night."

"That's one objection," Eleanor said. "Surely anyone with any sense would know a—a stunt like that would point directly toward persons of some education."

"Yes, there's that about it. But I don't know," Rocky said. "I'm surprised a lot of times at the way teachers and educated people are surprised at the things a lot of people don't know. Because they know a thing themselves they just take for granted that ever'body else does—or should."

Nancy smiled faintly. "That's true enough. I know Florence Newman—well, all of us—are always amazed and exasperated if the children in this town don't know what we're talking about when we refer to persons or events we think everyone must have heard of."

"It don't matter—right now. Eleanor's objection's a good one, but I can think of one or two ways to get aroun' it. For one thing—you aren't exactly what you'd call a congenial group, are you?"

"Show me any seven people working together who are!"

"I prob'ly couldn't. But usually when seven people work together an' don't like each other they don't have to go on seein' a lot of each other after workin' hours. You spoke about that yourself."

"Y-yes, I did. But that was before—"

"Before anyone got killed? Heath made a crack himself to the effect that you didn't all get on together as well as you might, didn't he? Well, there's a lot you don't have to tell me. You know Charlie Dyer? Your local trustee on the county high-school board? Charlie is a nice old guy, but he talks too much, and I've known him for years."

"I've met him. He's the one who insisted that Miriam be re-elected for this year."

"There's more to it than just the fact she got her job back. She got it when Kline didn't want to hire her again. I understand it's not so very often teachers are hired against a principal's wishes."

"That's true. But I wasn't here last year."

"Then maybe all this will be news to you," Rocky said blandly. "Charlie told me they damn near didn't hire Kline again. They think he's a good principal and all that, but some people thought Heath would be a better one. I said once that Merton people don't pay much attention to the teachers, but there's a small lot who do, and they make up in noise what they lack in numbers. Charlie held out for Kline because he said it looked to him like Heath had deliberately tried to stir up trouble an' get the job for himself."

"Of course every man who intends to stay in teaching wants to get a principalship. And of course the older men have to retire before the younger ones can move up. And I must admit the older men never know when it's time for them to quit."

"Kline had Fulton's support," Rocky went on. "Also Miss Newman's. They fired two women that were Heath's friends. You 'n' Miss Whyte took their places. I take it Miss Atkins was on Heath's side as much as she'd bother about takin' sides at all. Charlie Dyer said he didn't like it: he didn't think teachers ought to fight among themselves. He said Heath was too good to fire without a better excuse than they had, and he hoped this year things would be all right. If they weren't, both Kline and Heath would have to go."

"Well, that's fair enough."

"Is it?" Eleanor said. "Mr. Kline's a fairly old man. I've known teachers to be out of a job for two and even three or four years, especially some of the older ones. Of course Mr. Kline should be prepared for that. He's had a good salary for twenty years or more. And he could just teach; not hold out for a principalship. But from what I've seen of him I should think he is a man who's used to authority, likes it and would resent losing it. Would resent one of 'his' teachers being responsible for ousting him."

"He would," Nancy muttered. "He'd hate it like hell."

"You said he and Heath never had much to say to each other. They evidently weren't on any better terms this year than last."

"I don't know that they were. But Mr. Kline certainly should have had the advantage, Rocky. After all, he's the boss. He was evidently too stiff-necked to complain to the trustees about Paul last year, and he couldn't truthfully complain about his teaching. It was different with Miriam. But the recommendation a principal writes for you when you part from him to try to land another job is a pretty important thing. He could very thoroughly damn Paul with faint praise."

"Well, let that go for a while. Why did Jazz say Heath 'used to' run aroun' with the Fultons and Miriam Atkins? Why are Fulton and his wife always snapping at each other, and why weren't Heath and Fulton speaking to each other?"

"I can tell you that," Eleanor said. "Mrs. Fulton had evidently once been too much interested in Mr. Heath. Clarice gave that away yesterday. When Mrs. Kline spoke of 'our men,' Clarice said 'our Mr. Heath' was 'good.' Or something like that. She looked at Mrs. Fulton, for one, when she said it."

"Where did Heath live last year? Do you know, Nancy?"

"He boarded with the Fultons at the beginning of the school year. You can find that out easily enough. He left them at Christmastime. He did take Miriam to dances the first few months. She told me that. And the Fultons always went with them. Miriam didn't care—when he stopped going around with her, I mean."

Rocky let that pass without argument. "Then there's Miss Whyte, even if she had only known Heath a few months. Why did she say 'Make the arrows sharp, then,' when you said she ought to be Diana?"

"What if she did? What's wrong with that? Diana did carry a bow and arrows."

"Oh, of course. But it was kind of a funny thing to say. An' then she recommended Heath take the part of Mercury, not in very flatterin' terms."

"Oh," Nancy cried, "I do talk too much! I didn't realize all that would mean so much to you. Well, Lou detested Paul, and she'll be the first one to tell you so. They had a little argument about who should take a perfectly fiendish study hall and she got stuck with it. And Lou and I are very fond of each other, and Florence and Miriam quite often bore us to tears. I don't come in contact with Mr. Fulton enough to think much about him one way or another. Mr. Kline exasperates me terribly, but I don't dislike him. Will that do?"

"For you. I take it Heath just kind of ignored Miss Newman or gave her a careless pat on the head now an' then?"

"You don't miss much, do you? You might have warned me," Nancy said to Eleanor, seeing her smile. "Just as one girl to another."

"You told your story in your own way, my lamb."

"Well, I didn't mean to say so much, but I guess my artistic instinct ran away with me. I suppose you could dig up a lot of dirt around town anyway."

"No end of it," Rocky said encouragingly. "An' from a—maybe—more prejudiced point of view than yours. At least, it'd be prejudiced in the other direction." He got up, rubbing his unshaven chin regretfully. "I reckon if I've got to see all those people I'd better clean up some. I admit I don't know how to handle 'em. . . . That crack of Heath's about 'ox-eyed Io' was interestin' too. Miss Newman has got big and kind of cowlike eyes. . . ."

CHAPTER EIGHT
MR. KLINE IS APPALLED

Eleanor hung up the dishpan and opened the bath-room door. "Rocky—if you don't mind telling—what are you going to do now?"

Rocky came back into the kitchen buttoning the collar of a clean shirt. "Talk to all these people. The cor'ner hadn't got home yet so I left a message for him. But I'm pretty sure he won't come back here again till tomorrow. Miller's doing the—what he's got to do, this afternoon. So I'm free to start in on this game of questions an' answers. Nancy, I forgot to ask you Do you all have such things as personal records?"

"Is that the name for them on the railroad? We have what are called our 'papers.' They tell most of our life history and have pictures attached that usually make us look like escaped lunatics. The longer you've taught, the more recommendations and things you collect."

"How can I get hold of copies of them?"

"Mr. Kline has them—if he'll let you look at them. We file them with the commercial agencies and the California Teachers' Association and the placement bureau of whatever university we graduated from. Most principals keep copies after they've hired you. Of course Mr. Kline would. But I'll bet he won't let you see them."

"I'll take you up on that. I reckon he will."

"What do you want our records for?"

"To see how old you really are. No; just to get a line on all of you. I don't know how it is with the teaching game, but in railroadin' you get so you're never surprised at runnin' into someone you know most any place. Or you discover mutual friends or meet people who know people you've known."

"Well, we're always on the move. We work with each other for a year or two and then apparently say good-by forever. But in another two or three years we may find ourselves teaching together again. For instance, I taught with a girl who had taught the same place as Louise. And Paul knew someone who'd taught with Mr. Fulton someplace. I might leave here and go way down South and run into someone who'd known the Klines. You had something like that in mind, didn't you? That perhaps our—our relationships date back more than two or three years?"

"It seems like it would be possible. Do you know if Heath had any relatives and where they lived?"

"A mother and a stepfather. I don't think he got along well with either one. I've forgotten where they live. Some small town fairly near Santa Barbara, I think. But Mr. Kline will know. Rocky, have you—have you seen Jazz?"

"Again? I saw him early this mornin', you know. Yes, I saw him a second time. Just before I came over here. I didn't want to risk someone else buttin' in on him with the news. What became of that tie I wore last night, honey?"

"I suppose it's wherever you happened to throw it. No, I'll find it," Eleanor said. "It will save time in the long run."

Rocky looked at Nancy with a troubled frown. Jazz had taken the news of Heath's death very quietly—too quietly. It would have been better if he'd walked up and down and talked at the top of his voice. He had always been able to hit out at people or things that didn't suit him, and once he'd let off steam that way he was the easiest person in the world to deal with.

Right now there was nothing for Jazz to do but sit tight and wait. That might suit some people, but expecting inactivity from Jazz was about as reasonable as expecting the wind to stop blowing because you asked it to. Jazz always had to be doing something. He might manage to act sensibly for a while but not for very long. Especially if some well-meaning fool happened to think he should drop in to talk things over with him. . . .

"W-what is he doing now?" Nancy said.

"He's cleanin' house with all the frenzy of a man who expects his wife home any hour after he's been baching for a week. I told him to stay home. He didn't want to, but it's the safest thing for him to do. I don't know how long he'll mind what I said."

"Here's your tie. I don't know how it got mixed up with the bedclothes. Let me do it." Eleanor pulled the necktie into shape and kissed him lightly under the chin. "I wish there were something I could do."

"I wish I could take you with me. But it wouldn't be pleasant for you—right now or later on. I guess we'll have to hop back to Brookdale for a few hours tomorrow."

"We will if we're going to stay here very long. That's your last clean shirt."

Nancy apparently had not been listening to what they were saying. She said, "If you hadn't already seen Jazz I was going to ask you—won't you be dropping in there again? Will you—may I go with you?"

Rocky appealed to Eleanor. "Will you tell her why she can't?"

"I would if I knew. Why can't she?"

"A great help you turned out to be! You know why, an' it hasn't got anything to do with Em'ly Post. Look, Nancy—I knew I'd have to tell you this sometime. Your line from now on is to open up your eyes in kind of a baby stare—"

"I won't! I hate people with baby stares."

"It happens to be kind of effective lots of the time. Try it anyway: to oblige me—an' Jazz. You look that way and say, 'Oh, but Mr. Mitchell was never anything more than a casual acquaintance of mine—'"

"I will not say anything of the kind! What do you think I—"

"Oh, I don't think you're the kind to run out on your friends when they get in trouble. But if you insist on sayin', 'Mr. Mitchell was—was—'"

"'Madly in love with me,'" Eleanor supplied. "I begin to get the idea. Let's be journalistic. Then the headlines will say, 'OPERATOR SLAYS RIVAL, GIRL, FOR PRETTY TEACHER.'"

"You think of everything, don't you?" Nancy said ungratefully. "They wouldn't— You're—

you're serious, aren't you? You mean if I admitted Jazz had ever shown any sign of wanting to marry me that would strengthen the case against him?"

"It certainly would. An' don't think our county pros'cutor would mind puttin' you on the stand. The gen'ral impression may be that Jazz was pretty hard hit, but I don't know who can prove it except you—or him."

"And who else can prove that Paul Heath was—as Eleanor so touchingly puts it—a rival? Did Jazz say he was going to deny he ever—"

"Had any serious intentions? Just exactly. He'll keep you out of it if he can—so for God's sake try to help him do it! I'm going to get goin'," Rocky added more gently. "You stay an' talk to Eleanor."

He wondered, as he walked toward the high school, if Kline did any work in his office on Sundays. It would be a good deal more convenient to talk to him there. And the janitor's house was the first below the high school, and he wanted to talk to Barker. Louise Whyte boarded with the Barkers, so he might as well start from there.

Barker was pulling withered hopvines from a trellis in front of the porch. "Principal's up in his office now," he said in answer to Rocky's question. "I suppose he's locked the front door after him, but I can let you in." He fished a dirty plug of tobacco from his pocket and wrenched a piece from it with discolored teeth. "He's heard about Heath. Funny thing, ain't it? I never liked him myself."

"How long did Kline stay up there last night?"

"Hunh? You mean after the dance? The lights went off about two thirty-five," Barker said. "Mr. Kline told me I didn't need to stay up there because he'd be there to lock up. I like to get to bed early, and I knew I'd have to clean the place up this morning. But the wife, she stayed till it was all over. Woke me up and fussed around a long time gettin' ready for bed. Fin'lly she says it's after two-thirty an' the lights are still on up there. But Mr. Kline, he always has to see that everything's just right before he'll leave."

"Did Mrs. Barker see him come by here?"

"No, but she said the lights was out. That was just before she got in bed. Want me to let you in up there?"

Mr. Kline did not appear to have done any work, though he was seated before a starkly neat desk in the small, square office. "I would have come to see you this afternoon, Mr. Allan. Though no one had—officially—informed me of the appalling tragedy."

"I didn't have time to come to see you right away," Rocky said politely. Mentally he noted down the words "appalling tragedy." He must remember to tell Eleanor that some people really did talk that way.

"Oh, I know you have been very busy," Mr. Kline said grudgingly. "I knew that you would want to know the name of Mr. Heath's mother. She is a Mrs. Woody and lives in Santa Maria. I've written down her address for you."

"Thanks." Rocky accepted the small slip of paper. "But I'd like to have all your records on Heath—an' all the rest of your teachers."

"What? Why, that's absurd, Mr. Allan! What makes you think I would let you see those papers? Mr. Heath's, perhaps. I can see that there would be reasons why you would want those. But certainly not the others."

"Why? Is there anything wrong with them?"

"If you mean is there anything detrimental to the characters of our teachers in their papers—certainly not! Do you suppose I would hire anyone who hadn't a good record?"

"I wouldn't think so, but you refusin' to let me see the records makes me begin to wonder."

Mr. Kline settled his glasses more firmly on his long nose. "That is beside the point. Those papers are private and personal—"

"Oh, I don't see how they could be—very. They've been read by a lot of principals and the heads of agencies and the people who work in

them. The whole trouble, Mr. Kline," Rocky said
pleasantly, "is that you feel like I've got no right
to check up on your faculty. I hadn't heard of any
special immunity bein' granted to schoolteachers.
I can get copies of those papers by wirin' the agencies. You can slow me up by refusin' to let me have
them now, but I imagine the agencies will wonder
a lot about why a sheriff wants all the records on
the Merton high-school teachers."

Kline, frowning at him, seemed suddenly to realize that he was dealing with another adult and
not an insubordinate pupil. He said slowly:

"Of course I would always wish to aid the law
in every way possible. But I'm afraid I still don't
see the reason for your request."

"Don't you know that when anyone's killed it's
cust'mary to check up on all his—his associates?"

"Yes, I believe it is. But in this case—I understood that Mr. Mitchell—"

"I don't know who you been talking to. Not to
me, or you'd know I've got no notion of arrestin'
Jazz Mitchell."

"But I knew that he and Mr. Heath had some—
some words last night. I meant to speak to Mr.
Heath about it. I thought that he should have been
more mindful of his position here. And Mitchell
asked me if Mr. Heath had gone home and then
went out as if he intended following him."

"They walked the same way to get home. How well do you know Jazz—Gerald Mitchell, Mr. Kline?"

"Not very well. I met him last year when his orchestra played for a parent-teacher dance. And again this year when we were arranging for the music last night. He impressed me as being a very reckless and quick-tempered young man "

"I suppose he would. What would be your opinion of his cult'ral attainments?"

"His—his—what?"

"His cultural attainments," Rocky repeated solemnly, but his eyes twinkled because Kline was so obviously doubtful whether or not he had heard correctly.

"His— Oh, exactly. I'm afraid I wouldn't rate them very highly, Mr. Allan."

"Wouldn't expect him to be very well up on mythology, would you?"

"Mythology?" The principal's eyes narrowed a little. "No, I can't say that I would."

"Just offhand, would you expect very many people aroun' here to know the Greeks put a coin in the mouth of a dead person to pay his fare across the Styx?"

"I . . ." Kline picked up a pencil and began to draw meaningless figures on his desk blotter. "No, I certainly would not."

"I don't think very many people would remember a fact like that. They'd know who Charon was an' maybe that they did bury people with money. I remembered that much when the subject was mentioned, but not that the coin was put in the mouth. When I found Heath there was a coin in *his* mouth."

"Of course I know to what you are referring. I remember the conversation of which someone evidently has told you," Kline said, a gleam of cold anger in his deep-set eyes. "I wouldn't have supposed that anyone would relate a piece of mere— frivolous chatter "

"It don't sound quite so frivolous now, does it? It seems kind of stretching the long arm of coincidence out of joint to say it was nothin' but that. So you see why I want the records of your teachers."

"Yes, I see." Kline got up, opened a drawer of a small filing cabinet and from its neatly arranged contents took out a number of long double sheets with smaller papers clipped to them. "These are what you want. My own record is here too. I am not really supposed to have that, but a friend in one of the agencies made a copy for me."

"Have any of these people ever taught under you before this?"

"Miss Newman was with me for two years in the Willows High School. As there was a vacancy in her line here I asked her to fill it. We consider her a friend: she boarded with us when we had a larger house."

"You've been here two years, haven't you? This is beginning the third?"

"Yes. This is my twenty-second year of teaching," Kline said, "and in all that time nothing like this has ever occurred—not even a breath of scandal cast on any of my teachers."

Rocky seriously doubted that, but he said soothingly, "You aren't to blame if Mr. Heath got himself pretty well disliked by someone."

"I'm afraid he did—well, of course events have proved that. But I meant that I am afraid he was not of an entirely admirable character. I did not like him," Kline said with painful honesty. "No doubt you know why. I have taught too long not to know that the townspeople will gossip about their teachers."

"There's something more I wanted to ask you. Who was the last person to leave the building last night besides you?"

"Why—I think you and Mrs. Allan and Miss Towers were the last to leave. Miss Selby had gone out just ahead of you, you know. You left me in the gymnasium, but when I went in there I am certain there was no one in any other part of the building. I inspected all the rooms again after I'd

looked over the gymnasium and locked it, and I
saw no one then."

"Did that take you very long?"

"Perhaps fifteen or twenty minutes after you
left. I know that I reached home at two-forty, and
it takes me about three minutes to walk from here
to my home."

"The other teachers had all gone home?"

"They had," Mr. Kline said stiffly. "Miss Newman and Miss Atkins left with Mrs. Kline fairly
early. I told Mr. Fulton he could leave about
one-thirty because Mrs. Fulton had a headache
and wanted to go. I don't believe they left until
about ten minutes of two, though, because I saw
them again. I think Miss Whyte left when they
did. She had only a step to go."

"That's all—and thank you. I'll bring back these
papers soon as I can. An' I'll try not to bother any
of you any more than I have to. I suppose you'll
have to get someone to take Heath's place?"

"As soon as possible. I will have to wait until
tomorrow to telephone the agencies."

"I nearly forgot—but I'll have to look over
things in Heath's classroom. Which one is it?"

Kline frowned again but said, "The one nearest
this office on the left-hand side. You will find it
open: we don't lock the classroom doors."

When Rocky came back, empty-handed, from Heath's classroom to the main hall, Louise Whyte was just locking the big front double doors behind her. She said:

"I suppose you'd like to talk to me?"

"What makes you think so?"

"I thought you would. You've been talking to Mr. Kline. Would you mind coming into the domestic-science rooms? I have some work to do there. . . . Checking over dishes and silverware," she explained when they were in her classroom. "Whenever the P.T.A. uses the kitchen Mr. Kline always wants me to be certain none of them have tried to collect any of our valuable belongings."

"What did you think I wanted to ask you?" Rocky persisted.

"Any number of things. I know Jazz Mitchell well enough that I don't think he killed Paul Heath. If he didn't—we're all in the picture, aren't we? Besides, you might happen to know if any of us had known Paul before. It just happens," Louise said calmly, "that I had."

"Yeah? You'd taught the same place?"

"No. We were born and brought up in the same town: Santa Maria. It's a very pretty town fairly near Santa Barbara. It's large enough that you don't know everyone in town, but I did go to school with Paul Heath."

Rocky sat down on the edge of a kitchen table. "Tell me about him," he said.

"There isn't much to tell. He must have been about thirty-one or two. I'm thirty myself. His father ran away with another woman, and his mother got a divorce and married a well-to-do grocer. They sent him to Southern Cal and I went to California, so we didn't see anything more of each other until this year."

"Vacations?" Rocky suggested.

Louise hesitated. "Well, this sounds very snobbish," she said finally, "but you know there are social classes in all towns. The Heaths—or Woodys—weren't in the same one that we were. I hardly ever met Paul Heath—socially. Then, he didn't spend any more of his vacation time at home than he had to. The only time I ever saw him to talk to him in the summer was this last vacation. He spent two or three weeks at home I think."

"How'd you happen to talk to him this time?"

"Because the local paper printed an item about my coming up here to teach, and he came to call and tell me about the town. Very nice of him," Louise said unenthusiastically.

"What was his reputation aroun' home?"

"Well, his father had always been known as a chaser, and everyone said that Paul was just like his father. He left a trail of broken hearts behind him in his high-school days. I admired him from afar," Louise said casually, "but I got over that when we were older and met once or twice."

"Did he have any serious affairs?"

"Not that I know of—in Santa Maria."

"Weren't you in the habit of callin' each other by your first names? Doesn't anyone know you'd known each other before?"

"Oh, so far as names are concerned, I must be formal even with Nancy in school hours. But Paul and I had a slight disagreement almost at once. A little matter of who should take over the worst study hall on the schedule. I had to do it while he sat in the office while Mr. Kline was teaching and tried to read the private papers in the files. I really needed the time to keep things in order here, so I made a few sarcastic remarks which were returned in kind.

"So no one would have guessed we were old schoolmates by our manner toward each other after that. Mr. Kline must have known we came from the same town. It never occurred to me to ask if anyone else knew. I suppose they all know that the more I saw of Paul Heath the less I liked him."

"Any special reason?"

"I believe in supporting my principal," Louise said definitely. "And I don't like lady-killers or people who don't care what methods they use to get what they want. But I haven't any specific incident in mind to back up that statement."

"I might guess at one or two. Do you happen to know where Heath spent the rest of last summer vacation?"

"He said he was going to summer session at Berkeley. I think that was just an excuse to keep from having to visit his mother any longer. I was in Berkeley later on myself and I didn't see him. But I didn't go to summer session. Miss Newman may have run across him, but she also very easily may not."

Rocky gave her time to count a stack of saucers and himself to frame a cautious question: "Did you ever see Heath wear—or carry—any particular kind of—of charm?"

"Charm? What do you mean, something like a rabbit's foot?"

Rocky laughed. "No; not that. I've seen men wear funny things on their watch chains: gold nuggets or old gold pieces or some little thing they thought was lucky. . . ."

"I don't think he ever wore a watch chain. No, I never saw anything of that sort attached to him. Though of course," Louise added shrewdly, "you aren't being at all definite. On purpose, I suppose. Still, I think anyone could tell you he never carried any sort of odd token where it could be seen."

"You didn't stay till the last dance last night?"

"I stayed until people were out of here and the place was in order. By that time I was damn good and ready to go home. About all of the dance I saw was ham sandwiches and cake and coffee." Louise stopped to count a pile of nickel-plated knives and checked against a typewritten inventory. "The dear ladies were supposed to do all the work, but I was requested to supervise operations. I went home about ten of two, just ahead of the Fultons."

"You didn't happen to hear Mr. Kline when he went by, did you?"

"I don't know what time he left here. But I'd had too much coffee to go to sleep at once. I heard Mrs. Barker come in. She didn't look in on me," Louise said with an odd little smile. "I have the front bedroom with an outside door onto the porch. I heard a lot of people going home; then things quieted down, and just as I was going to sleep I heard someone pass by—someone alone. That's the best I can do for you."

"It's good enough. By the way, where does Miss Atkins live?"

"At Mrs. Fenners'. But you won't find her there right now. She's taken her car and gone somewhere—to Reno, I suppose."

"All alone?"

"She often does when she can't get anyone to go with her. Don't worry: she'll be back. She left the dance early anyway."

"She looked to be havin' a good time when I noticed her."

Louise chuckled. "Miriam was suffering from an embarrassment of young men, not the lack of them. She absentmindedly promised three of them that they could see her home, so she decided to avoid trouble by not waiting for any of them. Sundays in town bore Miriam. So do they all of us, but Miriam doesn't even do her own washing and ironing, and she never darns a stocking, so she's simply got to go places."

Rocky laughed and started toward the door, but Louise said, frowning over the list in her hand, "Mr. Allan, if you want to check up on me in Santa Maria, please don't do it through my parents. I suppose you wouldn't."

"I wouldn't—at all."

"You don't think you need to now, but you might find later on that you did. The chief of police has been there for years, and he can keep his mouth shut. My father is pretty old and has been sick for quite a while. I don't suppose he'll ever get any better," Louise said stoically. "Some men simply can't throw off the shock of changed circumstances. . . . But I wouldn't want him or my mother to be worried."

"I don't see any reason why they should be, or your police chief either. I'm glad you mentioned him because I might have to check up on Heath. Where is the Werners' house—where Miss Newman lives? They're new people in town—"

"It's one street over from this one. I've forgotten its name, if it has one."

"The same street Paul Heath lived on?"

"Yes; a corner house. About—well, about half a block from where Paul lives—lived."

CHAPTER NINE
"I SAW A LIGHT FLASH ON"

The house in which the Werners lived was not only just half a block from the cabin where Heath had died: its rear yard touched the same alley that ran back of Ma Jenkins' boardinghouse. Rocky whistled when he realized that; muttered, "Talk about bein' centrally located," and knocked on the front door.

Mrs. Werner, a round little woman shining with soap and starch, volunteered to "call schoolteacher." She did call, very loudly, from the foot of the stairs and then came back into the parlor and dusted the tables with her apron. Rocky's polite remarks about the weather were received with smiling bobs of a flaxen head, and when Miss Newman appeared, Mrs. Werner said, "Cake in oven," and left them alone.

"You wanted to see me?" Miss Newman asked.

Rocky had considerably revised his youthful ideas regarding teachers since knowing Nancy and meeting Louise Whyte, but he felt very much at home with Miss Newman. He expected at any moment to hear her say, "But why haven't you studied your lesson?"

He said hastily, "I did. I've been checking up on the times all of you got home last night. This mornin', I should say. I've been told you came home fairly early with Mrs. Kline and Miss Atkins."

"Yes, we left quite early. A little after one o'clock, I think." Miss Newman's tone said, "And what business is that of yours, my good man?"

"Haven't you been downtown this morning? Hasn't anyone told you—"

"I heard that Miss Selby was killed last night. But as I hardly knew the girl—"

"We didn't find Paul Heath till later on in the mornin'. But he was probably killed first. In that little cabin where he lived. Funny thing," Rocky said deliberately, "but there'd been an old coin stuck in his mouth."

"In his— No, I hadn't heard," Miss Newman said steadily. "I went downtown quite early and haven't been out of the house since then. I've been upstairs in my room, and Mrs. Werner is not well enough acquainted with her neighbors to have news carried to her immediately."

"Is your room a front or back one?"

"It is a back room. I can look down on the corner of the boardinghouse on the next street. Its back corner, I mean. I suppose the room there would be Miss Selby's. She spoke at Mrs. Kline's yesterday of sleeping on the ground floor with her windows open. Whenever I have glanced down there in the mornings the windows have been open."

Eleanor and Nancy had slipped up on that one, Rocky thought; though of course Eleanor would have remembered sometime to tell him about it. He said curiously:

"Did you hear any commotion down there early this mornin'?"

"I'm afraid I didn't. I am not accustomed to late hours, so I slept soundly once I was able to sleep."

"What time *did* you go to sleep?"

"I really don't know. It seemed a long time to me. But I didn't hear anything that— No; wait!" Miss Newman's even voice quickened slightly. "I had forgotten. I did doze off, but I didn't sleep soundly and my head began to ache. I got up and found some aspirin and took one. I was not entirely awake, Mr. Allan—you understand that? I did look at my watch, and I think it was four o'clock. I am quite ready to admit that I might have been mistaken in that or that I only imagined that for an instant—when I passed my window after I had turned my own lights off—I saw a light flash on and off in that other house."

"In Clarice's room, that would be? Was it like the lights in the room had been put on and off?"

"N-no—no, I don't think so. The light—if my recollections of it can be trusted—was not bright enough for that. It was more the type of light that a flashlight would produce. That seems very odd—now. Could someone have been searching for something?"

Rocky looked at Miss Newman's smooth hands, folded precisely in her blue silk lap. "Where did you leave Mrs. Kline and Miss Atkins last night?"

"We left Mrs. Kline at the first cross street after leaving the high school. Their house is on the corner there. Miriam left me here. She lives on this block on the other side of the street."

"I know where the Fenner place is. Had you known Mr. Heath before he came here, Miss Newman?"

"No. I had taught under Mr. Kline before. You know that? You've talked to Mr. Kline? Did you tell him what you have told me about the—the circumstances of Mr. Heath's death?"

"Yes. He admitted he remembers a certain conversation you all had about Greek costumes—and customs."

"I remember it too, of course. I am sorry I said what I did if you think the information I gave was—had any influence upon anyone. I don't see how that is possible unless the conversation were repeated elsewhere. Placing a coin in Mr. Heath's mouth seems hardly the action of a normal person."

"Do you think very many people know as much about things like that as you do?"

"I'm afraid not. I'm often amazed at the general ignorance regarding simple facts of mythology. The subject is not even taught in high school as it used to be. Neither is the *Aeneid* read by very many people. There is a reference in the *Aeneid,*" Miss Newman added, "to that custom of burying the dead with the necessary money for their fare across the Styx. The coin you spoke of was not by any chance Greek?"

"I don't imagine there's many of them floatin' around. No, it wasn't, though it was plenty old enough. Do you know someone who owns some Greek coins?"

"No; at least, no one who lives here. But I must say, Mr. Allan, that one fragment of conversation seems to me a rather poor excuse for investigating the movements of an entire faculty."

"You're human beings, aren't you? A good education ain't necessarily a lifelong safeguard against a desire to kill someone. I understand," Rocky said, "that you weren't exactly just one big happy family—"

"Miss Towers is very indiscreet, and I consider her conduct very unprofessional!"

"I didn't say Nancy had been talkin' to me. I can nose aroun' town and pick up all sorts of interestin' information. I haven't—yet. Mr. Kline admits he didn't consider Heath exactly an admirable character."

"If Mr. Kline admitted that—no doubt he had his own reasons for doing so. I am quite willing to be guided by him. But I really have nothing to tell you, and under no circumstances would I care to discuss the foibles of my colleagues."

"There's a little contradiction between the first and last of that sentence, isn't there? But I don't expect you to tell me anything along that line. You and Mr. Kline are the only ones I've told about that coin. I didn't warn him to keep still—"

"You most certainly did not need to! Mr. Kline's discretion—"

"I thought it could be relied on," Rocky said affably. "Especially in this case. It'd have a very bad effect on the school if people began wonderin' which of you killed Heath, and they might, if they knew everything. But I won't keep you any longer, Miss Newman. . . ."

He stopped at the back corner of Ma Jenkins' boardinghouse, looked up at the house he had just left and decided that Miss Newman might easily enough have seen a light in Clarice's room if she had been looking down from her own. Then he walked on to the next cross street and along that to the house the Fultons rented.

Either Mrs. Fulton was a superlatively bad housekeeper or someone had let an active and destructive pup loose in her living room. She did not appear in the least embarrassed by the disorder but set a chair on its legs again and told Rocky to sit down. She swept a tangle of blankets from the chesterfield to the floor and looked hopefully into a box that should have contained cigarettes.

Mrs. Kline had stood up when Rocky entered the room and said that she "must run along," but somehow when he sat down she was still there, perched uneasily on the edge of a big chair. Mrs. Fulton said wearily:

"You might as well stay. Mr. Allan probably wants to talk to you too. And I haven't any secrets after the way I've babbled to you already."

Mrs. Kline murmured deprecatingly and bent to pick up the cigarette stubs that had spilled out of an overturned smoking stand. She smiled distressfully at a litter of newspapers on the floor and said:

"I just ran in to talk to Gertrude for a while. Mr. Kline was so shocked! He just wouldn't talk at all. He went downtown for the mail and he heard—and then he saw Dr. Miller. That poor Miss Selby! She was such a nice girl, and just yesterday—"

"Just yesterday she was bidding four no-trump with only queen high," Mrs. Fulton drawled. "There don't seem to be any cigarettes here, Mr. Allan. I always forget to get them. Then Leonard tears up the house looking for a package that should be somewhere and never is. Have you— Thanks."

Mrs. Kline shook her head at Rocky's polite gesture. "No; Hamilton doesn't approve of smoking, though I tell him that's for everyone to decide for themselves. Of course Miss Selby did use too much lipstick—"

"Let's not talk about that," Mrs. Fulton said fretfully. "I know how I look without my makeup on."

Rocky felt that the conversation was escaping his control and grabbed at it hastily before it roamed any farther afield. "What time did you-all get home last night, Mrs. Fulton?"

"So that's it? Oh, sometime around two. I was bored to extinction, so I manufactured a headache, but then Paul Heath asked me to dance and

I did. That was the last dance but one, and Leonard scowled so much that I didn't finish it out. He was coming to a slow boil."

"Why?"

Mrs. Fulton flicked the ash from her cigarette onto the floor. "I must get hold of that Italian woman to give this place a good cleaning. Oh, because Paul had danced with me."

"Mr. Heath was only being polite," Mrs. Kline said quickly.

"That's not very complimentary to me. Well, as a matter of fact, it was mostly a duty dance. But he did like to see Leonard fume. Also, he was pretty mad at Nancy Towers, so he wanted to take it out on someone else. The biter bit," Mrs. Fulton said maliciously.

"I'm afraid," Mrs. Kline said, "that Gertrude's nerves are a little on edge. Well, I'm sure I feel very nervous myself. Like I was getting one of my headaches. I don't know when such a thing has ever happened in all the time Hamilton's been teaching. Of course you can't blame poor Mr. Heath. . . ."

"I guess people are quite often to blame for getting themselves killed. If they weren't just plain louses no one would kill them."

"You think Heath came under that class'fication?" Rocky asked.

"I guess you know he did by this time. Oh, there's lots like him. Every time a new woman came along he put his nose up like a dog scenting game. The people in town couldn't have realized that, or there wouldn't have been any talk about his being principal."

Mrs. Kline winced. "He wouldn't ever have been, Gertrude. Everyone knows what a good administrator Mr. Kline is, and he didn't take Mr. Heath seriously."

She didn't really smile all the time, Rocky decided. But you thought she did because the corners of her mouth were permanently turned up. At that, she must have been good-looking enough when she was younger: before hair and eyes were dulled and what must have been a slim young figure became only ungracefully flat.

"Well, he was making a damn good try at it," Mrs. Fulton insisted. She held out her hand for another cigarette. Rocky gave it to her, looking at the blankets on the floor. He decided that diplomacy was wasted on Mrs. Fulton in her present mood.

"Did either of you go out again after you'd got home from the dance?"

"Leonard went out and walked around the block about—well, we couldn't have been at it more than twenty minutes. About two-twenty, probably. He came back in five minutes. I heard him. I didn't see him."

"Why not?"

"I'd locked the bedroom door on him and thrown some covers out here. He didn't break the door in—this time."

"Gertrude! Why do you want to joke like that?"

"I'm not joking, Mrs. Kline." Mrs. Fulton smoothed a bruise on her white upper arm. "He did break one in last year. We had an awful time explaining it when we moved. The truth is that Leonard and I fight like hell over so often. And I mean *fight.*"

Rocky looked about the room, his glance lingering on the overturned smoking stand. "It must be kind of hard on the furniture," he suggested.

Unexpectedly Mrs. Fulton laughed. "It's grand. There is nothing more satisfying than to slam a few things on the floor. Leonard and I always get along very well for quite a while after we've had a good row. For one thing, I have some respect for him after he's hit me—well, not that he ever really hit me," Gertrude Fulton added thoughtfully. "Not what you'd call really hitting."

Rocky could not help laughing, though the idea that people like the Fultons threw furniture at each other was a rather startling one. Still, there were times when you could see why it would be a relief to sock a woman on the jaw, and he was willing to bet that Gertrude Fulton could very easily rouse that urge in a man.

"But you didn't make up last night?" he said.

"Not for a while. I locked the door on him, and I guess he went to sleep for a while and woke up in a forgiving mood, so he started hammering on the door and I let him in. I was cold. I suppose," Mrs. Fulton said, disregarding Mrs. Kline's magenta flush, "you'd say we made up."

"Well—where is he now?"

"Oh, we were eating breakfast—very peacefully, though I did burn the toast—when Mr. Kline came by with the glad news. That upset Leonard quite a bit, and when Mrs. Kline came up he said he had work to do in the shop. You must just have missed him if you've been at the high school. Of course the shop is at one side of it.

"I wouldn't be telling you all this if Leonard could ever lie worth a cent," Mrs. Fulton added. "But he can't, and he has such a hangdog expression when he tries that I don't think it would make a very good impression on you. I should have cleaned up this room: anyone with any sense could see someone slept here last night."

"All young couples have these little disagreements," Mrs. Kline offered brightly. "You should remember the two big bears—bear and forbear."

Rocky thought he heard Mrs. Fulton mutter, "Dear God!" but aloud she said patiently enough, "We aren't exactly a young couple after eight years of storm and strife."

"Hamilton and I have been married eighteen years, and I've never been away from him but one time."

"Well, believe me, if Leonard didn't control the purse strings I'd skip out of here as often as our dear friend, Mrs. Jordan. If he'd only get a school in some town of decent size. . . ."

Again Rocky brought the conversation up with a jerk. "What time did you get home, Mrs. Kline?"

"Oh, it was just about ten minutes after one. I looked at the clock and decided it wasn't worth while going to bed before Hamilton came home. I knew he'd be home about two-thirty, and I don't like to be waked up. I guess he was a little later than that but not much."

"About two-forty, he said."

"Then that's right. He's always very exact about things like that—or anything."

"Funny; I dreamed about a wedding last night," Mrs. Fulton said abruptly. "Doesn't that mean something? 'Dream of a wedding—'"

"'Attend a funeral,'" Mrs. Kline said. "Not that I suppose we will.—Attend a funeral, I mean."

Rocky got up to go but stopped at the door. "Were you expectin' me to come aroun' here, Mrs. Fulton?" he asked.

"I was hoping it wouldn't occur to you to do it, but it evidently did. It would have been nice if you'd just gone out and arrested young Mitchell. But since you didn't—I mean, since you're evidently making a real investigation of things—of course we'd be the first people you'd investigate. Are you going to talk to Leonard? Well, please don't tell him all I said. He wouldn't think some of it was funny."

Rocky silently agreed with this statement, but when he found Fulton smoking in the manual-training shop the man was very nearly as frank as his wife had been.

"Gertrude and I quarreled last night. It's been coming on for quite a while. These damn dissatisfied women! Can I help it if I have to teach in the sticks? Oh, she's a good scout most of the time, in spite of the way she talks, but the place gets on her nerves. Well, we got home about two, but she can't say I was in the house after two-twenty because she was in the bedroom and I went out and walked around the block "

"Meet anyone?"

"Not a soul. I saw some people farther down on our street evidently going downtown. I didn't see anyone on the street where Heath lives. But I didn't get any nearer than a block and a half to his place. I didn't go up that street: I went down it, toward town. I mean, toward Main Street. And I never even looked up the street toward Heath's place. Then I came back and slept in the front room for a while. Gertrude was in the house then, all right. I could hear her moving around. That what you want to know?"

"Some of it. Did you know Heath before you came here?"

"A little. We went to the same university— Southern California. It's a big place, but we happened to meet. Never could go him," Fulton said, shooting out his lower lip to bite at his mustache. "I played football, and he played in the band. Still, that's no reason. He never could leave other fellows' girls alone. . . ."

"Or their wives?" Rocky suggested.

Fulton glared at him and then smiled wryly. "Well, you'd know town talk. Everyone did talk when I kicked Heath out at Christmastime last year. He'd been rooming with us before that, and we'd gotten along pretty well. But I had to be up here at night a lot coaching basketball, and I decided Gertrude was finding him too entertaining. Not a thing wrong, but she was bored, and she's not above flirting with a good-looking man—and you know how he was.

"Then there was the way he always tried to gum up things at the high school and throw the blame on Kline. He was clever at it: I don't understand how he did it. Well; little things like telling the kids all unpopular rules were 'Mr. Kline's orders' with a kind of sympathetic smile. Then they'd go home and tell their folks Heath was a swell guy."

"You run into that kind of skullduggery in any kind of work," Rocky said. "There was an assistant yardmaster we had here once that was like that."

"A fellow can talk to you," Fulton said gratefully. "I get along with Kline, but we haven't much in common. I'm not strong on brains: had a hell of a time getting through college. I'm a good coach, and I can work with my hands. If the kids act up I slap them down, and they like it. I didn't kill Heath though. Not the way he was killed. I get sick at the sight of blood."

He smiled sheepishly. "I don't admit that if I can help it, but it's the truth, and a lot of people could tell you so. Oh, not just a nose bleed, but a lot of blood—and from what I've heard about Heath—"

"Yes; there was," Rocky said briefly. "Do you think Heath ever had any chance gettin' Kline's job?"

"Only God and a board of school trustees know what they *might* do. N-no, I don't think so, but he could have got them both fired. I don't suppose he'd have cared if he did. Kline shouldn't worry, but of course he's getting on, and there are a lot more competent principals than there are schools for them. He lost his savings in a bank failure a few years ago."

Fulton stopped, his fair skin reddening. "I shouldn't have told you that. Didn't mean to. I guess there's no doubt Kline would always get another job."

"Some kind of one. A man like him don't like to step down. You folks seem to be about evenly divided. Some of you want to know by what right I dare check up on you, an' the rest of you just take it for granted."

"Oh! Well, I supposed you'd check up on us. Be a fool if you didn't. I know Kline acted like he thought the whole thing was just a regrettable happening that would disorganize classes tomorrow morning. He'd heard people saying maybe Jazz Mitchell did it. And a lot that said they didn't think so. Well, I like Mitchell. I've met him quite a few times. I can get along with the men in this town all right," Fulton said complacently. "I wish Gertrude would meet a few women she liked. . . . Of course, as Kline said: Where does Miss Selby come into it? She and Heath were thick enough that he probably told her too much for her own good.

"I've probably talked like a fool to you, telling you so much. A fellow has to let off steam sometimes. Someway, I don't think you'll spread it around unless you have to. In that case you could dig up all I've told you without needing to talk to me to find it out. Maybe you'll count it a point in my favor that I've saved you a little trouble. . . ."

CHAPTER TEN
JAZZ PUTS ON HIS HAT

Tom Wright's face more than ever suggested that of a horse as he blew his lips out in a sound expressive of disgust. "And that's all you're going to tell me, Rocky?"

"What else did you want to know?"

"You haven't said anything except that Heath was found in the cabin he rented from Mrs. Pratt. People like details—preferably gory ones."

"You can add all the gore you want to." Rocky looked at his hands. He had scrubbed them two or three times, but where his fingertips had been stained red they still did not feel clean. "I happen not to want anyone to know just exactly how he was lyin' and how the room looked."

Wright lifted his shoulders resignedly. "O.K. Anything else?"

"Who was king of England about 1575?"

"Damned if I know. What's that got to do with things? Let's see. . . . 1575. . . ."

Rocky laughed. "It wasn't a king. I remember now: it would have to be Queen Elizabeth. For your information, 1575 is not the right date."

"What information? Not the right date for what?"

"Well—maybe I might tell you. . . ."

"While you're making up your mind whether you will tell me whatever it is, shall I say you expect to make an arrest shortly?"

"Hell no! Because I don't."

"That isn't supposed to make any difference. What do you think of Dud's idea?"

"Has he got one?"

"He's talking about homicidal maniacs and some Negro who carries a knife around with him."

"You know," Rocky said slowly, "that's a swell idea. I hope Dud keeps right on talking. I'd forgot all about this Buck Harvey in the excitement. We're keepin' our eyes open for him. He's wanted in Butte County for killin' Burns. The special agent, you know. An' he's wanted over in Utah for murder."

"Off the record, do you think he's in this part of the country?"

"Not to be quoted: I don't. But I wouldn't mind at all if people thought he was."

"I get you. When Fred Haynes gets back he'll probably be up here poking his nose into things—"

"An' yowling for an arrest."

"Inevitably. Now, what is it you're going to tell me about 1575 and Queen Elizabeth?"

"It's your own fault I'm not goin' to tell you after all," Rocky said with a grin. "I was, but when you mentioned that Dud has ideas I decided not to. As far as Clarice's death is concerned, you can hint delicately that her murder is linked up with Heath's. She was probably killed about 4 a.m., if that's any good to you. An' Heath was killed earlier."

"Do you know that for a fact?"

"I will when I talk to Miller again. You can check up on that tomorrow. I called up Sloane just now, and he won't be here till in the mornin'. But what I'm getting at: I'd like you to play up the idea that Clarice's murder wasn't any crime of passion but that she was killed because she knew too much."

"What?"

"You're a newspaperman: you ought to know how to suggest I know that, even if I don't. When we get the time of Heath's death pretty well fixed I can do better. You see, Clarice was the last one to go home from the dance except for Kline and Eleanor, Nancy and me. We went in the opposite direction from Clarice, an' Heath and Kline was quite a bit later leavin' than we were.

"I haven't got the times all correct yet so I won't bother you with 'em, but it does look to me like she may have met whoever it was that killed Heath just comin' away from his place. Or seen someone goin' in there. Of course that might apply to Jazz as well as anyone else, so I don't want it printed for a while."

"I hope you realize what a good guy I am," Wright said. "Well, I'll have enough to more than cover the front page anyway. Maybe I won't have to fill in with cute little items about how Mary Jane Jones entertained all her little friends with a party on her seventh birthday. That guy Leaman has been shooting off his mouth around town most of the day."

"I can't stop him, can I?" Rocky stretched his long legs out in front of him and sighed. "I'm going to get a car from Art Finley at the garage. I'm going to have to hire one permanently for the times I come up here in the plane anyway. I've been all over town three or four times today, and I'm tired."

"Should think you would be. There's Miller driving up in front of the town hall now. Probably looking for you. . . ."

"Well, we did a good job of it, Jordan and I together," Miller said. "Here; get in and I'll take you wherever you want to go."

"All right." Rocky got into the car. "When you've finished what you've got to tell me."

"Well, Jordan helped me, and whatever his faults, he knows his business. Of course we knew when Heath had eaten last. Jordan's got a pretty good layout rigged up, and we got through it all right. We don't want to fix the time too close, but he was probably killed about two-fifteen. You know he wasn't killed before two, and he might have been killed as late as two-thirty or thirty-five, but Jordan doesn't think so."

"Do you think the same kind of knife was used there as with Clarice?"

"Yes. It may not have been the same knife, you know. We couldn't swear to that, but it certainly was the same kind of knife. Of course Clarice was stabbed while she was lying down: a straight blow. Heath was evidently standing up when he was struck, and the blow took more of a downward course. Well, most people will strike down, you know."

"Mexicans usually aim to strike up and gut a fellow," Rocky said irrelevantly. "I guess you're right. Unless you were pretty short and had to strike up."

"This person wasn't, then. I couldn't say how tall he might have been from the location of the wound. Maybe some experts could."

"Would you say whoever handled the knife was lucky—to kill with one blow?"

"Not particularly. And no expert knowledge required, if that's what you mean. Clarice was stabbed beneath the breastbone, you know. She didn't die instantly, but too soon to make any fuss over it. They got Heath just under the heart. I won't bother you with the technical details. He fell and was probably stunned by that."

"Which reminds me again," Rocky said, "to tell you to keep your mouth shut on all details. I'm not puttin' out any more 'n I can help. I'd like you particularly to keep still about me findin' that coin in Heath's mouth."

Miller's china-blue eyes sparkled. "You mean you might be able to trick somebody into an admission about that when only one or two people are supposed to know about it? Sure, I'll keep still. But I supposed I'd have to tell about it at the inquest tomorrow."

"We'll see. I'll talk to Sloane. I don't suppose Jordan mentioned where he was last night?"

"He did, in a very offhand way. He was playing poker with Pat Healy and a gang of the boys."

"Then why was he so upset about Clarice's death?"

"Bad publicity for the hospital. And he really liked the girl. Besides—" Miller chuckled—"I suppose he saw right away he'd have to establish an alibi. He feels like it's a little bit beneath his dignity to have been playing poker with the town's leading bootlegger."

"Late lamented," Rocky corrected.

"Well, yes—with the town's late-lamented leading bootlegger and his friends. I suppose you've heard Jordan likes cards—likes to gamble, for that matter. He said he didn't care to go to the dance when his wife was out of town and didn't know what else to do with himself."

"He probably told Pat Healy to keep still about it. I've heard Mrs. Jordan don't like him to play cards with that bunch. Pat didn't mention Jordan being there last night when he talked to Dud. Well, I'm glad he was, because now I don't have to talk to him. I always felt like it would be just a waste of time—and probably tryin' to both our tempers."

"Well, I've got to get back to the hospital. Where do you want me to take you?"

"I've got plenty to do at home but— What time is it? Nearly five? I wonder if Miss Atkins would be home yet."

Rocky regretted mentioning the girl's name as soon as he had said it, for Miller was immediately and persistently interested.

"Miriam Atkins? You know, she and Heath did seem to have a case on each other when they first came here last year. It apparently didn't last long. I could go for that girl myself, but she won't give me a tumble."

"I've got nothing against her, but I've got to check up on all the people who knew Heath, and she happened to be gone earlier in the day."

"To Reno?" Miller accented the two words so peculiarly that Rocky looked at him sharply.

"Yes. Why?"

"She certainly does go over there an awful lot. I'll—well, I'll tell you something funny. I said I could go for her, and I wanted to take her over there to a show once or twice, but she never would go. That's all right, but then I'd hear she'd gone off there by herself. Sometimes she'd have someone with her, but not very often. Well, one time I was going over there in the evening and I said to Miss Towers I'd like to look her friend up and try my luck again.

"Just joking, you know, because I knew she'd gone over earlier. Miss Towers laughed and said Miriam always stayed at the Riverside. I looked for her there and then at the Golden, and she wasn't registered at either place. So I got kind of curious, and I went to all the hotels any girl by herself would be apt to stay at. And I never did find her."

"Well?" Rocky liked Miller, but he thought the doctor would be an awful gossip by the time he was forty. Perhaps it came from having so many women patients. "Maybe she has friends over there. Ain't her life out of school hours her own affair?"

"To me. But probably not to you right now. Or to her board of trustees, I suppose. But you're the only one I ever mentioned this to. She told me she didn't have any friends in Reno. But the reason I happened to think about it right now is because Heath was in Reno himself that same week end."

"Oh! Yes, that is kind of—interestin'. Well, somehow I don't imagine she's back yet, so you can take me over home an', if you don't mind waitin' one minute, bring me back to Jazz's place."

Eleanor said, "Yes, I'll have supper ready by the time you can get back to eat it. Nancy has gone home, and I don't expect her to come back, so why don't you bring Jazz with you? You can't expect him to sit there and think things over forever."

"I'll try to bring him," Rocky promised. "It's a good idea, but I don't know if he'll come."

Jazz was just buttoning his coat and putting on his hat in a spotlessly clean parlor bedroom. That was a bad sign: Jazz, like Rocky, wore a hat

only on very special occasions. Even more omi-
nous were the two white streaks along the sides of
his nostrils.

"Goin' somewheres?" Rocky said casually.

"I am going," Jazz said, "to settle accounts with
that dirty bastard who's been shooting his mouth
off all over town—"

"Leaman? Was he in here?"

"No, but Art Finley took it on himself to come
in and tell me all Leaman has been saying. Well, if
he'd kept his dirty tongue off Nancy, I'd swallow
the rest of it. But I won't take that."

"If you beat up on Leaman people will say there
must be some truth in what he's sayin'."

"Yeah? You'd figure it out that way if it was
Eleanor he was talking about, wouldn't you? You'd
do just what I'm going to do."

"Eleanor wants you to come over to supper,"
Rocky said tactfully. "You'll probably feel better
after you've had something to eat."

"Eat? Did you ever try to eat when you felt like
everything inside of you was up in your throat
trying to choke you? I'm going! And if you want
to throw me in the can afterward, it will be worth
it!"

Rocky sighed and stepped between Jazz and the
door. "I hate to do this, but you ain't goin' any
place. You'll stay right here an' think it over."

He ducked hastily. Jazz had a swell left hook, and this one missed his jaw by about half an inch. He said, "You're a damn fool to—tackle a guy weighs thirty pounds—more 'n you—do," and felt one corner of his mouth begin to bleed.

That was a little too much. Rocky whirled Jazz around and sank his fist squarely in his stomach. Jazz grunted and turned a sickly green, shook his head dizzily and split the skin over Rocky's cheekbone with another hard left.

"All right," Rocky said breathlessly, "you asked for it," and let him have it full on the point of the chin.

He looked for an instant at the huddle on the floor that was Jazz, walked out to the kitchen and wet a handkerchief at the faucet before he drew a glassful of water and, returning to the front room, threw the water in Jazz's face.

"Maybe that'll cool your hot head a little," he remarked, picking him up and putting him on a chair.

Jazz coughed, opened his eyes and closed them again. "Christ, my jaw aches!"

"It ought to," Rocky said unsympathetically. He dabbed at his cut lip with his dampened handkerchief. "An' you ought to be right thankful I pulled that punch some, or you'd still be hearin' the birdies sing."

"You've got a kick like a mule in that right of yours—not that anyone needs to tell you so. You're no modest violet," Jazz said. "Anyway, I was too mad to cover up."

"Wide open. Well, you made me look pretty, an' that bum wrist of yours . . ."

Jazz grinned wanly. "There's nothing wrong with my wrist any more. It would have been good enough to lick Leaman with. Well, I can see reason now. I'll try to leave him alone—till I get another brain storm. How do you know I didn't kill Heath in a fit like that?"

"With a knife? I can imagine you lickin' the pants off him, but that's as far as my imagination will take me. You ought to know what other people will say if you start runnin' around town giving them a sample of that temper of yours. I'd like to hit Leaman on the snoot myself. Is my cheek bleedin'?"

"Not now. Tell Eleanor you walked into a door, will you? She'll—she won't like that and—I guess I won't go with you anyway."

"I guess you will. Nancy isn't there, if that's what you're thinkin' about. By the way, when was the last time you really talked to Nancy?"

"At the dance last night, if you want to call that talking. All we did was fight. Before that? Last Monday, I guess. That was when we talked about the dance and having supper together. Thursday night I got a snippy little note—"

"That's all I wanted to know: that she never had a chance to repeat a conversation to you that happened Tuesday. Why," Rocky said, grinning, "did you bother to put on a hat to go see Leaman?"

"Damned if I know. To make it more formal, I guess. Where is my hat?" Jazz got up and picked it off the floor. "I'll go with you, and it's damned good of you—and Eleanor. Hell! I don't—"

"You'd better wash your face first," Rocky said hastily.

Jazz looked at him and smiled crookedly. "I guess I had," he agreed. "I'll be with you in a minute."

Every one of the half-dozen men they met on the street spoke or nodded very cordially. Perhaps Jazz thought they were too markedly offhand with their "Hi-ya! How's tricks?" Because of a certain nervously quick grace of movement he had often been credited with a "swaggering walk." At this moment such a statement would have been well justified. But he dropped his pose of bravado when they reached Mariposa Street and Eleanor met them at the front door of the house.

"I'm so glad you came, Jazz. And supper is almost ready. But—but Nancy just came back to get a purse she left here. I don't know what you want to do. She doesn't know you're here, and I can shoo her out the back door."

Jazz's face went blank. "Do you think she'd rather have it that way? It'd probably be the best thing "

"No; she wanted to see you, and we told her she couldn't start people talking by going over to your place. And you needn't glare at me like that, Rocky. He might as well know the truth."

"Yes, and as long as she's here, he might as well talk to her. I don't suppose it matters, and I'm not too certain she won't get a brain storm herself and pay no attention to what we said. So if Jazz has no objections—"

"None at all," Jazz said politely.

Eleanor put one hand impulsively over his. "Please don't be like that, Jazz. You can't keep her out of it entirely, you know. And if your positions were reversed you'd want to see her. She hates to have anyone think she'd run out on her friends when they get in—in—"

"A jack pot? Sure, I know. I suppose I would feel the same way. Where is she?"

"In the kitchen. But I have to look after things in there so I'll send her out to you. Sit down."

Jazz did not sit down: he thrust his hands rigidly into his pockets and was standing by the window when Nancy came in. He said, "Well?" uncompromisingly.

"Well—really!" Nancy's golden-brown eyes sparkled dangerously. "You act as if I were some sort of pursuing female who'd been chasing you all over town and finally caught up with you!"

"I didn't mean to," Jazz said with an unwilling smile. "But what do you expect me to do? Go on from where we left off? It can't be done."

"I don't see why not. You haven't done anything."

"Sure of that?"

"Yes, I am sure!"

"That's— Of course I like to hear you say that. . . ."

"You don't sound as if it sent you into spasms of joy."

"I don't—I don't like to have to be grateful to you for telling me I didn't kill Heath or Clarice. I suppose you can't understand that."

"Yes, I think I can," Nancy said slowly. "You don't like to be grateful to anybody for anything and particularly to me. Why don't you resent Rocky's championship, then?"

"That's different. Oh, I can't explain how. But he doesn't—pity me."

"Neither do I! Not one damn bit! Not when you act the way you do."

"Nancy, if you cry—"

"What will you do?" Nancy said hopefully.

"Call Eleanor to come in here and make you behave."

"'Fraid-cat!" Nancy tucked her handkerchief back into her sleeve. "I'm not going to cry. You just make me furious, that's all. Jazz, where has your sense of humor gone?"

"I don't believe I ever had enough to go very deep. Rocky always said I took everything too seriously. But I think," Jazz said grimly, "that no one but a fool would laugh about this. Of course, there was the man who said hanging certainly would be a lesson to him—"

"Please! Don't talk like that."

"I thought maybe that was the sort of attitude you wanted me to take. Just what did you want to talk to me about, Nancy?"

"I guess I did have some idea of murmuring coyly, 'I believe in you,' and then you would thump your chest and say resoundingly, 'As long as you have faith in me, nothing else matters.'"

"I'd like to say that, Nancy. And don't think I'm not—glad that you're sure I'm in the clear on this. But just that isn't enough. Men—men don't build their lives on what one woman thinks about them. I've behaved myself pretty well in this place. It's the best assignment I ever had, and it's good for a long time, because I'm one of the few operators that can handle such a hot trick. I wanted to settle down after packing a blanket roll up and down the canyon and out onto the desert for five years.

"Well—this town is broad-minded, but it doesn't forget. If this thing isn't cleared up it'll always be remembered against me. And if they bring me to trial or even before a grand jury, I might as well look for another job."

"If you did, there are lots of things besides telegraphing that you could do. Play in a dance orchestra—"

"I've been around the Musicians' Union down in San Francisco and seen a lot better than I'll ever be waiting around for jobs. I'll stick it out here till it's settled one way or another, because I won't clear out and leave Rocky holding the sack. But if we never find out the truth I'll be traveling again."

"Alone?"

"You don't think I'd ever take you with me—if you'd come. And I want to keep you out of this. I've heard you say teachers can't risk scandal."

"Pooh!" Nancy snapped her fingers. "*That* for my reputation! I can always get a job in an office."

"Your people—"

"Paul Heath and I had one bond in common: stepfathers. Mine's very nice—so nice that he occupies Mother's mind to an extent that she doesn't fuss over me. Jazz, there was another thing

I wanted to ask you. It's—it's worried me so, thinking of you being all alone. You've brothers and a father you could send for."

"I suppose the old man would come. But he's working on the D.&R.G. out of Denver, and I wouldn't ask him to do it. I suppose he'll hear about it before long: you have no idea how fast news can travel out over the line. I wouldn't call on my brothers if I was already sitting in a death cell. They'd say the whole situation was due to my mother coming out in me."

"D-didn't they like your mother?"

"Like? I suppose they did—more than that. She was a lot younger than the old man. She ran away with a fellow her own age when I was about ten. They stuck together and are married now. But the boys think Dad is a swell guy—which he is—and they never even spoke about her again. There's nothing in their makeup to make them understand people can't help doing things like that some-times. I look like her: they're big and raw-boned and towheaded. I guess that kind of got on their nerves."

"And you are like her . . . ?"

"I suppose so. She was crazy about music. The old man didn't like that. She tried to persuade him to let her have me, afterward, but of course he wouldn't. He made me go through high school, but he saw to it I was made—learned to telegraph—over on the D.&R.G. He was probably right. But there was too much older brother, and I cleared out. So I can get along without any mourners at the funeral."

"I see," Nancy said in a low voice. "I see—oh, a lot of things you probably didn't mean me to."

"I didn't intend it to be any sob story," Jazz said brusquely. "You asked me, and I told you."

"Of course. There's nothing more to say except that I'm sorry I couldn't forget what Paul Heath said to me soon enough to—to act reasonably. If I hadn't made you so angry you wouldn't have rowed with Paul so that everyone knew about it."

"I probably would have called him on the way he was playing that sax," Jazz said frankly. "I guess I deserve my reputation for being a hotheaded fool. I admit I lose my temper too easily. But even so, when some fellow makes you mad it seems to me hitting him and having it out right then is as good a way as bickering back and forth for months. I've fought a lot of fellows that were my friends afterward—and I've taken my medicine when I tackled the wrong fellow."

He touched his chin reflectively. "But that's different from killing anyone. I couldn't do that. Most people want to live; they want like hell to live."

"You're thinking of Clarice," Nancy said.

"Yes. You don't suppose she wanted to die, do you? Or Heath. Clarice got a lot of fun out of life. It's hard to realize she's dead."

"You—you liked her quite a lot, didn't you?"

"Yes, I did. I wanted to tell you that. Can't you imagine liking some man a lot: too much not to go on being friendly with him, but still never wanting to marry him?"

"Yes, I suppose I can. Sometimes I liked Paul very much. He was amusing and so calmly unscrupulous about some things that it didn't seem worth while to argue with him. I'm afraid I can't produce anything more than conventional regret for him."

"I'm glad you got off so lucky. I'd like to know who killed Clarice. From what Rocky said—that maybe she ran into whoever killed Heath—it may've been my fault she did. She stayed too late trying to argue with me to keep me from acting like a fool. She may even have gone home by his place to see that everything was all right."

"It wasn't her place to try to interfere," Nancy said sharply. "If it hadn't been for her we'd never have quarreled. If she—"

Jazz said without raising his voice, "Don't talk like that," and Nancy stopped abruptly. Then:

"It's very well for you to feel you owe her some regret! You don't bother to ask yourself if you owe me anything or what it is.—No, I'm going home! I'm sorry I bothered you, and I certainly won't do it again!"

CHAPTER ELEVEN
HENRY AND MARY

"It sounds to me," Rocky said, "like someone left in a hurry an' banged the door hard enough to crack it. I'm afraid your matchmakin' schemes ain't working out so very well."

"Rocky! I did not have anything to do with Nancy's coming here just now. Have you been suspecting me of sending her a message to come over at once? And whom would I send?"

"I didn't know. Sit down. Jazz will come in here when he gets good an' ready. It seems to me there's an awful lot of people in this town who're always fightin'."

"Are there? Would you mind kissing me?"

"Not at all. It's a pleasure. But why?"

"Because I'm so sorry for Nancy and Jazz," Eleanor said logically. "Rocky, when I'm fat and forty will you still let me sit on your lap?"

"By that time I may not have any lap left for you to set on. I've got an awful lot to talk over with you, sugar. . . ."

Eleanor got up hastily as Jazz pushed open the kitchen door. He had lighted a cigarette and smoked it determinedly, but she thought he looked white to the bone. She said casually:

"Do you want a drink, Rocky? I'll put dinner on the table."

"I could do with one." Rocky got a bottle and glasses down from a shelf; pushed one toward Jazz. "Sit down."

"Thanks. I suppose you heard Nancy leave? You couldn't very well help it. It's all right, though: I'm glad we got it over with."

"Over with? Don't kid yourself. A woman's last word is usually just the last one she can say before she has time to get her breath an' start in again."

"Are you going to let him get away with that, Eleanor?"

"He's only trying to be funny." Eleanor sat down at the table and unfolded her napkin. "Besides, a man's way of thinking there is nothing more to be said on a subject that hasn't been half talked over is just as exasperating."

"Don't you two ever fight?"

"You know how hard it is to quarrel with Rocky. And that's exasperating too." Privately, Eleanor thought, these moody, intense men may be very interesting, but I'm glad I didn't marry one of them.

Jazz and Rocky probably thought she hadn't noticed Rocky's cut cheek or the bruise on Jazz's chin. It would be too bad to disillusion them, particularly since Jazz was doggedly talking over railroad affairs with Rocky and eating enough to satisfy any but the most demanding hostess.

"Is that second trick operator to be trusted?" Rocky said presently, lighting a cigarette. "I had to send a wire this afternoon that I don't very much want to be spread aroun' town."

"He's all right. He'd better be. He knows all Western Union business is strictly confidential." As first trick operator Jazz managed the Western Union attached to the railroad telegraph office. "He won't talk, and that's more than you can say about some of the telephone operators in this town."

"That's just what I was thinkin' about. I know Goldie Thomas listens in whenever she can, and somehow or other what she hears always leaks out. I had to wire Heath's mother," Rocky said. "And there was a question I wanted to ask her at the same time. How good are you on history, Jazz?"

"I know a list of the Presidents and that old rhyme about the kings of England. You aren't consulting me as an authority, are you?"

"No. . . ." Rocky hesitated, put his hand in his pocket and drew out a round, flat object that he tossed onto the table. "I'll let you two see this. No one else has got a good look at it but me."

"It's very old, isn't it?" Eleanor said, examining the coin eagerly. "It's hard to tell what it is; silver, maybe. Two uncrowned heads facing each other—1565. . . ."

"Can you read the Latin on it, honey?"

Eleanor turned the coin to follow the letters circled within its outer edge. "HENRICVS & MARIA D. GRA. R. & R. SCOTORVM.'—They make their *u's* just like *v's*.—'Henry and Mary, by the grace of God, King and Queen of Scotland.' Isn't that it? It's Scottish, then. Mary of Scotland and Henry Darnley."

"That's what I figured. I could make out the Henry and Mary part of it and that it must be of Scotland. Look on the other side."

"The arms of Scotland, I suppose. I don't know what they look like, but I do remember the Scotch thistle. There are two little things here that might be thistles. 'QVOS DEVS COIVNXIT HOMO NON SEPARET.' Oh, I know! 'Whom God hath joined let no man put asunder.' Mary insisted on making Henry king as well as her prince consort, and a lot of people didn't like that or want her to marry Henry Darnley in the first place. Elizabeth of England didn't, because Darnley had some claim on the English throne. But I don't suppose that's important."

"I don't see how it could be. What is interestin' about it is the fact that Heath's name was Paul Henry. I looked at the first page of those records of his, an' that was the first thing that hit me in the eye. So I looked through the others, but there's no Mary among 'em."

"Miriam is the nearest to it. You mean he may have given this to some woman as a sort of keep-sake or remembrance? It's had a little hole drilled through it so it could be worn on a chain. I sup-pose he could have worn it attached to his watch chain, but I never saw him do it. It would take a very thin chain to go through that hole."

"No one ever saw him wear it, an' he didn't wear a watch chain. I asked his mother to let me know if he owned a coin like this. She'd certainly know if he'd had it very long, and it might've been a fam'ly keepsake. I don't imagine there are very many of them except in collections. It very likely would be worth some money."

"But where did it come from?" Jazz said. "What's so important about it?"

"I didn't tell you that, did I? Well, I reckon you might as well know. . . ."

"I don't think my worst enemy could picture me going around dropping sixteenth-century coins into people's mouths," Jazz said when Rocky had finished. "But why not just put it in his hand?"

"That's where it gets mixed up in mythology. An' that leads straight to the faculty."

"All of them?"

"Not Nancy. She's the only one that lives over here on this street, and that's about as far away from where Heath lived as you can get. An' she left the dance late, with us. You don't need to scowl at me," Rocky said pleasantly. "I never considered Nancy. But it's a fact that if Heath was killed between two-fifteen and two thirty-five she couldn't have got over there to do it. She and Eleanor talked quite a while after we got to the place where she boards."

"I'm glad of that," Jazz muttered. "It will make enough stink as it is, if all the teachers are going to get in the newspapers."

"I'd like to get this thing settled before we get any reporters up here. With only one train it isn't so easy for them to get here in a hurry, but I'm afraid they'll be comin' up before it's ended. I've really not got anything against anybody. Before this I've always had ever'body under suspicion right under my nose where I could watch 'em. The only thing to do now is sit tight and pray somebody will make a mistake—where I can catch them at it."

"It looks to me like whoever did this would be too smart to make any mistakes," Jazz said.

Rocky opened his lips, closed them again and finally said, "I'm not lookin' for this murderer to be smart," but he did not amplify this statement. "What I'm hopin' for is that he'll try to cover up—try to be too smart. I often wonder why there ain't more murders in this town. It'd always be easy enough to kill someone in the dead of night with no police aroun' and the streets so badly lighted. An' with no trained police force to check up thoroughly afterward."

"This is certainly not in the usual tradition of sudden death in Merton," Eleanor agreed. "They usually just shoot it out in the public square. You aren't going, Jazz?"

"I'd better. I know Rocky's got a lot of things to think over, and I'm keeping him from talking to you about them."

"As soon as it gets dark I'm going to drag Eleanor out for a walk aroun' town."

"To reconstruct the crime? Well, I won't wait for that. I'll hole in," he added as Rocky went with him to the front door. "And try not to run against any red boards again."

"I wish to God you would manage to keep calm," Rocky said fervently. "I've got my hands full without taking you on too. You know you've got a lot of friends in this town. Art Finley probably is one of them even if he didn't express himself very tactfully this afternoon about Leaman. Probably he just didn't know what to say."

"I don't believe he did," Jazz admitted. "Art's all right."

"He or Orin Roberts weren't ever especially friendly with Clarice, were they? I haven't talked to either of them."

"Of course all four of us played together for about a year. They both liked Clarice, but that's all. Orin goes with that fat dame from the laundry, and I don't think Art ever went for any woman. You—" Jazz was closing the door as he said it— "you tell Eleanor I think she's a—a good scout."

Rocky did tell her, as she sat at the table staring at the heads of Mary Stuart and Henry Darnley as if she thought they had some secret to tell her. She smiled maternally.

"I pity men. They can never take down their hair and have a good cry. What are all those papers?"

"The personal records we were talkin' about. Kline refers to them as papers, and he squalled like a catamount about lettin' me have them. That other bundle is some letters of Clarice's. I tell you— Do you have to wash the dishes right away?"

"Well—I won't. What do you want me to do?"

"You read the letters. You might get more out of 'em than I would. I'll go over the records and see what I can find out from them."

"Have you a pencil and paper? I'll clear the table so we can write if we need to. . . ."

"Well, what have you got?" Rocky said half an hour later, raising his head to look at Eleanor across the table.

"Not very much. I've been waiting for you."

"It took quite a while to get everything down. I'll start with Kline. He's forty-five: younger 'n I thought. He's been teaching twenty-two years. I waded through all his recommendations, and he seems always to 've been spoken of very highly. He's stayed at least three years ever' place he's been except one. That was five years ago, when he just stayed one year in a little place called Aden, up in Modoc County. He went to Willows, which 'd be a better job. None of these people but Miss Newman ever taught any place where he was.

"She's the next oldest: thirty-seven. She's been at it fifteen years. Name is Florence Anna. She's got good recommendations too. She never crossed trails with any of these people. Two years with Kline in Willows and came here with him. Miriam Rachel—"

"I always suspected her of having Jewish blood," Eleanor said. "She's one of these oriental beauties, you know. Of course it must be on her mother's side."

"Well, I shouldn't have taken her next because she's only twenty-five and this is the only place she's taught. She lives in Berkeley an' went to California, but later than any of the rest that graduated from there. What recommendations she has seem to kind of evade the question of whether she'd be a good teacher.

"Heath an' Fulton are—were—both thirty-two and went to Southern Cal at the same time. They taught different places before they came here, Heath last year and Fulton when Kline did. No connection with Louise—just plain Louise—Whyte. She's thirty, but she went to California.

"Like she told me, she and Heath were born in the same town and went to high school together.

"Nancy's twenty-five. She must've been brighter than Miriam Atkins, because she got out of school in time to teach a year longer. I suppose they were at college the same time but never met each other or she would have spoken about it."

"Not much good, is it?" Eleanor said doubtfully. "Of course there's the fact that Miss Newman has known Mr. Kline for so long. But I've guessed from things Nancy has let drop that she probably admires him very much."

"I got that myself from talking to her. I don't know that it's necessary for any of them to have known Heath any longer a time than they appear to 've done. You can get to hate a person even in a few weeks. I did have an idea he might have known some of them before and turned up here knowing something he could politely blackmail them with. But I guess that's out. Let's hear what you have."

"Three of these letters are from stores in the city about some dresses Clarice had sent up here. One is from a girl in Oakland whom she'd evidently worked with at one time. There's only one interesting thing in it. It's written last January, and the girl says:

> *"So you broke off with the boy friend and no hard feelings on either side? That's the way it ought to be. You wouldn't want to marry a telegraph operator and settle down in that dump, and you can pass the time away with that teacher till you meet that millionaire you're always talking about.*

That might help Jazz a little.

"Then there's a letter from Paul Heath, written from Berkeley last summer. He says he was surprised to hear from her: that he thought she never wrote letters and he very seldom does himself. Then he says:

> "It was nice seeing you. Too bad you can't get down here more often. Your scolding me for my habit of kissing and telling is very amusing. You always stand up for your own sex, which is more than most of them do for you. Still, I suppose a good many of them have suffered more or less at your hands. I guess we're just two of a kind, my dear. I was a little drunk that last night or I wouldn't have talked so much. The affair's over now, and I still insist it was very amusing, for reasons you don't seem to appreciate. Also, I'm still faintly surprised that it happened. However, all things considered, I'd just as soon you'd forget what little I told you."

"Is that all?"

"No. Then he says that it won't be long before he'll have to be back in Merton and that he wishes vacations would last forever. The end is—well, I'll read it:

"I'm afraid you took my romantic de-claiming too seriously. Or isn't it roman-tic for a young man in his cups to declare moodily that he feels he will never live to have a gray beard? As a matter of fact, I have no desire for a gray beard.

"No, dear child, as you so aptly put it, no one is out gunning for me. But truth-fully, someone might hate me enough to kill me. Don't worry about your friend Mitchell. He is really a sentimentalist at heart. I wonder why no one realizes that and that he is painfully sensitive. He might remove a good deal of skin from my face, but I always hope to avoid that. I will really try not to ride him—quoting you again. I realize that it is beneath my professional dignity.

"Of course I do a great many things that a molder of young ideas should not. But I'm a great deal better off than the rest of them. You wouldn't know anything about repression, would you? I don't sup-pose you ever repressed one little natural desire in your life, and more power to

you. You'd be surprised at what people who have might suddenly be capable of doing after years and years of a perfectly blameless existence.

"Damn it, Clarice, I think I've had one too many again. The fact is, I feel lonely as the devil tonight and like talking a great deal to someone. You know, if I ever found a woman I thought I could trust, I'd marry her. Of course that would be hard on her. I hope you make a habit of burning letters, but I doubt it. There's no harm done if you don't, and I'm not going to waste this unusual effort by destroying it."

"He certainly had both Jazz an' Clarice pretty well figured out. I can see," Rocky said thoughtfully, "how he might have been kind of interestin' at times."

"Yes, though I doubt if Clarice really appreciated that letter. He'd had an affair with some woman in Berkeley and told Clarice about it."

"He didn't def'nitely say it was in Berkeley last summer."

"N-no, but he'd evidently told Clarice about it when they met down there, so it must have been recent enough to be on his mind. Even if it started before, it must have ended last summer. I wonder what he meant by saying it was 'amusing, for reasons you don't seem to appreciate'?"

"I wish I knew. I suppose he had an idea Miss Newman didn't like him."

"All that talk about people repressing their natural desires, you mean? Yes, that certainly would seem to point to her. Still, he doesn't say that he's referring to a woman. There's Mr. Kline."

"And Mrs. Kline. Well, why not? She seems to be mighty proud of the old man. I don't imagine she'd thank Heath for makin' trouble."

"No, of course she wouldn't. I suppose she is a possibility along with everyone else. But I certainly would swear she wasn't cherishing any hopeless passion for Mr. Heath."

Rocky laughed. "I didn't have any such idea. Do you think Heath's letter hints that somebody might be? Well, maybe it does. It does such a lot of hinting that you could argue about it all night. You know, he might've meant Miss Newman had this hopeless passion you talk about—for Mr. Kline."

"Well, there *was* that remark of his about Jupiter and Io. But why would that be dangerous to Mr. Heath?"

"It wouldn't, unless she thought so much of Kline she'd obligingly get rid of Heath for him.

Or unless Heath could actually prove something between them. I can't see that Heath's death is gettin' Kline anything but a lot more grief. You'd expect either Miss Newman or Mrs. Kline would realize that's the way it would be."

"Would you say Mrs. Fulton was repressed?"

"Her? Hell no!" Rocky laughed again and told her about his conversations with the Fultons. "If she ever comes out in public with a black eye I'll be pretty sure he gave it to her. How about puttin' on your coat and coming for a walk up to the high school, and I'll tell you some more."

"But we're going out of our way if we're headed for the high school," Eleanor said suddenly, stopping on a street corner. "I was listening to you and didn't notice. This is Wilson: we've gone two blocks past Pine."

"I know it. But I've got something to tend to before we go on up to the high school and start from there. I'm going in here." He laid his hand on the Leamans' front gate. "I won't be a minute."

"Rocky, that's just exactly what you've been telling me you wouldn't let Jazz do."

"This is different. I ain't going to hurt Leaman. You stay out here unless I give you a distress signal. That'll mean Mrs. Leaman's pullin' my hair out and I want you to come in an' settle with her for me."

Rocky was relieved to find Leaman alone. The man attempted an ingratiating smile that only made Rocky want more than ever to drop him into a tub of hot water and take a cake of strong soap to him.

"I thought you might be coming around to talk to me after all," Leaman said. "Just a little hasty, wasn't you?"

"I reckon I was. I should have waited this mornin' to say what I've got to say now. That is: You keep that tongue of yours still."

"This is a free country! I got as good a right to talk as anybody else, I guess. Ever'body's talkin'—"

"They don't all spend the whole day paradin' up an' down Main Street or standing in the pool halls talkin' against just one man."

"I guess I know my duty as a citizen—"

"An' I guess if you're such a damn valuable witness, you'd ought to be locked up so's you can't tell everything you know to everyone you meet. If you were to be called as a witness, any smart lawyer could make a fool of you an' shoot that story of yours full of holes in ten minutes. Then when that was over Jazz might want to bring action against you. Or even if you never got a chance to talk on the witness stand. There's a law against defaming character, you know."

Leaman was unable to argue this point. There were so many laws against doing so many things that he was not at all certain he had not broken one today. He laughed weakly.

"I guess there's no law against tellin' what I know. I don't see how I'd be defaming Mitchell's character—"

"I heard he wasn't the only one you had a good deal to say about. I don't s'pose," Rocky said speculatively, "that Jazz would ever bring a legal action against you. He'd rather take it out of your hide. It'd be quicker an' easier."

"I'd have him up for assault and battery if he did! I'd—"

"You listen to me," Rocky said in his softest drawl. "You keep your mouth shut, or you'll land in jail. Dud Williams don't like you either, and he'd be very glad of a chance to give you a good goin' over. I doubt if anybody'd listen to you much if you did yell you'd been framed. Is that all clear?"

"I've got friends in this county! I can make things hot for you. You don't need to worry," Leaman said sullenly. "I'm called out at ten o'clock. But," he added with a malicious smile, "I guess you can't shut the wife off." And then, with gloomy conviction, "I guess no one could do that."

CHAPTER TWELVE
"PAUL HEATH WOULDN'T HAVE TOLD"

"We are now on the front steps to the high school."

"Obviously," Eleanor said. "So what?"

"Well, most ever'body that walked started out from here to go home. So did the people in cars, but they don't matter. I'm goin' to take two-fifteen for the time of Heath's death," Rocky said. "We'll see for ourselves how long it takes to walk to his place. Look down this street here: Pine Street—"

"I'm looking. Grove is the first intersecting street, and the Klines live on the corner of Grove and Pine. Mr. Kline told you it took him three minutes to walk home, which is not very fast walking. The Fultons live on the corner of the next intersecting street: Pine and Sierra."

"Yes. They'd all go straight down Pine to get home. Louise Whyte lives right there." Rocky pointed to the Barkers' home, just below them. "She and the Fultons, Mrs. Kline, Miss Newman and Miriam Atkins left here before the dance was over. Any of the last three would have time to get over to Heath's cabin before he did."

"There would always be people standing right here on the steps until the dance was over. Still, Louise could have gone out the back way without being seen," Eleanor admitted. "And so could anyone else. They'd have to do that if they didn't want to be seen, because there were a few people going home all the time."

"There's plenty of convenient back doors and alleys. Yes, Louise Whyte could have beat Heath to his cabin. But I don't see how either of the Fultons could have if they told the truth about going home from here. If either of them did it, Heath was probably killed a little later than two-fifteen. They must've met people going home: I'll try to find out. The biggest crowd went home between two and two-ten. I don't see how anyone could risk goin' over to Heath's without being seen at that time. Either before or after that would be the best bet."

Rocky looked at his watch by the rays of the flashlight he carried. "Come on: we're Heath, goin' home."

"Are we? I don't believe he took as long strides as you do," Eleanor said, catching at his arm. "I think he'd consider it beneath his dignity to hurry too much to get away from Jazz."

"All right: is that better? Here's the Klines' place. We turn and go along Grove—an' remember this is the same way Clarice came."

"Yes. And we come to Grove and Marin, where Miss Newman lives—"

"Five minutes," Rocky said, stopping. "Remember that, will you? And on to Heath's place will be about one minute more."

"So he should have been home by two-eleven at the latest. If he was killed at two-fifteen someone was waiting for him."

"It looks like it. I don't see how Jazz could have gotten here before two-sixteen."

"I'm afraid that isn't going to do him any good."

"Not with anyone who wants to make a case against him. To me, it means he came by this corner just about the time Heath was being killed. I wanted to get that straight. Clarice was about five minutes behind him, and she wouldn't walk so fast. She wore high heels and kind of minced along: I noticed that. She should have passed here about two twenty-five; maybe a little earlier. Well, that would do—"

"You mean it would be about the right time for her to meet anyone who was coming away from Mr. Heath's cabin? Yes, I suppose it would, and by that time there wouldn't be anyone on the streets. Oh, what about Mr. Fulton?"

"Well, if he told the truth he was just going back into the house at that time. Let's leave him out of it for a while. Clarice had to come by here to get home. And any of the people we've been talking about had to pass this corner to get home. Even if they sneaked through the alleys they'd have to cut across Grove Street somewheres." Rocky pointed down the street. "Miriam Atkins lives just about half a block down there. There's no use arguing they—he—might have made a circle way over to the edge of town and then sneaked back. That would be foolish. Well, none of that proves anything to anybody's satisfaction but my own. I'm not workin' on this with the open mind you're supposed to have. I'm tryin' mostly to prove Jazz didn't do it because someone else did."

"I suppose if Clarice met someone hurrying to get home she wouldn't think anything about it then. Or mightn't she have seen someone going toward Mr. Heath's place instead?"

"That's always a possibility."

"She'd probably speak—because of course she'd know whoever it was—and they'd know that later she could place them on the scene of the crime. But there was plenty of time to dispose of her in a less public place. . . . It's very quiet and dark now where Mr. Heath lived."

"There's not so many houses up there," Rocky said. "Mrs. Pratt lives in her kitchen and never lights up the front part of the house. She was in bed a long time before the dance was out. The people who live in the three houses across the street are all middle-aged and go to bed early. There's a vacant lot the other side of Mrs. Pratt's."

"Yes, I see there is. And then the Christian Science church, and the only street light is beyond that. Rocky, didn't Mr. Heath have any letters—or other interesting documents—in his room?"

"I looked through his things in a hurry, but I didn't find anything but bills and business letters. There was nothing but school papers in his desk in his classroom. I want to go over his cabin again. Do you mind comin' in? It's all right."

"I see Mrs. Pratt doesn't go in for gardening," Eleanor said. "But why spread crushed gravel all over the place?"

"To keep the dust and mud under control. She hates dirt like poison. Spends half her time sprinkling down the road when it's dusty. It was probably some of the damp earth aroun' her place that got scraped off on Clarice's window sill. Mrs. Pratt didn't like to have the old man aroun' the house because she said he made too much cleaning for her to do. So she built him this nice little doghouse."

"It's very nice and cozy," Eleanor said when Rocky had turned on the lights. "He could have a fire, and most boarders freeze to death unless they sit out in the front room with the family."

She looked around the room; down at the woven rag rug and quickly up again. "I forgot about that," Rocky said. "Or hardly noticed it."

"It's hardly noticeable. I wonder if Mrs. Pratt will ever be able to rent this place to anyone else." Eleanor sat down on the day bed at one side of the room and watched Rocky go through the drawers of the table that Heath had used as a desk.

"He kept his affairs in order. There isn't a thing here that does us any good. I suppose Kline will want these papers he corrected." Rocky turned over a pile of red penciled examination papers; took a small black cat fashioned of some heavy metal from the drawer and weighted the papers down with it.

"That's cute," Eleanor said, looking at the cat's complacent smirk. "Nancy has one like that, but hers was white. There's someone coming, Rocky?"

"You *can* hear steps on that gravel. Oh, good evenin', Mrs. Pratt. I was just looking things over again."

"I hope you get through sometime. I want to clean this place up." Mrs. Pratt was a gaunt female with slippery hair and a long, agile mouth that seemed to throw words at you. "I must say Mr. Heath was neat—for a man. He never kept a lot of junk around like most men do."

"Did you clean in here for him? When was the last time you did?"

"Yesterday, when he was up to the high school in the afternoon. Friday was my usual day, but I put it off."

"You looked aroun' in here this morning, didn't you? Did anything seem to be missing?"

"Not a thing. He used to tell me to go through everything: that he never kept anything around he'd mind his landlady seeing. He was a great joker."

"He must've been," Rocky said solemnly. "You're sure you were sleepin' at the time he came home? We were just noticin' that you can hear steps pretty plain on that gravel."

"I know you can. But I wouldn't have heard him if I'd been awake—which I wasn't—because my room's the other side of the house. Which it seems to me I told you. Is his folks comin' up here? If they don't someone will have to pack up his things."

"Somehow I don't imagine they'll come. I ought to have word by tomorrow mornin'."

"Well, when can I have the use of my own place?"

"Maybe sometime tomorrow; maybe Tuesday. I don't know. I can tell you more after the inquest."

Mrs. Pratt sniffed discontentedly. "Well, I s'pose that'll have to do. Don't you lose that key. I think it was a tramp did it. Believe me, I lock my house up tight at night. You wouldn't believe the number of bums I have to turn away every day. Yesterday there was one looked like he'd as leave murder me as eat."

She turned to go. "And don't you leave them lights on and run up my electric bill on me."

"I won't. I'm all through here anyway," Rocky said. "You wouldn't happen to know if Heath was careful about lockin' up?"

"I warned him about it two or three times. I s'pose he always locked up at night, but he'd leave the place open in the daytime so's I had to watch it." The heels of Mrs. Pratt's bedroom slippers flapped against the gravel underfoot as she led the way around to the front of the house. "I'm just taking a look-see to be sure no one's hanging around. If they are, they'll get a load of buckshot in the pants. Good night."

"You said Mr. Heath had his key in his pocket, didn't you? And you thought that meant he hadn't had time to lock his door before he was killed?"

"That's what I really think, but I can't prove it, sugar. And I may not want to."

"Why not?"

"Because," Rocky said exasperatingly. "Anyway, who knows anything about it? It's all a matter of habit. Heath may've been in the habit of lockin' his door just before he got into bed instead of as soon as he'd come in."

"Had he had time to start undressing?"

"He was dressed like he was at the dance. But he may not have wanted to go to bed right away."

"You said you were going to take two-fifteen for the time of his death, and now you seem to be trying to prove that he was killed later than that."

"It's an ace in the hole, honey. I might want to say he was killed a little later, so I might as well keep all the arguments in mind. It doesn't look, offhand, like that'd do any good, but it might. I was thinkin' about what Barker, the janitor— Jesus Christ!"

He swung Eleanor half off her feet and back against him. A small roadster came hurtling up Grove Street, turned widely and at full speed at the corner and skidded to a stop in front of Florence Newman's boardinghouse. The car's headlights were dark, and the front right-hand fender grazed the front of Eleanor's coat. She said shakily:

"I'm all right. I didn't see it at all. Rocky, you aren't going to—"

"I sure as hell am!" Rocky said, striding over to the car. "Anybody who drives like such a damned fool ought to be put—"

"Oh, I'm so sorry! I was in a hurry, and I'm afraid I'm not a very good driver. I didn't hit anybody, did I?"

Rocky looked at Miriam Atkins in the dim light, swallowed twice and discarded several pungent phrases before he answered:

"I agree with you on that proposition of not bein' a good driver. If you didn't hit anyone it wasn't your fault. Do you always drive without lights?"

"Lights? I guess I just forgot to turn them on. But you see they aren't very good so I didn't miss them. And I was in a hurry."

"Going somewheres?"

"I wanted to talk to Florence. Louise doesn't seem to be home. So I— Oh, Mrs. Allan, I'm sorry! I didn't see you at all. There's never anybody on the streets—well, not very many people, at least. I ran through a red light in Reno today," Miriam said sadly. "But they let me off when I explained I was from California and didn't know their laws."

"I thought a red light was a red light whatever state it's in," Rocky said uncompromisingly. "I want to talk to you. But let us get back on the sidewalk before you start to drive down to your place."

"Oh, now you're just being mean," Miriam said cheerfully. "All right." She kicked at the starter. "Darn this thing! It never does works right."

"Shall I come with you?" Eleanor whispered. "I can go on home if you'd rather."

"No, you come along." Rocky winced as Miriam stopped her car in front of the Fenner house with grinding gears and squealing brakes. "It's a crime for people like her to be let drive a car. Is it all right for us to come in and talk to you here?"

"I don't see why not. The Fenners will be at church. And of course they've let the fire go out," Miriam said petulantly. "They always do."

She opened the door of the big circulating heater in the Fenners' neat living room and looked helplessly at the coals inside. "As if," Eleanor said later, "she could start the fire again by looking at it coaxingly." Rocky said:

"Here; I'll fix it," opened the dampers and poured coal into the stove. "They may not like that, but it'll burn."

"I don't care if they like it or not." Miriam loosened her coat and opened a door off the living room. "This is my bedroom. Now maybe I can get it a little warm before they get back. Honestly,

I don't blame Gertrude Fulton for complaining
about the cold—"

"Have you seen anyone since you got back to
town?"

"Oh, you mean have I heard about Paul Heath?
It certainly is terrible, isn't it?" Miriam said placidly. "I heard in the drugstore. I stopped there
when I got in. Then I went up and talked to the
Fultons, but they didn't have very much to say, so
I thought I'd see Louise or Florence. I knew Nancy
wouldn't talk. But what did you want to ask me?"

Rocky looked at her rather helplessly. What
could he ask her and be certain of getting any
helpful answer? According to Nancy she didn't
bother about what was going on around her, and
she wouldn't be apt to give them any new light
on Heath's character. He knew what time she'd
left the dance and when she should have reached
home. But that car of hers had missed Eleanor by
about six inches. He said:

"Where do you stay when you go to Reno?"

"I just went over for the day."

"Well, where do you stay when you do stay all
night?"

"Oh, at the Riverside. I do like a lot of service
and steam heat and hot water. Hot water!" Miriam
said dreamily. "Mrs. Fenner acts like it was worth

its weight in gold, and I'm sure I don't run it any more than—"

"Do you ever stay at any other hotel? Or with friends over there?"

"N-no. Just at the Riverside."

"Then I suppose they ought to know you there by now."

"An awful lot of people stay there and come and go. Why? What difference does it make to you?" Miriam asked uneasily. "Why do you care where I stay when I go over there?"

"You do go there quite a lot, don't you?"

"Well, I have to go somewhere. What has that to do with Paul Heath or Clarice Selby being murdered?"

"Heath used to trot over to Reno quite a bit."

"Oh! Well, that's not so, and I know who put it into your head! That tubby little Dr. Miller. He told me he'd looked all over the city for me one night and he thought maybe I'd gone places with Paul. I never saw Paul at all when we happened to be there at the same time, and that night I—well, Dr. Miller just didn't happen to find me, that's all. He had a nerve to try to."

When Rocky did not answer she got up and threw off her coat, delved in her purse and found her lipstick. "You—you aren't going to investigate the hotels and things in Reno, are you?" she said finally.

"I might. Don't you want me to?"

Miriam painted a small face in red on the back of her hand and returned the lipstick to her purse. "No, I don't. Because then you might— Damn! I can't help it. Mother says no nice girl swears, but there are times when you've got to. Well, I'll just have to tell you. I'm married!"

"M-married?" Rocky echoed uncertainly.

"Yes. I met him in Reno, and he runs what he calls a dude ranch near there. His name is Ted Lowell. You can find out all about him easily enough, but just two friends of his know we're married. People think I just stay over there now and then."

Rocky looked at Eleanor. She said, "But do you have to keep it secret?"

"Oh yes. We got married last Christmas vacation. Down in Los Angeles, so none of these old ladies who read all the Reno papers would be able to see about us from the marriage licenses. I was down in L.A., and he came down. But you see, I couldn't have had my job back again this year if they'd known I was married. And my grandfather's going to give me ten thousand dollars to go to Europe on when I've taught two years."

"Are—are you going to Europe?" Rocky said inadequately.

"Of course not. I'm going to put the money into Ted's place and make a real fashionable resort for divorcees out of it. All he needs is a little capital so he can put in a swimming pool and things, and hire some more cowboys from Hollywood."

"Don't your grandfather want you to get married?"

"We-ell, I don't think he'll mind. But he's a man of his word—he says so himself—and he's determined I'm going to earn my own living for two years. After that he won't care how much money he gives me. But even if I never get any more, ten thousand will be plenty. He's a Jew," Miriam said irrelevantly. "Calls himself Rose, but it used to be Rosenheim. I do hope you aren't going to tell on me. I've had a hard enough time of it. Ted gets furious because I won't quit my job, and last summer I had an awful time pretending I was at Tahoe when I wasn't."

"I won't let anyone know unless I have to," Rocky said briefly. "I s'pose you know your husband was home all last night?"

"Goodness, you don't suppose he'd come clear over here, do you?"

"It's a routine question," Eleanor said, smiling.

"Oh. Well, I do know he was home, because they had a dance there and I'd wanted to go over for it. And I never talked to him about Paul Heath because he's very jealous."

"Any cause to be?" Rocky said.

"I think you're mean! Of course not. He doesn't need any cause to be jealous: he just is. I did go around with Paul some when we first came here, but that didn't last long. Oh, we liked each other, and I never quarreled with him, but we just didn't click. He started flirting with Gertrude Fulton, and then he met Clarice Selby. And this year it was Nancy. I do think he would have made a better principal than Mr. Kline, but I didn't care about that one way or the other. I just agreed with whatever Paul said and was perfectly nice to Mr. Kline too."

"That's one way to keep out of trouble."

"I think it is," Miriam agreed. "So you see I wasn't—and aren't—very much interested in anybody here. All I want is to get this year over and be able to go live with my husband. I'm not half as fond of buying clothes in Reno as I pretended, but I have to have some excuse for going over there so much."

"I think I've met Lowell. I've heard of his place. He's about my height, isn't he, and has kind of reddish-yellow hair?"

"Yes; that's him. He's a lamb, but he is—" Miriam sighed—"terribly jealous. As if there were anyone in this town for him to be jealous of! And he isn't very practical. Well, I'm glad that's settled."

Rocky raised his eyebrows. "I suppose it is—in a way. But—do you think Heath had any idea you were married to Lowell?"

"Goodness, why should he? He—well I don't know," Miriam said slowly. "He did used to try to tease me about going to Reno every week end I could. Wanted to know why I didn't go home instead and what fun could I have over there all alone. Unless I knew someone over there."

"It probably wasn't a husband he suspected you of having there," Eleanor said.

"You mean— Well, I suppose he would think that. Even if he did accuse me of being old-fashioned. I guess I am," Miriam said virtuously. "Too old-fashioned for Paul Heath, anyway. I don't know; when he was in Reno the same time I was he might have found out where I went. He was curious as a cat."

"And suppose he had found out?" Rocky said.

"Oh, he wouldn't have told—I don't think he would. Well, if he had, I don't suppose they would have fired me in the middle of the year."

"They made a teacher down at Brookdale resign at Christmastime when it came out that she'd got married in the fall."

"Oh, did they? I didn't know." Miriam flushed under his disbelieving look. "Well, yes—I did know that. But I still say Paul Heath wouldn't have told on me."

"Didn't he know all about your grandfather and the money you're supposed to get? I suppose he wouldn't have minded havin' a little extra money himself."

"He was always saying he wished he had more. He was very extravagant— Oh! He wouldn't black-mail me, and I wouldn't let him if he tried it! Not for a thing like that. I—I think you've got an evil mind!"

"This business don't have a tendency to make you think just the best of ever'body. But I haven't any more questions to ask you. You can go an' call on Miss Newman."

"Oh, I don't think bother. If I get into the bathroom before the Fenners get back there isn't anything they can do about me using the hot water for a bath. . . ."

"Well, what do you think?" Eleanor said when they were outside.

"What do you?"

"Of course she must really be married. There wouldn't be any point in making up a story like that. In some ways she isn't as stupid as I thought. And yet—some of the things she admitted . . ."

"That may be another sign she ain't as stupid as you thought. Are you too tired to walk down to the telegraph office? I told the operator to hold any wires there if the messenger boy didn't find us home. I didn't want to risk havin' it stuck under the door. There's a chance there might be a wire from Heath's folks."

Mr. Hiram Woody had sent his wire collect and not bothered to count his words carefully.

MRS. WOODY'S HEALTH DOES NOT PERMIT COMING TO MER-TON. UNABLE COME MYSELF AC-COUNT BUSINESS. SHIP HEATH'S BODY HERE. ALSO PERSONAL EF-FECTS AND PAPERS. BELIEVE HE BANKED IN MERTON. PLEASE AD-VISE. COIN YOU MENTION WAS VALUABLE FAMILY HEIRLOOM. GIVEN TO HEATH BY MRS. WOODY. PLEASE INCLUDE AMONG PER-SONAL BELONGINGS.

"Why, the hateful old—"

"I agree with you," Rocky said. "I begin to think it might not have been all Heath's fault he didn't get along with Woody. That wire just reeks of 'good riddance to bad rubbish.' Can't wait to get his hands on anything Heath left. Well, we'll go up by the town hall an' see if they've been telephoning any more from Brookdale, and after that I think it's about time we called it a day."

CHAPTER THIRTEEN
NANCY IS STUBBORN

Mrs. Logan did not "have to take a boarder: in fact, I really lose money on it, but I like to have someone in the house when Dusty's out on the road." But Dusty Logan liked to play poker with his friends in the crying room down at the station. Dusty's luck was notoriously bad, and Nancy had noticed that Mrs. Logan preferred to receive her check for board when Dusty was absent.

However, Mrs. Logan was a leader in the small Christian Science church of Merton. Tonight, without admitting that she imagined Nancy to be in need of consolation, she suggested several times that she "had ought to go to church. Mrs. Weaver is going to sing a special solo."

"Edwin's mother? But I understood that she has a very bad cold," Nancy said innocently. "Edwin said she couldn't speak above a whisper on Friday."

"I'm sure she will sing just beautiful," Mrs. Logan said firmly. "Well, if you're sure you don't want to go . . . There's an awful good detective story I got from the library. It's about—oh, maybe you wouldn't want to read it. You don't care so much for detective stories."

"I'll find something to read."

"Of course you will. Maybe you've got school work to do." Mrs. Logan put on last summer's hat and a pair of mended tan cotton gloves. Then: "You know, dearie, I'd just as soon stay at home if you're going to be lonesome," she said.

"I'll be all right. I'll probably go over and talk to Miss Whyte. You're—you're very sweet to think about it, and I'm sorry I talk the way I do about—"

"Now, you didn't say one thing," Mrs. Logan insisted. "Not one thing. And you know none of your—our friends would ever do anything he—they shouldn't. And if you get hungry there's some apple pie in the cupboard and the cold roast pork."

When Mrs. Logan had gone Nancy went into her bedroom, put up a window and smoked a cigarette out of it. That window was a blessing, because it was a back one and faced an unseeing and uncritical growth of scrub pine. Poor Louise often spoke feelingly about her front room and Mrs. Barker's keen sense of smell. . . .

Any girl would lose her temper when she had virtually thrown herself at a man's head and he'd

told her she couldn't make up to him for the opinion of all the rest of the world. Nancy felt her
cheeks growing hot. Insufferable little prig, expecting to be overwhelmed with gratitude because
she was willing to tell Jazz she "believed in him."
Of course he wouldn't play up—and she liked him
for it. But who would have expected their positions to be so neatly reversed? One would suppose
he would be more than ever the suppliant.

Of course, suppliant was far too extreme a term
for Jazz at any time. But he had done the asking
and she the refusing, and now he had gone noble
on her and wouldn't even promise to kiss her if
she cried.

It was queer about men like Jazz—well, and
Rocky too. Very likely, Nancy thought a little maliciously, Eleanor had been surprised to find that
at times men didn't consider women very important. At least, they wouldn't let anything a woman
could say or do influence them from any decision
they had made.

Eleanor was a darling, but her air of superior
wisdom was rather trying at times. Of course it
was only that of any woman who had been very
happily married for so short a time that she still
felt she was the first discoverer of the married
state.

"That sounds very well," Nancy muttered. "I ought to go look for someone to say it to. Now I'm beginning to talk to myself—I wonder if Lou is home. But the Barkers would be there, and probably Mrs. Barker would want to talk things over."

She lighted another cigarette. If she could go back just one week and be walking with Jazz down by the painted red-and-yellow bushes along the river, when he said, "Will you marry me, Nancy?" she would say, "Yes." And later on: "Clarice doesn't matter."

At least she would try to. Then Jazz wouldn't have quarreled with Paul Heath and would have taken her home after the dance and taken a good long time to say good night, and then he would have had an alibi. For Paul's death, at least, so that things wouldn't be quite so bad. What could Rocky do? Theorize and ask questions of people who were used to evading questions they didn't want to answer. . . .

Nancy got up, very carefully disposed of her cigarette stubs and looked for the book she had been reading earlier in the week. It took her several minutes to remember that she had had it with her in the domestic-science rooms during Friday's lunch hour and had left it there in Louise's locker.

"Well," she said, "then I'll correct papers. Oh, damn it! I forgot to bring them home too."

The papers really should be corrected, Nancy decided. She could discuss them—caustically—with their perpetrators, and that would help to pass away what were going to be rather trying class periods. All the students would be talking, and heaven only knew what they would do with those in Paul Heath's classes.

She slipped into her coat, found her keys and pulled a beret down over her curly hair. When she discovered that her flashlight battery had burnt out she hesitated for an instant. The most direct route to the high school from Mariposa Street was by the rutted road that crossed the no man's land between the high school and the end of Mariposa. You really needed a light to walk over it comfortably, but except for that it was safe enough. She simply could not stay in this house alone with nothing to do but think. . . .

There was no light in Louise's room, so if she was at home she would be in the living room with the Barkers. Nancy went on to the high school; unlocked and locked the big front doors and fumbled for the light switch near them. She heard the switch click, but the hall remained dark.

She remembered, then, that the main switch was in Mr. Kline's office, and of course he would turn it off over the week end; just as inevitably as he would always lock the office door. He was constantly warning them to be careful not to lose their keys and to lock the front doors after them when they had to come to the high school alone after school hours.

This was the first time she had been here alone at night, but Nancy thought she knew her own classroom well enough to find the papers she wanted. She explored her coat pocket and found a paper folder of matches. Only four, but those should be enough to light her way to Louise's locker in the domestic-science room.

She felt her way past the corner just beyond the principal's office and turned into the corridor that ran at right angles to the main hall. The commercial room was at the end of it on the right-hand side. Luckily Mr. Kline did not insist that classrooms be locked, so she could get into Lou's room without a key.

The corridor smelled of oiled wood; her classroom of chalk dust and the cloyingly sweet powder Genevieve Thomas had spilled on the floor late Friday afternoon. Nancy stumbled against a chair, but she found her desk and the pile of papers on it. A classroom shouldn't have any ghosts, but there was one there now: Paul Heath sitting on the edge of her desk and saying, "But why blame me, Nancy? You've still got me, you know.

And you'd really like to smile and stop pretending you're correcting papers. . . ."

He walked out of the room with her and down the hall. He often caught up with her as she was starting home, with: "Another day can be marked off the calendar. What future President have you started up the path to glory today?" But now he said, "I know you didn't love me, Nancy, but you might be a little sorry for me. I didn't want to die. . . ."

Nancy jerked one elbow closely against her side. She felt as if cold fingers were touching it lightly. But of course there was no one there. Her footsteps were little and lonely in the black hall. By day so many careless, hurrying feet passed over these oiled boards.

She managed to save herself from slipping with one hand thrown out against the corridor wall. Mr. Barker had evidently oiled the floor today, and she realized now that she had been very nearly running.

She stood still, taking purposely slow and deep breaths. There was nothing to be afraid of, but she whispered, "I am sorry, really." Now surely it would be all right. She could go on to Louise's classroom and find *Shining and Free.*

Around the corner in the main hall someone had moved. Or was that only a ghost too: the same

one that had walked down the hall with her? Nancy
hugged the thick sheaf of bookkeeping papers to
her; holding onto them to keep her hands from
trembling. She said, "Lou, is that you? It's Nancy." And then: "Mr. Kline! Mr. Barker!"

There was no answer. She shifted the papers to
one arm and finally managed to light one of her
precious matches. The tiny flame lasted until she
reached the main hall. The central light just over
her head was a contorted bulk that threatened her
for an instant and then faded into the dark as the
match burned out. But there was no one in the
building but herself, and she was going to get the
book she had come after.

She must go up six steps, and then the door of
Louise's classroom would be just a few paces beyond. Nancy counted the steps; put her foot out
firmly but with the feeling that she would plunge
into space when she did it. The floor was in its
proper place, and her fingers finally touched the
knob of the door.

She was not so familiar with this room as her
own, but another match showed her the cutting
tables and the lockers built into the wall on one
side and a glimpse of the kitchen on the other side
of an archway. She hoped Louise had not locked
her locker: she kept nothing valuable in it and let
Nancy leave odds and ends there. It was the first

one at the top of the third row, but it was almost impossible to locate it in the dark.

The third match flared and went out. The last one burned her fingers, but she had her hand on the locker door before she let the match and paper booklet drop to the floor. An odor of stale bread and ham made itself evident. She had the right locker because she had left an uneaten ham sandwich there on Friday. Spools of thread, a pin cushion that pricked her fingers, rolled-up wads of cloth, and finally the hard edges of a book.

She thought rather highly of Nancy Towers as she tucked the book under her arm. She hadn't let herself be frightened away, and in an instant she would be out of the building. She wanted to get away from this room. Last night it had been crowded with long tables, and Clarice Selby had sat at the end of one of them to eat supper with the strong light overhead making her red curls look more than ever as if they were lacquered.

Where the lockers ended was a large closet in which Louise kept stacks of paper towels, brooms and a mop. After that would come a corner where she would turn and in a few steps more find the door into the hall. The closet door was a little ajar. Nancy remembered suddenly that she had hung the outside sweater to a twin set there several days ago. If she could find it she had better

take it home now. That and her red skirt would do
to wear tomorrow.

She had hung it near the front of the closet.
It should be on one of the first hooks if Louise
hadn't moved it. One hook was bare, but her fingers touched soft wool hanging on another one.
She thought: My breathing sounds so loud in here.
I'm getting jittery again. If I walk out very slowly
and quietly—

She tried to scream and could not, for the hands
were like a steel necklace around her throat.

Dud Williams' prominent eyes had a rather
glassy look, but, as was usual with him when he
was a little drunk, he was ponderously polite.

"Set down there, Mrs. Allan, ma'am. Are you
sure you're comfor'ble? I was just gettin' ready to
go home. I begun to think you wasn't ever goin' to
look over those bums I dragged in, Rocky."

"The— Oh yes." Rocky winked at Eleanor with
the eye that was turned from Dud. "I'll go in an'
look them over now."

"I'm afraid Mrs. Williams will be waiting dinner for you," Eleanor said solicitously, though she
knew quite well that Mrs. Williams would be doing nothing of the sort.

"I just get myself a snack every now and then,
and Dud can look after himself or go without.

I gave up waiting for him to come home twenty years ago," was the way Mrs. Williams put it.

"I guess she'll wait," Dud said firmly. "When you're married to a man in the public service you got to learn to put up with little inconveniences. I guess you know that, ma'am. I always say to Mrs. Williams, 'Well, a wife has got to do her part.' It's kind of late, though, so I may just get me some ham and eggs at the Greek's. I ain't unreasonable: I don't expect her to be able to keep things warm forever."

"Those guys you rounded up look harmless enough to me," Rocky said, returning from the jail. "None of them has any record that I know of, an' they all swear they just got in this mornin'."

"Then I'll turn 'em loose."

"Send them out to prey like the locust on our fair city?"

"I don't know about that. But there's a freight east at ten." This was an angle of Dud's job that he knew perfectly. "They'll go whether they want to or not. If somebody kicks them off the freight that ain't my business."

"I doubt if they want to go," Rocky said, grinning. "They look right comfortable. They ain't the sensitive kind that mind a few cooties, and the nights are gettin' mighty cold."

"I fed 'em once, and that's enough. Jail didn't use to be so popular a few years back. That was when we just had a kind of big iron cage where this place is built," Dud explained. "Except for the summer months that place wasn't popular with the bums. No privacy, either, you might say. Of course we didn't ever put anybody in there in wintertime."

"I'm sure that was a credit to your humanitarian instincts," Eleanor said sweetly.

"I thank you, ma'am. There was a message from Brookdale, Rocky. I wrote it down." Dud produced a dirty scrap of paper covered with straggling hen tracks. "I've forgot what he said—old Sloane, I mean."

"This seems to be in some kind of forgotten language. Is this right? Sloane says he'll be here in the mornin' and—" Rocky murmured profanely. "And he's just heard Freddie Haynes will be back on the early mornin' train an' I can probably expect the pleasure of his company tomorrow."

"He didn't say anything about it bein' a pleasure. Haynes' company, I mean. But that's right: he did mention him. Mrs. Leaman's been yellin' about somebody stealin' a leg of lamb off her back porch. Let her yell, I say. Then one of those guys from your office in Brookdale called up. He ain't located that guy's been passin' rubber checks, an' someone went and busted into a grocery store last night and got away with some canned goods. They didn't find it out till this afternoon."

"As soon as the inquest's over I'll have to hop to Brookdale an' deal with their crime wave," Rocky said ironically. "I suppose Cy Rand— I'll take it, Dud."

He reached for the telephone. "Hello. . . . Yes, this is Allan. . . . Who? . . . Yes, I think I get you. You don't want . . . Well, never mind. I can come up and talk to you. . . . Yes, right away."

He put the telephone back on the desk and lighted a cigarette. To Eleanor his nonchalance seemed rather overdone, but Dud only said, "Somebody?"

"Yeah. It was—Ma Jenkins. She wants to talk about Clarice's fun'ral. Are you usin' your car for a few minutes, Dud?"

"Keep it all night. I'm goin' to get somethin' to eat, and I only live two blocks away. I can get the car if I should need it before you get back here tomorrow."

"I'll get it back here early in the mornin'. Good night. Come on, honey."

"But what does Mrs. Jenkins really want to talk to you about this evening?"

"She don't. It wasn't— Damn it? Is this car ever going to start? It wasn't Ma Jenkins," Rocky said above the stiff roar of a cold motor. "I think it was Louise Whyte. Whoever it was didn't want to tell me anything. Must've known the operator would be listenin' in. But she said to come to the high school right away."

"At the rate we're going now we're practically there," Eleanor said. "What do you suppose— You're sure it wasn't Mr. Kline?"

"It was a woman's voice, and it sounded like Miss Whyte. She has a kind of crisp way of talkin'. But I don't know." He stopped the car in front of the high school. "Come on in if you want to," he said over his shoulder. He was halfway up the steps to the entrance doors before Eleanor could get out of the car and did not hear her:

"All right, Big Chief, your squaw will trail along behind."

The lights were on in the hall, and Louise was walking nervously back and forth near the front doors. She wasn't the sort of person you'd ever expect would cry, Rocky thought, but her thick, sandy lashes were wet. She drew her arm impatiently across her eyes.

"Thank heaven I found you so easily. I didn't know where you might be, but I took a chance. And I'm so glad you brought Mrs. Allan with you. Nancy wouldn't let me call a doctor—"

"Doctor?" Eleanor said. "What—where is she?"

"Come down this way. I found her in my classroom. Someone evidently tried to strangle her. Oh, she's really all right now."

Louise pushed open a door marked "Teachers." Nancy was lying on a slippery leather couch with a damp towel wrapped about her throat. She sat up and said hoarsely:

"I told Lou she shouldn't let everybody know about this. I wanted—" She swallowed painfully.

"Let me see. Oh, that isn't so bad," Eleanor said with a sigh of relief.

"It looks bad enough to me," Rocky said, looking grimly at the red marks on Nancy's throat.

Nancy smiled wanly. "They didn't choke me much. Just a little bit. Unfortunately, like Anne Boleyn, I have such a little neck. Lou, you've been crying."

"Sheer helplessness. What would you expect? I came up here to get some sewing I'd left in my room. With a flashlight—something Nancy apparently did not bring with her."

"Oh, I know I was foolish. Don't look at me like that, Rocky. I did have four matches—"

"Don't talk," Eleanor said. "Let Louise tell us about it."

"Well, I had my flashlight, but the lights in the building were turned off at the switch in Mr.

Kline's office. There's nothing to tell except that I went into my room and found Nancy lying just inside a big closet there."

"I wasn't really unconscious," Nancy croaked. "I knew I was going to be able to get up a little later, but I just didn't want to right then."

"You didn't seem to," Louise said dryly. "I carried her in here— Oh, I'm strong, and she's light as a feather. I admit I was crying and swearing and generally acting like a fool. You see, I was afraid to leave her alone, but I couldn't get in the office to use the telephone. So I threw water on her—"

"You certainly did," Nancy said ungratefully, touching her wet coat.

"And she came to quickly enough and wanted me to take her home and say nothing. But I wouldn't do that. I must admit that when I was over being frightened I didn't want Mrs. Barker to know all about it. That would be the same as a radio broadcast. So it was pure luck that Mr. Barker should have decided to come up and see if they were going to need to order fuel oil tomorrow. He has a key to the office, and he turned on the lights, and I telephoned you."

"Papa Kline's going to think he should have been notified before anyone else was," Nancy remarked.

"I suppose he will, but I just don't see it that way."

"Can Barker keep his mouth shut?" Rocky asked.

"He's had a lot of practice listening and saying nothing, and it's a principle of his never to tell Mrs. Barker anything. I think he can—except that Mr. Kline will have to know about this. He—Mr. Barker—would insist on that. Luckily Mrs. Barker didn't know I was up here because I'd been walking before I came in."

"Isn't anyone going to listen to me?" Nancy said fretfully. "Oh, I'll be brief. I went to Lou's room to get a book. I'd been in my own, first, and when I got near the end of this corridor I did think I heard someone in the main hall. By the time I got my nerve back, lighted a match and turned the corner, there wasn't anyone there."

"Dodged back into my room and into the closet, I suppose."

"Yes, though of course he—she—*it* may have been there all the time, Lou. If I hadn't decided to get a sweater out of that closet nothing would have happened. I'd used all my matches by then. Well, the closet is large, so I didn't brush against whoever was at the back of it, but they—oh, damn pronouns!—they must have been afraid I knew they were there because these—those hands got me around the neck before I could stir.

"Choked me until I was seeing red-and-yellow flashes, and after that it was perfectly safe to dump me down on the floor and get out. I suppose that's what was done with me. There's a minute or two somewhere I can't account for."

Eleanor said, "Poor child," sat down beside Nancy and put her arms about her with a foolish and consoling murmur of words.

"Just what she needs," Louise said to Rocky. "A little mothering. My maternal instinct is slightly underdeveloped."

"But you act quick in an emergency. What time was it when you found her?"

"What time is it now? Nine-fifteen? Then I must have found her about five or ten minutes of nine. I can't be certain. But when I was walking up Mariposa Street it was a quarter of nine. I stopped to see if Nancy was at home and then came over here."

Nancy raised her head from Eleanor's shoulder. "I don't know how long I was wandering around in the dark, but I'm sure it wasn't any later than a quarter of nine when I started into that closet. I looked at my watch before I started up the front steps, and it was eight-thirty then."

"What makes you so set on keeping this quiet?"

"Well, imagine what effect it would have on all the kids. They'd all be staring at me and whispering—and before long everyone would be insisting the high school was haunted. Maybe it is. Anyway,

I'm not going to have this spread all over town," Nancy said. "If you want to know the truth, I don't want Jazz to know about it."

"That's what I thought. I wanted to be sure. Suppose you don't feel like teaching tomorrow?"

"I will wrap a strip of flannel around my throat and say I caught cold."

Rocky laughed. "All right, sister. But don't you pull a stunt like this again."

"I won't. I've had some of the seven years bad luck Mrs. Kline predicted for me when I broke my mirror. You haven't asked me if I know who was in that closet."

"I didn't suppose that was the kind of information you'd suppress just for the sake of suspense."

"Well, I don't know who it was: man, woman or child. Maybe it was one of my loving pupils," Nancy said cheerfully. "They often look at me as if they'd like to strangle me. Anyway, it was someone who had a key to the high school or a way of getting one." "And Jazz," her face added very plainly, "doesn't come under that classification."

CHAPTER FOURTEEN
"A VERY SHARP KITCHEN KNIFE"

"Yes," Rocky said, "someone certainly did have to unlock the place to get in. I'm goin' to look aroun'. I'd like you to come up to your classroom, Miss Whyte, and see if you can find anything missin' there. Eleanor can take Nancy home and put her to bed, and I'll walk."

"I'll wait for you there," Eleanor said. "Or come back for you."

"No; I'll stop by Mrs. Logan's if the car's still out in front. I suppose all of you've got keys to this place?" Rocky said as he and Louise started down the corridor.

"We all have keys to the front door, and Mr. Fulton and I have keys to the outside doors to the gym. Mr. Barker has a complete set to all the doors, and so has Mr. Kline, of course."

"Do they lock the doors between this part of the building and the gym?"

"No, there's no point in doing that. Mr. Kline did talk of it, but Mr. Fulton and I begged off. There's enough locking and unlocking to do around this place as it is."

"I suppose you're careful of your keys?"

"You don't know Mr. Kline," Louise said sadly. "I'd do almost anything before I'd go to him and admit I'd lost my keys. I did lose the one to the gym this year, and I got along without it until I could have a duplicate made from Mr. Fulton's. Oh yes, we guard our keys with our lives."

She switched on the lights in the domestic-science rooms. "I don't know how on earth to tell you if there is anything missing from here. It doesn't seem to me there could be anything in either room that anyone would want. The girls' lockers are all locked. I leave mine open so Nancy can use it, but there is nothing but odds and ends in it."

"What about that closet?"

"Well, take a look for yourself. That's the sweater Nancy wanted, and there are the bookkeeping papers she dropped on the floor."

"Paper towels, a broom, another sweater and a couple of aprons. No, I reckon whoever it was just got in there because it was a good place to hide." Rocky turned on his flashlight and got down on his hands and knees on the closet floor.

"I have always wanted to see a detective do that," Louise said pensively. "If you only had a magnifying glass."

"As a friend of mine said on a sim'lar occasion, I left my magnifyin' glass at home this time. It would be nice," Rocky said, rising to his feet, "if someone would drop a few hairs or a han'kerchief or leave a nice, distinct footprint aroun' where I'd find it. Tomorrow you be sure to notice if anyone misses anything that ought to be here when you all are workin'."

"That might happen. I'm not teaching cooking until next semester," Louise said, stooping to pick the burned matches and paper folder from the floor before passing through the archway into the kitchen. "So this room isn't used as much as the other one just now. We—the teachers—eat lunch in here usually—"

"What's the matter?" Rocky said as she stopped suddenly and stood looking at one of the long kitchen worktables.

"This drawer isn't closed all the way. Yes, it *is* important. It gets on my nerves to see a drawer not closed tightly, and I always slam them shut." Louise jerked the offending drawer open, and her thin shoulders tensed. "Do you see anything interesting?"

"I see a very sharp kitchen knife lyin' on top the rest of the stuff in the drawer. Shouldn't it be there?"

"It should—and it shouldn't. I didn't mean to keep this from you. I simply forgot all about it. That knife," Louise said, "is one I had Mr. Fulton sharpen out at the shop Friday afternoon. I had to help serve supper here Saturday night. We were having ham sandwiches, and," she said with a fleeting grin, "I knew the P.T.A. ladies would want to cut the ham very thin. I didn't have a carving knife, so this had to do. We used tinned baked hams—"

"Did you miss the knife last night, then?"

"Yes. I was slicing ham for a while, and then someone called me to give my expert opinion on the state of the coffee. That was after the first rush was over. Pretty soon I came back and found Mrs. Kline working with a very dull knife. I looked for the other one, but when I couldn't find it, I didn't give the matter much thought."

"I suppose you wouldn't—then."

"If you'd ever cooked you'd know how things that you have in your hand one minute will seem to have taken wings and flown away the next. Of course I should have thought about it afterward. But you didn't tell me—and I'm only guessing now—that you didn't find the knife that was—was used."

"Well, we didn't. I suppose the reason you think there's something funny about finding it is because you checked over things this mornin'?"

"Of course. I was surprised that the knife didn't turn up then. I thought someone would find it last night and put it with all the other things on the table."

"Who among you," Rocky said bluntly, "had a chance to take that knife?"

"All of us. Yes, I mean that. If you think Mr. Kline wouldn't be in here—well, I repeat, you don't know Mr. Kline. He ate rather late, and then he came in and paid his compliments to the kitchen force and looked around to see if we were doing things the right way. Leonard Fulton was with him, and they both stopped to talk to Mrs. Kline."

"Was she cuttin' ham right then?"

Louise frowned. "I can't remember. It seems to me she was buttering bread at the other end of the table. Frankly, when she said this knife was missing I thought she'd mislaid it herself. She's rather careless and absent-minded. The kind who never finds anything she needs at the moment she needs it. Of course she had about the best chance of anyone to take the knife and plenty of clothes to hide it in.

"But there was a little while when the knife was lying there not in use, because I'd cut quite a few slices of ham before I stopped. And I remember wishing to heaven people would stop crowding into this room. Miriam and Mrs. Fulton came in and made polite offers to help which were politely refused. And Florence did help, cutting cake and serving for a while. Nancy was the only one who didn't come in here at all. I'd told her to stay out and not bother me."

"I'm going to take that knife, though I don't know any way to prove it's the one we've been lookin' for. It does happen to be about the right size. I wonder," Rocky said slowly, "why it was necessary to bring it back here."

"So do I. Why not dispose of it in some other way?"

"Or just keep it."

"No. . . ." Louise picked the knife up by its blade and turned it over to show Rocky the small M. H. S. scratched on the bone handle. "I did that to protect high-school property. It wouldn't be perfectly safe to keep a thing like that and claim it was yours, though you could easily miss seeing the initials at first glance."

"Then how does this strike you? Someone knew you'd miss that knife and sooner or later you might connect it with these murders an' begin to ask yourself who could have taken it. Your answer'd be the same as you've already given me. But if you just found it here tomorrow, you'd think it'd been mislaid and you hadn't noticed it when you checked things over."

"Why, I think that's darned good," Louise said with a not very flattering note of surprise in her voice. "Of course it was a rather foolish thing to do."

"If murderers didn't do foolish things once in a while we'd never get a break. It was arguin' a little farther ahead than was really necessary, maybe. Murderers hardly ever leave well enough alone. The ones that're caught don't have the guts to sit tight an' do nothin'. Still, if Nancy had been a little easier frightened you might just have found that knife—"

"And I would have thought it had materialized in the way kitchen utensils so often do. At least, I think I would. Wouldn't that bone handle take fingerprints?"

"It would—and you don't expect anybody would leave any on it, do you? This knife had to be cleaned, you know. But I'll make sure when I go to Brookdale tomorrow." Rocky put the knife in his pocket; took a last look about the room. "I'll take these papers back to Nancy's room and then see if I can find Barker. You go on home and lie like hell to Mrs. Barker if you have to."

He found the janitor just coming out of the gymnasium. "I was lookin' for you. I been taking a good look around. The windows are all O.K., but there's something I wanted to show you. That is—" Barker hesitated—"if you can keep still about it if it don't turn out to be important."

"I can keep still if you can," Rocky said significantly.

"I got to keep my mouth shut or I wouldn't have my job very long with old Kline being principal. Of course he'll have to know what happened to Miss Towers—"

"I expect to tell him. What've you got to show me?"

"This door here." Barker led the way across the gymnasium floor to the stage, past the one tiny dressing room on the left side and several pieces of unnaturally bright stage scenery. "This door here," he said, opening it. "It's got steps down—see? It faces the shop, and there's a path leads over to it. Well, it ain't got a Yale lock, and I always had my suspicions about it."

"Suspicions?"

"Yeah." Barker spat neatly out over the wooden steps below them. "It's hell to work around a place where you can't spit except in the furnace. Well, this door ain't supposed to be used, though it'd be the nearest way for the boys to get to the gym from the shop. Fulton's got a key to it and so has Kline, but it's supposed to be locked all the time except when they give a play. Mr. Kline don't want nobody to be able to sneak in here."

"And you think some people have?" Rocky said impatiently.

"You know how the kids are in this town. Anybody could get a key that'd fit this door. And one time about four years ago a tramp got in some way and cut a square out of their stage curtain for a blanket. I guess I'll have to speak to Kline about it," Barker said reluctantly. "But I spend half my time locking up as it is. Anyway, this here door was unlocked tonight."

Rocky whistled. "It was? Well, s'pose you keep that under your hat for a while. No; don't even tell Kline. He'd just blame you—"

"He would," Mr. Barker agreed gloomily.

"We may never need to tell him about the door bein' unlocked tonight, but it might come in very handy that it was. Later on you can speak to Kline about it without sayin' you ever found it open. When's the last time you looked at it?"

"I dunno. Sometime last week, I guess."

"O.K. Open the main entrance doors for me, will you?"

"I s'pose so." Barker grumblingly dug his keys out of his pocket. "Though why you want—"

"I wanted to look out an' check up on my g'ography. I suppose it wouldn't int'rest you that these

doors to the gym face a lot of baseball field and
vacant lot? And a path that leads over the hill to
Marin Street?"

"What street's that? The one where Heath lived?
He never walked that way at night. Not many people do: it's too dark."

"That's just what I was thinkin': that it'd be
good and dark. Whereas the front entrance to the
high school proper is pretty well lighted. Did you
see Miss Whyte or Miss Towers go by?"

"I set in the kitchen when I'm home. I ain't
interested in who goes by."

"Well, you can lock up here," Rocky said. "I'm
going to use your phone in the office, an' if Kline
wants me to, I'll go down and talk to him."

What really "appalled" Mr. Kline, Rocky decided with rather sour amusement, was not so much
that someone had attacked Nancy but that it had
been done inside his sacred halls of learning.

"I can't understand it," he said flatly. "And I
can't believe . . ." He did not say what it was
that he could not believe. "I did not think anyone
could break into the high-school building, but it
must be possible in some way to do so."

"Through a window, maybe," Mrs. Kline suggested.

"Barker looked at the windows. He said they were all right, and they're all so high off the ground you'd need a ladder to climb in them."

"I suppose one would," Kline admitted. "I am grateful that Miss Whyte and Miss Towers acted so sensibly, though Miss Whyte certainly should have called me at once. But our entire program would be disorganized if this came to be known among the children."

"It may have to be known all over town," Rocky said shortly. "You can thank Miss Towers that it isn't common gossip now."

"I was just going to say that I don't think you seem to appreciate what Miss Towers has been through, Hamilton," Mrs. Kline remarked, smiling nervously. "Of course I know you're just worried about everything, but Mr. Allan may not realize that."

"Oh—oh, of course I am very much concerned about Miss Towers. But Mr. Allan tells me she has suffered no real injury. It was foolish of her to go up there without a light. What did she want?"

"A book she was reading an' some papers to correct. She had a few matches with her, but I'll have to agree she was foolish to do it. Or it seems so now."

"What," said Miss Newman abruptly, "could there be in the domestic-science room that anyone would want?"

She had been with the Klines when Rocky arrived, and Mr. Kline had insisted that she stay. "Miss Newman," he had added, "is always the soul of discretion." But he moved uneasily in his chair as Miss Newman was indiscreet enough to ask a question he had so far evaded.

"Apparently there wasn't anything in there of any value," Rocky said. "Can you think of anything that would be? No? Neither could Miss Whyte. Maybe there's some very simple explanation for someone being there and not wantin' to be caught. You can try to figure it out for yourselves."

"Hamilton went to church," Mrs. Kline volunteered. "I didn't. I was lying down with a headache until Miss Newman came in just before he did. Then I thought I'd just make myself a cup of tea—"

"You didn't go to the Christian Science church, did you, Mr. Kline? The one up there a little past where Heath lived?"

"I went to the community church," Kline said stiffly.

The community church was farther down this street, close to the business section of town. "I suppose," Rocky said, turning to Florence Newman, "that you've talked to Miss Atkins?"

"I didn't know she had returned from Reno. She didn't come to see me. Did she intend to? I've been at home all evening until I came here." Miss Newman smiled frostily as a sign that she knew quite well what was the real significance of Rocky's question. He said:

"She got in a while ago. I guess that's all, so I'll be getting along." Rocky stood up, brushed against an overburdened table and just managed to catch a small vase before it rolled to the floor.

"I'm sure you must be very tired," Mrs. Kline said. "Maybe nothing else unpleasant will happen. Knock on wood! I think I'll go make some tea for all of us. Won't you stay and have some, Mr. Allan?"

"No thanks! I mean—my wife will be waiting for me. I'm sorry you don't feel well, ma'am," Rocky said guilelessly. "You must've worked too hard last night."

"Oh, I only helped out where I could. I'm sure Florence did a lot more than I did, but I do feel tired."

"Did Miss Whyte find the knife that was missing?" Miss Newman said unexpectedly. Rocky tried to look blankly uninterested, but he thought: She's smart, all right. She knows what I was driving at. . . .

"What knife? Oh, that one. We looked all over for it and never did find it. I'm afraid Miss Whyte thinks I mislaid it, but I'm perfectly certain I didn't. I never used it at all. She was using it, and I was buttering bread—"

"Does it matter?" Mr. Kline said impatiently.

"Why—Hamilton! It really isn't like you to be so cross. I don't know that it matters, only you're always so careful of school property. And I did see the knife lying there on the cutting board when Miss Whyte went to look at the coffee—because Mrs. Thomas thought it was getting to be a *little* too weak—and then when I went over to cut some ham the knife just wasn't there. I did the best I could with another one, but it was very dull. I wonder if Leonard would see to sharpening some of our knives. But I hate to ask him, because Gertrude says he simply won't bother to do hers, so she never has a sharp knife in the house either. But I'm sure Miss Whyte's found that knife by now."

"If any of the school children had been in the kitchen, I would think," Miss Newman said, "that one of them might have taken it. We have had odder thefts than that."

"I wonder," Kline said, "if, in spite of my many cautions against doing so, some of the teachers may have lost keys at some time. Young Mitchell has known Miss Towers since the beginning of the school year."

"So he stole one of her keys so's he could go up to the high school whenever the notion struck him?" Rocky said derisively. "That won't wash. If you want to pin this on Jazz you'll have to argue he did it without plannin' any farther ahead than after he squabbled with Heath. There's no place for keys to the high school in that the'ry. Anyway—was Jazz ever in the kitchen last night, Miss Newman?"

"No; or if he was, I didn't see him. I don't believe he ate supper at the high school."

"I'm sure all of the teachers are very careful not to mislay their keys. You know you *are* very particular about them, Hamilton. Not just your own. Well, Miss Towers was very foolish. I wouldn't think of going up to the high school alone at night. Of course I couldn't get in unless I went with Hamilton. I haven't been up there for quite a while until last night, though I like to go up to walk home with Hamilton, and I always thought how quiet the place is when the children have gone. But Miss Towers is a determined little thing. Oh, are you going, Mr. Allan? Well, if you won't stay and have a cup of tea . . ."

Rocky felt that he needed something a great deal stronger than tea as he walked wearily back to the high school and then over to Mariposa Street. Well, at least he never forgot a conversation, and perhaps when he wasn't so tired he would be able to decide what had been said that was important and what was not.

He thought that Eleanor would probably have gone home by this time, but Dud Williams' car was parked in front of the Logans' house and Eleanor met him at the door.

"Mrs. Logan came in, but she's gone to bed," she whispered. "Nancy buttoned up her coat so her throat didn't show, and Mrs. Logan thinks I'm just talking to her. Nancy says to come in: she wants to ask you something."

"As long as Mrs. Logan knows you're here it ought to be all right. What's on your mind now, Nancy?"

"Keys," Nancy said huskily. "Eleanor and I have been talking about them."

"They're very much on Mr. Kline's mind too. He's afraid some of you haven't guarded them as you should've."

"And I was afraid that was what he would think. Well, I will solemnly swear I have never either lost or mislaid mine for one minute. And you can tell that to Papa Kline or anyone else who wants to know."

"I more or less gave Kline to understand I didn't think anyone outside the faculty could get hold of a key to the high school." Rocky did not mention the unlocked door off the gymnasium stage. "He began tryin' to figure out how Jazz could've got a key from you."

Nancy sat up in bed. "He's got an awful nerve." She flushed and pulled the covers hastily up to her chin. "I've got a good mind to stay home to-morrow and let him get along without me just to teach him a lesson! The man's a monomaniac. All he cares about is running his high school the right way. Well, to hell with him!"

"The ayes have it. But you'd better go to school if you can. If Jazz found out someone tried to throttle you, he'd start chasin' all over town tryin' to find out who did it. Also, he'd call me names because I don't know who did and can't do any-thing about it."

"I know that." Nancy lay down again. "He has enough on his mind without adding that. But I shall be cool and distant with Papa Kline—and I hope he'll realize that I am."

"We'd better go home and let you get some sleep. There was just one thing I wanted to ask you. Did you have a paperweight made like a little cat with a grin on its face?"

"How did you know? It was white with a blue bow around its neck. Awfully cute. Paul Heath gave it to me. He had three."

"A black one—"

"Yes, and a yellow one. He gave me my choice. I had mine at the high school, and it was among the things that have disappeared this year. All the youngsters liked it so much that I don't wonder I didn't keep it. Paul thought one of the McGees took it, but we couldn't prove that."

"Was he in the habit of givin' his lady friends things like that?"

"Oh yes. He gave me a blotter with a funny elephant on top of it and one of these figures of a drunk leaning against a lamppost—which I couldn't put on display. It's on the table over there. Yes," Nancy said, "he did have a habit of handing out perfectly worthless trifles like those."

"For your information, Mr. Allan, things like that make a hit with a woman," Eleanor said.

"Is that so? I was going to give you one of those real jade rings from Chinatown for your birthday, but if you'd rather have something unique I've got the tooth of a bear I killed once, and I can have that made into some kind of gadget."

Nancy giggled; then said soberly, "Paul always said, 'It's the sentiment that counts.' Meaning to be funny, of course. Were you wondering if he'd be apt to give that coin to someone for a keepsake? It would have been just like him."

"That's what I thought. Come on, honey; let's go home." Rocky reached over and patted the top of Nancy's curly head. "Don't you tell anybody one least little detail about what happened tonight. Promise? An' don't have nightmares. Nobody meant to kill you, an' it won't happen again. . . .

"Are there very many things you want from Brookdale?" he asked, climbing into the car. "Because if you think you can let me bring back what you want, would you mind stayin' here tomorrow?"

"Not particularly. I'll have to write you a list, and you'll make hay of my bureau drawers. I'll draw a diagram. 'Rear left-hand corner of second drawer from top—socks. May be identified by characteristic shape and appearance.'"

"Now, sugar, I do know a sock when I see one, but you keep changin' the places you put 'em. I thought I might take Jazz with me to Brookdale. Keep him out of mischief an' do him good."

"Yes, it will. But do you think— What will they say in Brookdale?"

"Who cares? He don't have to go into town. He probably won't want to. He can stay out at the

field and watch the plane. There's hardly ever anybody aroun' there. I'm only going to be in Brookdale long enough to bawl hell out of those so-
called deputies."

Eleanor smiled into the darkness as they went
up the steps to their own house. Those two men in
Brookdale—Cy Rand and Al Sully—who had until now pronounced Rocky a "good-natured kid,"
were going to have the surprise of their lives tomorrow. At a certain stage in any investigation
of this kind Rocky, in his own idiom, "got a full
head of steam and blew up." He was probably getting ready to do that now. . .

She switched on the lights and picked up an
envelope that had been thrust underneath the
front door. "Well, this *is* funny. Mrs. Fulton wants
to know if I won't come over and keep her company tomorrow afternoon. I wonder why?"

"Maybe she wants to try to pump you."

"Oh, you have an evil mind!" Eleanor said,
mimicking Miriam. Atkins. "Listen; she says, 'I
suppose you won't think I'm asking you just because I like you and get fed up with this town and
most of the women in it. Don't come if you don't
want to, and if you do we won't talk about anything but clothes.' I think I'll go."

"I reckon it might be a good thing if you did."
Rocky walked into the bedroom and stood looking

down at the bed. "The sight of this makes me feel poetical. 'Oh bed! reasonable bed, precious bed, long-sought bed, invaluable bed, coveted bed, necessary bed—'"

"Why—Rocky!"

"Honey, my mamma used to read *Water Babies* to me by the hour, and those were the biggest-sounding words I'd ever heard. I've got no hankering after 'backstairs,'" Rocky said, sitting down and attacking his boots, "but I sure as hell have after a little sleep."

CHAPTER FIFTEEN
MR. HAYNES SAFEGUARDS JUSTICE

For fifteen minutes Cy Rand had been sulking fatly in one corner of the sheriff's office in the courthouse at Brookdale. Al Sully had put on his hat and, without being ordered to do so, had gone down to the jungle to try to trace the canned goods that had been removed from Gray's Food Emporium on Saturday night.

"You know," Rocky said presently, putting a rubber band around the letters he had just read, "you guys don't need to send me an SOS every time somebody swipes a can of beans. With all your experience you can handle things like that by yourself."

Cy was ready to consider this a compliment and resume conversation. "Well, I guess I ought to be able to handle 'most anything. That time me and Jake Thompson chased them auto bandits halfway across Nevada after they'd killed two fellows—"

"Lorenzo broke all records on today's inquest," Rocky said hastily.

"That so? How'd Merton like that?"

"They didn't. It's their murder, an' they'd like to know all about it. Like to have a weapon to look at and other interestin' exhibits."

"I noticed you goin' over that knife for fingerprints. I guess there wasn't any? I never took much stock in fingerprints myself. Me 'n' Jake—"

"Heard from him lately?"

"Other day. He says he's happier now he's quit Richardson Springs and drinkin' that min'ral water, though it may've been good for his rheumatism. He asked after Freddie Haynes."

"I was just goin' to ask after Freddie myself."

"He breezed in here this morning with a carnation in his buttonhole. He only got in about seven, but he was here at eight. Wanted to know all I knew about the case. I told him," Cy said rather maliciously, "that you hadn't told any of us anything. He wanted to know had you made a arrest."

"He would. How'd he get his information? I haven't seen a city paper, but it seems to me yesterday was a little soon for the news to be in them."

"I don't think it could've been by the time Freddie left the city last night. I tell you—" Cy did not care any more for the public prosecutor than did Rocky or Jake Thompson—"I think your J.P.

in Merton—old Bartley—tipped him off. They always been thick as thieves. So when he couldn't get anything out of me, Freddie lit out for Merton."

"The hell he did!"

"Didn't you see him?"

"I'll bet he took damn good care I didn't. He wouldn't have got to Merton before the inquest started, and he knows what Lorenzo's inquests are like. I went straight from the mortuary out to the flyin' field. I suppose he's still up there talkin' to folks."

"Kissin' babies!" Cy said. "That's how he gets elected. And them punk cigars he hands out so free. What I say, he ought to stick to his own department and let us run ours."

"He's got the right to investigate—unfortunately. He can—"

"Speak of the devil!" Cy muttered, and became very busy cleaning his antique pipe.

Mr. Frederick Haynes entered the office with an air—the air of one who was already bowing his appreciation of the applause of a crowded courtroom. The carnation in his buttonhole was a trifle wilted, but his fawn-colored spats and stiff white collar were still spotless.

"So I caught you here? I was afraid you would have started back to Merton."

"You must've come back pretty fast. It ain't noon yet."

"I drove," Mr. Haynes caroled. "Oh yes, I drove. Of course I have not conquered the airways as you have. Well, Allan, I think I have our man."

Rocky had stood up when Haynes came in, but now he backed hastily away and sat down again. Haynes was one of these fellows who couldn't talk without tapping you on the chest and blowing his breath out in your face. Rocky was always thankful that the top of Haynes's head came somewhere under his chin, but it was just as well to sit down when you talked to him, because he would chase you all over the room if you were standing and tried to keep away from him.

"It's right nice of you to bother," Rocky said. "What do you think I been doin' these last twenty-four hours?"

"I attempted to discover that." Haynes turned arid looked at Cy Rand until even that gentleman's thick skin was pierced. He mumbled "see what Al's doing" and went out.

"Yes, I tried to find out what you have been doing," Haynes continued. "From what I gather you have been annoying the high-school faculty: the educators of our youth and future citizens—"

"And voters. I'm only one vote, Haynes, and that one won't ever be for you. Come down off the platform. If you begin on the great American eagle you'll have me weepin'.'"

All Haynes needed to look like a turkey gobbler distended to full capacity was a pair of wings scraping the floor. Rocky stopped to admire this phenomenon before he concluded, "Let's have it. Who is it you want me to arrest?"

"You know that as well as I do. Gerald Mitchell. The case against him is open and shut."

"You've got an open an' shut mind, you mean! It opens up a crack and then shuts up tighter 'n glue." Rocky fumbled in his pocket for cigarettes and lighted one slowly. He must not lose his temper again: that wouldn't do Jazz any good. And he couldn't claim to have an open mind on this subject himself. "Let's hear your case," he said evenly.

"Motive: Mitchell hated Heath and had—improper relations with Miss Selby. He wanted to marry Miss Towers, and Heath was his rival for her affections. He had to get rid of both Heath and Miss Selby to succeed with Miss Towers. I'm not saying that she was connected in any other way with these hideous crimes that are a blot on the character of our fair county—" Mr. Haynes stopped, swallowed and checked his winged oratory in mid-flight. "I mean, I have no idea she even remotely guessed how far Mitchell would go."

"That's nice of you. Let's take up your points one at a time. You can prove Jazz didn't like Heath and maybe that he had what you call improper relations with Clarice Selby. You can't prove he wanted to marry Miss Towers an' you can't prove Clarice was tryin' to hold onto him. Just the contrary is what you'll find out if you try it."

"Oh! Then you have investigated those points? Well, I will take your word for that," Haynes said nobly. "We have enough against him in the way of motive without it. I found by talking to various people that Heath and Mitchell quarreled at the dance Saturday night and that Mitchell left with the idea of following him home to—to settle with him. And Mitchell was seen leaving his cabin at three-thirty—"

"Clarice Selby was killed at four o'clock. And Leaman—who saw Jazz—saw him goin' back into his place, not comin' out."

"You can't prove that he didn't leave it again."

"Can you prove that he did? He can't prove he didn't go straight home after the dance, but neither can you prove he didn't. Can you?"

"I haven't yet found anyone who saw him at the scene of the crime at the proper time. Uh—what was it, by the way?"

"Between two-fifteen and two thirty-five, for Heath's death."

Mr. Haynes frowned ponderously over this information, then: "Well, those things can be ironed out when we have assembled our evidence."

"Listen, Haynes: I'll admit if you're the kind that thinks any old arrest is better 'n none, you've got enough against Jazz Mitchell to arrest him. You can get out a warrant, and I'll have to serve it. You might even bring him to trial, though it's no sure thing you will unless you get a grand jury packed with Brookdale people."

"Do you dare to insinuate—"

"I'm not through talkin'," Rocky said gently. "If you do bring him to trial you're goin' to be the laughing stock of the county. You ought to know evidence: think yours over. With a good lawyer—an' I'll see he gets one—he'll get off."

"What lawyer?"

"Well, how about old Gregory? He used to live here, so he'd just be a home-town boy who'd made good and come home."

Haynes smiled unhappily. He had no desire to match his courtroom technique with Gregory's. "If you have other evidence . . ."

Now, Rocky thought, he *was* on a blind siding with no phone. All Haynes wanted right now was an excuse to play along with him. But would the evidence he had be enough to convince him? No: he could probably twist some of it around to fit

Jazz. There were some points he had to suppress, anyway, to leave himself an out. And it wouldn't be safe to tell Haynes much of anything.

Give him a few facts, and he'd start chewing on them like a pup would a pair of rubbers. They'd be about like the rubbers when Haynes got through: pieces scattered everywhere and none of them looking very much like they had in the beginning. On the other hand, Freddie's tender vanity was going to be very much wounded if he wasn't confided in.

"Well, I'll tell you, Mr. Haynes—I don't like to speak too soon against anybody, so we'd better let it ride for a while. I admit I've been talking to the faculty up at Merton because those people were Heath's friends an' we may find out something more about him from them. But I promised to spare them all the publicity I can till we know something definite."

Rocky knew as soon as he had said it that he should not have used the word "publicity." Haynes snapped, "I am quite as regardful of all that as you could possibly be. I doubt if you know anything at all. Bluff. . . ."

"Oh, I've learned one or two kind of int'resting facts. You can ask the cor'ner if you think I'm just bluffing. He didn't see any use letting his jury know everything."

Haynes did not look as if he cared for the idea of going to Lorenzo Sloane for information. "The trouble with you, my boy, is that you're getting too big for your boots," he said, reverting to the vernacular. "You think because you were a fool for luck on two occasions no one can tell you anything. But both your criminals cheated the gallows."

"And you out of a trial. I thought you were elected on an economy program, so you shouldn't mind that."

"Ten to one," Haynes said, "this precious evidence of yours points against Mitchell. I know he's your friend. You had him to dinner last night, didn't you? Well, it won't do, Allan. I, at least, will safeguard justice in this county."

"'Liberty,'" said Rocky pensively, "'what crimes are committed in thy name.' Don't you forget the voters of Merton, Haynes. A lot of them—not the ones you talked to—like Jazz Mitchell. They'd hate to see him arrested on suspicion. So would the railroad if it turned out you'd been too hasty."

"I won't make any new move until tomorrow," Haynes said slowly. "I'll give you that long. Then, if you don't prove to me with evidence that Mitchell could not have killed that fine, upstanding young man and that—that girl, I must take some action."

Rocky grimaced unconsciously as he accepted this ultimatum. He didn't dare yield to his impulse to tell Haynes to go lay an egg. There were probably enough people who would applaud his action that Haynes would feel he dared to chance the arrest. Though that remark about the railroad had made him stop and think for a minute. . . .

"I suppose," Rocky said with suspicious meekness, "that you'd accept the real criminal in place of Jazz?"

Haynes snorted. "Bluff again! Why don't you settle down to business instead of dashing around the county in an airplane? It's not necessary: I haven't any plane."

"Mine's my own, and I pay for the upkeep. Tell you what: I'll let you use it all you want if you get a license to pilot it."

Mr. Haynes hastily mentioned his high blood pressure. "And you might try to apprehend other dangerous criminals. That Negro, Harvey—I heard he was down in the jungle here last week. But was he captured? No—"

"I got to congratulate you, Mr. Haynes. There's nothing slow about you. How'd you know that n— was workin' his way East? You go right to the point, don't you? Now if we can just get hold of him before he gets too far away from Merton . . ."

A complacent smile erased Mr. Haynes's momentary look of bewilderment. "Anyone would have known he must have gone to Merton from here. He couldn't hop a freight here: it's not on the main line. That's elementary."

Rocky choked and said hastily, "I inhaled the wrong way that time. Go on."

"Elementary. Of course," Haynes said with an uneasy look at Rocky, "the Negro is only one possibility. I never overlook one. It occurred to me— but of course he had no motive."

"Oh, I don't think he could've done it. Like you say, he hadn't any motive, though he does carry a knife with him and he's classed as a kind of homicidal maniac. But I don't see how it could've been him."

"I don't suppose you would. You'd rather pursue some more romantic theory. I advise you not to miss what is right under your eyes. I'll see you tomorrow? Good morning. . . ."

"Well, he brought it on himself," Rocky muttered. "He can't say it was my idea, and I told him what I really think only he didn't have sense enough to know it." He went to the door and shouted, "Cy! O Cy! Yes, His Nibs has retired to his Holy of Holies. Run me around to the house, will you—and then out to the flyin' field?"

Jazz was sitting on the grass with his back
against a wing of the plane, strumming on the guitar he had brought along "to pass the time away,"
and singing "The Eyes of Texas Are upon You" as
Rocky and Cy came up. He grinned at Rocky and
began:

*"Pa'don my Southern accent; pa'don my Southern
drawl . . ."*

"You sound just about like most of the Yankees
that sing that."

"Do you know, 'She's Only a Bird in a Gilded
Cage'?" Cy said.

Jazz laughed, but he sang it, with a very satis-
factory nasal quaver on the chorus.

"That's swell. I was nuts once about a girl went
and married a rich guy. Nice day, ain't it?"

Jazz said it was a nice day and as if he meant it.
He looked younger and less haggard this morning.
Rocky found himself wishing they could keep on
going once they were in the air, but there was no
use thinking about that. In twenty-five minutes
he'd be setting the plane down on the Merton flying field again.

The car he had rented from one of the garages
was still parked to one side of the road that ran
past the airport. "What are you going to do now?"
Jazz said, tossing his guitar onto the back seat.

"I wish you'd tell me. I don't know anything in partic'lar to do. I'm at a dead end."

"I hear Clarice's funeral is going to be tomorrow."

"Yes, it is. Ma Jenkins an' Pat Healy and Dr. Jordan made all the arrangements."

"I'm going," Jazz said quietly. "You wouldn't expect me to hide out until it's over?"

"I s'pose not. Will you go with us?"

"If you want it like that. People will begin to say you're keeping me under your eye. Oh, I don't care about that. It was—I'm glad you took me with you this morning. It was good to get out of town and away up above everything. You'll have to finish teaching me to fly when you get time for it."

"I always said I would. What made you stop takin' lessons in Reno? You got in quite a bit of flyin' time over there, didn't you?"

"I had a little disagreement with the instructor. He didn't like the way I like to take off."

"You won't take off in any climbin' turn when I'm with you," Rocky promised. "So get that off your mind." He stopped the car in front of the town hall. "Come on in an' see what Dud has to say."

The first five minutes of Dud's conversation dealt with Mr. Frederick Haynes, his character and probable ancestry. Rocky gathered that Dud

entertained serious doubts of the morals of Mr.
Haynes' mother, as well as a deep distrust of anyone who wore spats.

"So he says to me, 'You 'n' me can work together to advantage, Williams. You can help me out
a lot with my investigation.' And I says, 'What
investigation? Was you investigatin' something? I
thought you was a lawyer.' Then he give me a long
spiel about how he was responsible for seein' justice done in this county, and I says he'll have to
excuse me because I got my own rightful work to
look after and believed in doin' it instead of med-
dlin' in other people's business."

"He's within his rights, Dud."

"Is he? Well, I don't care about that. Then him
and old Bartley put their heads together. Bartley
was here, but he was already so soused he had to
go home a hour ago, so I don't guess he was much
help to Haynes. After that I heard he went out
and listened to all the dirt anybody'd tell him,
and there's plenty who got nothing to do but talk.
'Specially if you want to buy them a drink. I also
heard he went to see the principal and he referred
Haynes back to you."

"Good for old Kline. But I don't suppose he'd
want to waste his time on a school day going over
things again. Haynes didn't mention that."

"Oh, you saw him in Brookdale?"

"He high-tailed it back there," Rocky said with a sidewise glance at Jazz. "Yes, I saw him. We had quite a talk. He ain't going to do anything for a while. Did you say anything about that n— to him, Dud?"

"I mentioned him. I told Haynes I was doin' my part keepin' an eye out for any dang'rous characters that hit town."

"That's why he was so receptive to the idea, maybe," Rocky said obscurely. He reached for the telephone. "Have you had dinner, Dud? You have? . . . Say, Nick, trot two orders of whatever you've got that's good over to the town hall. . . . Hunh? . . . Sure, that's all right. What kind of pie do you want, Jazz?"

"Apple," Jazz said absently. "Won't Eleanor be expecting you?"

"Make it apple, Nick, and plenty of coffee. . . . I told her not to get dinner for me. It's after one now, and she's going callin' this afternoon. You haven't seen anything aroun' that looks like a reporter, have you, Dud?"

"There ain't been any."

"I didn't suppose there would. And, thank God, there's no train leavin' the city till this evenin'. I guess Tom Wright must've played down the story he wired to Sacramento."

The telephone rang, and Rocky answered it. "What? . . . All right, I'll send someone out right away. He hasn't got a gun, has he? . . . Oh, just a bed slat! O.K." He turned to Dud.

"Morelli, out at the mill, has gone on a toot again and wants to beat up his wife with anything handy."

"That damn wop! It's that vino he makes himself. I can drink most anything, but that stuff of his would eat your guts out. Who phoned?"

"His wife's locked herself up in the front room, where their phone is. She wants to be rescued before he breaks in a window and gets to her."

Dud grimaced. "I've rescued that dame before. If I beat up on her old man doin' it, she gets sore. Or she changes her mind and don't want him put in the can. Well, I'll go. . . . Hell no! I don't need any help. I can tie that wop in knots any day."

He held the door open for the small Greek whose name no one could either spell or pronounce and went on out to his car. "Good roas' bif with gravies," Nick said proudly, putting his tray down on the desk and whisking away the napkin. "With zoup, with potatoes, with apple pie. You eat it all, hanh? I come back for the tray sometimes. No—you pay me when you come in rest'rant next times. I know who I trust: Mr. Mitchell and Mr. Allan I trust all times."

"He's a good egg, even if you can't tell his roast beef from any other kind of roast," Jazz said. "Rocky, what did—"

"I know what you're goin' to ask me, and if it's all the same to you I'd rather eat in peace. I'd rather you would too. If you leave any of that stuff on your plate, Nick will say what he did to me once: 'This is not for look at: is for eat.'"

Jazz smiled dutifully, but his question waited only for the last bite of apple pie. "What did Haynes really say?"

"That he wouldn't make any move till he'd talked to me again tomorrow."

"And after that?"

"I don't know. Generous guy, ain't he? Gives me half a day to produce another—to find out—"

"To produce another suspect," Jazz said.

"I reckon that's one way to put it. I don't think he'll arrest you, though. Because I haven't told him anything, so far, and that's got under his skin. If I give him all the evidence tomorrow he'll probably think different about things."

"You mean about that coin and all the rest of it? You don't want to tell him, do you? He'll mess things up if you do." Jazz looked about the small room. Rocky believed he was thinking, A cell isn't even as large as this. But he said, "Well, don't tell him."

"That's—you'll have to let me make up my mind about that, Boy Scout," Rocky said, deliberately casual. "It isn't just because I think he'd mess up things that I don't want to tell him all my myth'logical an' historical researches—yet. I've got another reason. Are you goin' back to work Wednesday?"

"I'm supposed to. But I won't if things are like they are now. If I'm going to be arrested I don't want to be dragged away in the middle of clearing a train."

"It'd probably be better if you stayed off duty till things are cleared up. All I want is a little time," Rocky said, scowling at the desk. "And that conceited pip-squeak won't give it to me. He's got me where the hairs are short— What the hell's that?"

"Somebody seems to be kicking up a row in the jail. . . ."

CHAPTER SIXTEEN
WANTED FOR MURDER

The sole occupant of Merton's bastille was seated on a rickety cot trying to demolish two tin plates by beating one against the other as accompaniment for the weird noises that came from his throat. It might be yodeling, Rocky thought, or he might just be a champion hog caller out of a job. He said mildly:

"I didn't think there was anyone left in here. What's the matter with you?"

"I told you I'd make a noise if you dragged me in here! I haven't done anything— Oh, you're not the same fellow," the youngster said, looking up at Rocky through the bars on the upper half of the door.

"I'm not the guy that put you in here. Didn't you want to come? Dud fed you, didn't he?"

"I don't want to be fed in jail. I'm no bum: I'm a 'bo," Dud's prisoner said indignantly. "I'll work any time anyone will give me anything to do."

Rocky studied the boy and decided that he was probably telling the truth. He could not be more than eighteen and had the weedy look of a plant that had managed to grow under difficulties. There was a sparse stubble of yellowish beard on his chin, but his hands and the back of his neck were clean.

"What'd Dud pull you in for?"

"Nothing—nothing at all. I was offering to wash dishes at one of the rest'rants for a bowl of soup or some coffee. I told him I'd work, but he wouldn't listen to me."

"He's heard that story before, you know." Rocky produced the official keys and unlocked the door. "Come on out if you want to, but you might find it a lot more comfortable to stay here tonight."

"I'm not used to sleeping in a jail. Anyway—" the boy scratched himself vigorously—"those cots are lousy."

"So I've heard. They do delouse once in a while, but considerin' what kind of guests we have it's kind of a waste of time. What's your name?"

"Jim Somers. They call me Slim."

"Come on in here. Slim," Rocky explained to Jazz, "don't care for our hospitality. He'd rather work."

"I'm a bindle stiff, but I'm no bum," Slim repeated. "Sure, I'll work—if anyone will let me."

"I'll let you if you're sure you won't faint at the sight of a woodpile."

"The acid test to determine whether a guy's a bum or a hobo," Jazz murmured, but his hand was going mechanically toward his pocket when Rocky frowned at him. "You're kind of young to be on the bum."

"There wasn't enough to eat at home. I'm eighteen, anyway. I'll chop wood for you. Where is it?"

"In the woodshed back of my place. Do you know the town? Well, it's on Mariposa: the last street over. A log house with a stag's head over the front door. I'll give you a note to my wife, though I don't think she'll be there. You can show it if anyone asks what you're doin' there."

He turned over the papers on the desk until he found a memorandum pad. "It's up to you. If you want to do the work, come back when you've had enough and I'll pay you whatever— What's the matter with you?"

The boy was staring at one of the printed circulars that had been turned face up on the desk. "Is that fellow wanted for m-murder?" he said.

Rocky looked at the official photograph of Buck Harvey. "Twice over, kid. Did you ever see him?"

"I never saw him, and I didn't know he was wanted for killing anyone. But he's been down in this jungle—"

"The hell he was! When? Whereabouts was he?"

Slim squirmed away from the pressure of Rocky's hand on his shoulder. "I don't know exactly where he hung out. Not where I or very many others ever saw him, I guess. But there were some bums down there last night—I got in last night—two of them: tough eggs. Maybe they're wanted too. I steer clear of that kind usually, but they gave me something to eat. Afterward I was lying by the fire half asleep, and they were talking and didn't know I listened."

"Well! What did they say? And get it straight! This is important!"

"I just heard a few words at first. They were talking about a Negro who carried a knife and was dangerous. I mean, they seemed to be afraid of him themselves. One of them said you couldn't tell what he'd do and it was better to stay away from him. I heard one of them say 'hiding out,' and that they'd been watching the freights too close."

"How long had he been aroun' there?"

"I don't know. Oh yes, they said something about Saturday night 'uptown' and that 'he was taking a chance, but he had to eat.'"

"Mrs. Leaman lost a leg of lamb off her back porch sometime before yesterday mornin'," Rocky said softly. "Go on. . . ."

"But he isn't in the jungle now. I got that much. Because they finally mentioned someplace that used to be a station but isn't any more—"

Jazz and Rocky looked at each other. "Alder Creek?" Jazz said.

"There was a Creek to it. I began to really listen then, because they said a lot of freights had to stop at a siding there and it was an easy place to hop one."

"That's Alder Creek," Jazz said. "It always was that way."

"And you think that's where Harvey's hiding out?"

"Where he *was* hiding. I don't know about now. They didn't say, but they spoke like he might just have left and headed for there last night. They cleared out this morning."

"It's five miles. Here!" Rocky shoved a five-dollar bill into Slim's hand. "That's for your information, and it may be worth a lot more. There's a reward for that guy. Go chop wood if you want to, and after that I'll see if I can get you a job. Go on; scram!"

"Why all the gratitude?" Jazz said. "Do you want the Negro that bad?" He studied the circular. "'This man is dangerous . . . .' Six foot one and two hundred and ten pounds. He ought to be able to take care of himself without a knife— He looks good-natured enough. What are you loading that gun for?"

"You just read the answer to that. I'm goin' after him, and I'm not waiting for Dud. Like to come along?"

"Why not?"

"It might be good policy for you to. Can you shoot?"

"I couldn't hit the broad side of a barn at five feet," Jazz said cheerfully.

"Then I won't trust you with a gun. You might hit me. Come on."

"Of course," Jazz said as they crossed the bridge at the end of the town, "I can see why you want to get your hands on him, but why will it be good policy for me to come along? And why the unusual excitement?"

"Public opinion is a funny thing," Rocky said, watching the needle on the speedometer climb up to fifty. "If we can bring back this n— maybe we can both be heroes. I could give you a black eye and claim you got it by overpowerin' him."

"No thanks." Jazz stroked his chin reminiscent-ly. "I'd rather run into a door, and nobody would believe you anyway. Sa-ay! Are you going to claim this fellow killed Heath and Clarice?"

"Why not? I'm a very practical person," Rocky said modestly. "I b'lieve in using whatever comes handy in an emergency. Dud's already got the idea he might have. So has Haynes—mainly because I put it in his head an' then told him I was sure the n— couldn't have done it. We've got that kid's evidence Harvey was here Saturday night and went uptown. Maybe he did take Mrs. Leaman's meat off the back porch. That'd make the Leamans of some use for once."

"But—"

"Hell! I don't think he did it. Why do you s'pose I didn't want to tell Haynes anything more anyone else knows? That'd spoil things. A few people would know Harvey ain't the killer, but they'll give me time to work things out. It can't hurt Harvey. They've got a clear case against him for killin' Burns in Oroville, and he can only hang once."

"It's damned ingenious," Jazz admitted. "Yes, I can see how you might put it over with most people. What about motive?"

"Does a guy with his record—'suffers from delusions of persecution'—need a motive? I can fix it up to prove Heath may've delayed locking his door for a while and didn't know the person who killed him; that for all we know the n— saw the light and busted in. Then ran into Clarice going

away from there, watched to see where she lived
and disposed of her afterward. Or just climbed in
the window an' killed her on general principles.
Oh, there's plenty of embarrassing questions that
can be asked. But no one will, for a while. Well,
by that time—"

"We'll have gone in the ditch," Jazz said, clutch-
ing the side of the door as they skidded. "Suppose
he'll still be down there?"

"Christ, I hope so! But I don't know. The old
station's boarded up, but there was a kind of storehouse back of it that's just falling to pieces. That's
where the bums hide out. You can't watch that far
out of town all the time."

"You're a lucky stiff if you happen to catch him
from what that kid told you."

"Things do happen like that. You've got to
get a few good breaks in any game. An old timer
wouldn't have told us what that kid did, so I reckon you can call that luck."

"This is the first place I ever worked on this
road," Jazz said presently, looking out at the
boarded-up, faded tan station house. "That was
eight years ago. They never did really need a station here. I've got good reason to remember that
storehouse you spoke of—climbing up- and down-
hill to it."

"It doesn't look to me like anyone's meddled
with these boards," Rocky said. "It's a wonder

they haven't been torn off for fires. Let's go down to that shack."

The front of the station faced the railroad tracks. In back the ground fell away steeply to the sluggish thread of water that was Alder Creek. For some reason a small storehouse had been built close to its bank instead of on the hill beside the station.

"I think they had some idea the agent's food supply would keep cooler down by the water," Jazz said. "They're letting the place fall to pieces."

"It's been in use." The door creaked on its rusty hinges as Rocky thrust it open. "Somebody got hold of enough boards to knock a bunk together."

From among the assortment of empty tin cans on the floor he picked up the stub of a candle and then a crust of bread. "This is still pretty soft. Someone's been here not so very long ago."

"I don't doubt that: this is a great place for bums to hang out. They can sneak up the hill and hop a freight in the dark. But you don't know it was Harvey who was here," Jazz said pessimistically. "And if he was, he's evidently cleared out by now."

"Maybe. There was a freight called east at ten last night, but that didn't do him any good because it went the other way. You'd think he'd want to head east, but maybe he's finding that pretty hard to do. He might've decided to go down the canyon again."

"I heard Boomer Jackson whistling out early this morning," Jazz said. "I suppose that was an extra west. I remember thinking they'd have to meet Number Six somewhere."

"Would he dare to take a chance in the day-time? If I was in his shoes I'd wait till I got a chance to grab a ride at night. I'm going out and look up and down the crick," Rocky said. "Better come along."

"It's a waste of time. I'll wait here."

"Better not. He might come back."

"Nuts! He's nowhere around, and he wouldn't come back if he was. He could hear the car drive up and us walking down the hill. I'll yell and run if I see anything."

Rocky shrugged impatiently. "You're probably right. But I'll take a look aroun' anyway."

Anyone who had sense enough to crouch down in the underbrush along the stream and nerve enough to keep still, could hide there for a long time, he thought. Or get across the creek in one jump and disappear into the brush on the other side of it. He had been a fool not to wait to draft half a dozen men to cover the ground thoroughly.

In spite of all Jazz's reasoning to the contrary he thought—no, he felt—that Buck Harvey was not very far away from the deserted storehouse. Jazz would laugh if he said, "Fee, fi, fo, fum! I smell the blood of an Englishman!" but the feeling was something like that.

He turned back finally, after having gone several hundred yards up the stream. It wouldn't do to go too far in one direction: he had better try going downstream for a ways. And he didn't particularly like to leave Jazz alone.

He walked a little faster. It was lonely down here. Nearly all mountain streams chattered and laughed, but this one was dumb. And that station house looked like an old blind man peering down at him.

He pushed the door to the storehouse open and for one instant stood stone-still. Jazz was a motionless sprawl on the dirty floor, and an enormous, hulking figure bent over him, fumbling with black hands for a knife thrust through the waistband of filthy blue jeans.

Rocky jerked at his gun; discovered a sharp, quick voice that did not seem to belong to him: "Put 'em up, n—! I've got you covered!"

Harvey spun about to face him, drew his head down between his shoulders and came at him with the insane charge of a whirling dervish.

Rocky was utterly unprepared for that mad rush. He threw his gun up—some deep-rooted aversion kept him from shooting at the fellow's stomach. In another instant the gun was wrenched from his fingers, and he heard it thud on the floor and had time to think, "That was a fool stunt," before the Harvey's immense arms locked about him.

They went to the floor with a crash. Rocky got one arm free and jabbed uselessly at a heavy jaw and chest. He knew then that for once he had taken on more than he could handle. The man was strong as a gorilla, and far back in his eyes was a flickering red light. . . .

He was fumbling at his waistband again with one hand. Rocky brought his knee up into the man's stomach, but he had iron muscles there too. He only grunted, and twisted Rocky's left arm savagely behind him, but in that instant's pause he managed to get a grip on the man's right wrist.

He could not keep him from getting his fingers around that knife: a short knife with discolored handle and gleaming blade. He could only fight to hold it away from him, and each moment he lost a precious fraction of those few inches of safety.

He put every atom of the strength of his own powerful muscles into holding that black hand away. He felt sweat running into his eyes; the torturing pressure on the arm twisted behind him. And it was no good: in another instant that knife was going to slice through clothes and flesh.

The nearness of thick lips and foul breath was nauseating. He set his teeth: this was for Eleanor, this last endurance of a relentless pressure that could not be endured. . . .

He saw, across the Negro's shoulder, Jazz raise his head dizzily and begin to crawl toward the gun on the floor. His right arm bent a little; straightened for the last time. Harvey's mouth was wet and drooling, and he was beginning to laugh. Rocky thought, If Jazz just has sense enough not to try to shoot. He can get him on the back of the head.

It was queer that three men just breathing could make so much noise. Rocky lay flat for an instant before he managed to drag himself to his knees. His left arm felt as if someone had torn it loose at the shoulder and his right half paralyzed. Jazz slumped suddenly down on his stomach again, but he kept his hands on the gun and his eyes on Buck Harvey, breathing stertorously with wide-open mouth.

Rocky tried twice and finally found his voice. He said, "Thanks, Jazz."

"Thanks yourself. But why in hell didn't you manage to shoot when you had a gun in your hand?"

"That was plain damn foolishness on my part. I didn't suppose he'd come at me with a gun pointin' at him, an' then I couldn't make up my mind to shoot him in the belly—soon enough. This'll be a good lesson to me. I'm not fast enough on the draw to take a chance like that. How many times did you hit him?"

"Plenty. Funny; it flashed through my mind how hard they say a d—'s head is."

Rocky tried standing up, and after one heave toward him the floor subsided to its proper place. He produced handcuffs with a wry smile, rolled the Negro over and twisted his arms behind his back.

"Me startin' out all prepared to say 'stick 'em up!' and just lead my pris'ner in! The way I feel about it now, I'd like to tie his legs together. There's some rope in the car. Here; I'll take that gun now. Can you walk?"

"Walk? Why do you suppose I crawled? He must have stamped all over me when he got me down. My hip feels like it's paralyzed."

"I'd be obliged if you wouldn't pass out on me right now." Rocky got his hands under Jazz's armpits; pulled him up and got him over to the rickety bunk. "Thank God you're a lightweight. I don't know how we're goin' to get Buck Harvey in the car. Wait a minute; there's some whisky out there, and I'll get that rope."

Jazz looked better when he had taken a stiff drink from the bottle Rocky handed him. "I don't think he knew we were here. He jumped me from the door. I thought it was you coming back and stepped over to it. I might as well have tried to fight a steam roller. I guess he knocked me out and then kicked me two or three times. Wh-what was he doing when you got here?"

"Fumbling for that knife of his. If you'd been able to put up a real fight he'd have gone after it sooner. I couldn't have held him off more than about a minute longer. He's comin' to. This is going to be fun," Rocky said. "You can't drive the car, so I'll have to, but I don't think he can do much damage this way."

Besides handcuffing the Negro's wrists behind him he had tied his arms so that he could not move them. Now he prodded him ungently with the toe of his boot. "Come on! Get up an' walk!"

"Mistuh, I ain't done nothin'."

"You'll get credit for tryin', smoke. Come on; get up! An' don't try to run, because there's nothin' I'd like better than to put a bullet through your leg."

The Negro mumbled incoherently. Rocky jerked him to his feet, the gun against the small of his back. He stooped and picked up the gleaming knife and put it in his pocket.

"Ain't it nice that this little toy is just about the right size for what we want? Can you walk at all, Jazz? I can't take him out to the car first and leave him."

"I can try it." Jazz's face twisted as he took a painful step forward. "If I can hang onto your arm a little."

"Catch hold. We'll make it all right."

They were a long time reaching the car, but their prisoner showed no desire to fight or to try to escape. He seemed still half dazed, though he kept talking disjointedly to himself. Jazz did his best, but he was hardly able to bear his weight on one foot and collapsed limply onto the running board of the car when they reached it.

"Take another drink." Rocky rubbed his arm where Jazz's fingers had bitten into it and motioned toward the back seat of the car. "Get in there, Joe Louis. Don't sit on that guitar! Well, there's one guitar less in the world now. . . ."

He handed the gun to Jazz, dug a coil of fine wire from the toolbox and laced it around Harvey's ankles; rolled the car windows shut. Then he picked Jazz up and put him on the front seat.

"Keep that gun trained on him. I don't think he can move enough to make any more trouble, but I'm not aimin' to lose him now. I hope," Rocky added thoughtfully as he climbed into the car and put his foot on the starter, "that Tom Wright will be aroun' town when we get there and has that camera of his in workin' order."

CHAPTER SEVENTEEN
JAZZ WOULD RATHER NOT BE THANKED

"Of course, Leonard is right," Gertrude Fulton said over her second gin fizz. "If I had a youngster to look after I wouldn't have time to wonder whether I was bored or not. But twins run in both our families, and that makes quadruplets. I'm not going to have quadruplets just to get in the newspapers and please Mrs. Kline."

Eleanor laughed. "Does she recommend motherhood?"

"Oh, strongly. She thinks it 'would make you more contented, dear.' That gets my goat. What time is it?"

"Three-forty."

"Well, since she hasn't dropped in so far this afternoon, we're probably safe. I'll have to whisk this cocktail shaker out of sight if she does appear. She's used to seeing me smoke, but she and 'Hamilton' feel strongly on the liquor question, and I've had my orders from Leonard."

"What has anything you do got to do with them?"

"Oh, you wouldn't understand. A teacher can lose his job because 'we don't feel his wife is all she should be.' It's really a wonder the Klines haven't said that about me. But I think she's really fond of me, and I know he is of Leonard. He ought to be: Leonard never shirks any of the dirty work. By the way, would you like to buy two tickets to the P.T.A. bridge party tomorrow night?"

"I didn't know they were having one."

"Unfortunately, yes. As usual, Leonard brought home tickets to sell, though he knows I never do. It's for a worthy cause," Mrs. Fulton said, grinning.

"I'll take two for that reason, though I don't know if I'll be here for it. And I'm quite certain Rocky won't go with me."

"Does he play bridge?"

"Oh yes, though not according to rule. But he has a fine memory for cards, and he always holds good ones. So it never seems to matter unless he gets a partner who obeys all the conventions. He prefers poker, and so do I. I'm rather surprised they haven't postponed this affair."

"Mr. Kline said the tickets had been out too long and we must carry on. Or so Leonard said this noon. I gathered we are to hold our heads high and act as if nothing has happened. By the way, what did happen up at the high school last night?"

Eleanor hesitated; then shook her head.

"Oh, if you can't tell me it's all right," Mrs. Fulton said agreeably. "Leonard made a break at lunch that let me know something had happened. He isn't supposed to tell me what it was, but I'll get it out of him."

"I'll bet you will," Eleanor said with some conviction.

"Why not? Does he have to try to prove another alibi? He was out walking between eight and nine—that was when he left that note at your place—and I was here alone. But I promised not to talk about things like that. I do think I should say that Leonard is always going out for walks. He should have married someone like Louise Whyte. He adores exercise, and I loathe it. Well, that may be because he's pretty burly, and nothing in the world would ever make me fat."

"It's odd how so many men think exercise is a virtue in itself."

"Not exercise at one end of a vacuum cleaner," Mrs. Fulton said darkly. She looked around her orderly living room. "Did Mr. Allan tell you how this room looked Sunday morning and why? Oh, don't be embarrassed. I know he did tell you."

"He said something about it."

"Well, my child, you wait until you've been married eight years and you may get bored enough to give your husband some cause to be jealous."

"Suppose it was the other way around?"

"It sometimes has been. Contrary to general opinion, there are quite a few good-looking women teachers in this state, and Leonard's taught with a lot like that. Last year the commercial teacher was a good-looking gal and fancy free. That's one reason I was willing to flirt with Paul Heath. Besides," she added thoughtfully, "I'm no doormat—like Mrs. Kline."

"Is it really that bad?"

"Oh no—and she loves it. I'd get pretty tired hearing Papa praise Miss Newman. I know dear Florence thinks she'd make a lot better first lady than Mrs. Kline—and she would. I prefer Mamma Kline myself. But she doesn't seem to mind. She thinks he's George Washington and Abraham Lincoln rolled into one. I don't know how far she'd go for him—"

"You aren't suggesting she'd go as far as murder?" Eleanor said bluntly.

"No, I don't think so. When you put it that way it does sound pretty impossible. I think what I really meant was that I thought she'd protect him if *he* ever kicked over the traces."

"I think I hear someone coming up the walk."

"Grab those things off the table and stick them in the kitchen, will you? Better put them inside the dish cupboard. You never can tell."

When Eleanor came back to the living room Mrs. Kline was saying that she "just ran in to ask if you'd bake a cake for the party tomorrow night. I was talking to one of the ladies on the refreshment committee, and I don't think we'll have enough cake."

"You know what mine are like: very depressed in the middle. I'll make one if you think the guests can stand it."

"Well, if you don't have good luck—but I know you will—we can see that some of us get that cake."

"I was afraid of that," Mrs. Fulton said. "I'd rather donate some coffee, particularly if they'd promise to use all of it to color up the usual hot water."

"I'll make you a cake tonight," Eleanor said. "I'm quite certain I'll be here that long. And I'll pay you for those tickets now, Mrs. Fulton."

"I'm so glad you're coming to our party. We don't have the crowds that we should when it's for such a worthy cause. How is Miss Towers?" Mrs. Kline said. "I—I heard she had a bad cold."

"I saw her this morning. She has a very sore throat, but she was feeling better than she did last night."

Mrs. Fulton looked at them with uplifted eyebrows. "I'm very sorry to hear about Nancy's— sore throat. Here are the tickets. They'll be at our table if you use them, and if you can't come we'll fill in with someone else."

"Of course we'll change back and forth between tables," Mrs. Kline promised. "I think that makes it more interesting, don't you?" Mrs. Fulton did not look as if she did. "Hamilton always likes to play with Leonard and Miss Newman. There are eight women who belong to a club and they come, but they play contract and won't mix with the rest of the crowd, and that makes it difficult. But we'll manage."

"Who's at the head of this thing?" Mrs. Fulton said.

"Mrs. Thomas. And Miss Newman is helping her."

"Which means Miss Newman is running things. And doing most of the work: I'll give her credit for that. You don't have to go, Mrs. Allan."

"I'm afraid I should. It's after four, and Rocky should have been home long ago."

"If you're going I'll just walk as far as the high school with you. I must ask Mr. Kline about the folding chairs for the card tables."

"Here comes Miriam," Mrs. Fulton said as she held the front door open for them. "I wonder how she got out so early?"

"She isn't supposed to leave until four-thirty, but I think she does sometimes. When she has noon duty and can't get her mail then. I think," Mrs. Kline said, "that there must be a young man writing her letters. Goodness, she does drive so recklessly."

Miriam stopped her car to the usual sound of tortured brakes. "I've just been downtown," she said. "What do you think? They've caught the man who killed Paul Heath and Miss Selby. Mr. Allan and Jazz Mitchell went out and brought him in and nearly got killed doing it—"

Eleanor's purse struck the top porch step and disgorged coins, compact, comb and keys. The tinkling sounds they made rolling down the steps filled her ears for an instant. Then Gertrude Fulton said:

"You little idiot! Haven't you any sense at all?"

"Oh, but they weren't killed. Mr. Allan wasn't even hurt. It was Jazz Mitchell. But they had a terrific struggle before they— All right," Miriam said sulkily. "I just thought you'd want to know. Because it was a great big Negro, and he carries a knife around with him and has already killed half a dozen people, and I thought it would be a relief to you to know everything's settled."

Mrs. Kline was laboriously picking up pennies and keys and stuffing them back into Eleanor's purse. "I'm all right now," Eleanor said, shaking

off Gertrude Fulton's supporting arm. "I must—
Don't bother about those things, Mrs. Kline. I'll
get them."

"It isn't any trouble at all, and you're white as a
sheet, dearie. Miriam just didn't realize how she'd
frighten you. Here; I think I got everything."

"Were Rocky and Jazz still downtown when you
were there?"

"I don't know, Mrs. Allan," Miriam said in a
subdued voice. "Someone said they'd gone home.
I heard that funny-looking constable had already
started off to take the Negro to the county jail."

"Then I'll go home. You'll drive me over, won't
you? I don't care," Eleanor said, stepping into the
car, "how fast you go this time. And for heaven's
sake, Miss Atkins, don't break the news to Nancy
the way you did to me. It would be just as well if
you didn't break it at all."

"I thought she'd want to know, but if you think
I'd better not . . . She went home at three-fifteen.
Mr. Kline took her study hall. Anyway," Miri-
am said as they skidded around the corner into
Mariposa Street, "it certainly is a relief that they
caught that man. Now there won't be any reason at
all why Mr. Allan will have to tell anybody about
Ted and me, will there?"

"I can't think of any. I think you can rest easy
on that point. Thank you. I won't ask you to come
in. . . ."

She was out of the car and halfway to her own
front door before Miriam could answer. There
were two cars parked in the driveway: one of them
was Dr. Miller's blue roadster. Of course Miriam would never get anything right: all she could
know was what she had heard on the streets, and
she wouldn't be able to repeat even that correctly.

Rocky said, "Honey, you aren't going to cry
now, are you? I was just going over to the Fultons
an' get you. I didn't think anyone could've told
you—"

"You promised—"

"I know. I promised to take Dud with me if I
went lookin' for that n— down in the jungle. He
wasn't in the jungle, but that don't make any real
difference. Dud wasn't here, and I couldn't wait
for him. So I took Jazz along. You're going to forgive me this time, aren't you?"

"Wh-what do you think?"

Rocky held her more closely; kissed her mouth
lingeringly. "I thought about you, Redhead. I—I
wondered if you'd pick out something peaceable,
like a poet, for your second husband—"

"Rocky! How can you!"

"Well, I won't joke about it if you don't want
me to. You—you know that wasn't what I thought.
I wanted like hell to be able to come home to
you."

VIRGINIA RATH

"Then he did nearly kill you. . . . No, don't talk about it now. Just kiss me. . . . Who is that?"

"That stuff you put on your hair still makes me dizzy sometimes. Oh; from the sound of it, that'll be Jazz cussin' the doctor."

"And I thought Miriam Atkins was a self-centered little brat just now. I forgot all about Jazz."

"He's all right. Did they have him nearly killed too? I take it you got your information from Miss Atkins, an' she got hers downtown. I brought Jazz here, since we've got an extra bedroom and he wouldn't go to the hospital."

"Aren't you going to tell me anything at all?"

"I haven't had time. Sure, I am. . . ." Rocky carefully eliminated all details that might give the color of reality to his story and told it in a dozen sentences. "So then Jazz crawled across the floor, got that gun and hit Buck Harvey over the head with it, and we lugged him out to the car and brought him back here," he ended.

"Then I'm to thank Jazz—"

"I don't care how much you do thank him. I was a damn fool. Maybe Freddie Haynes was right when he said I'm gettin' too big for my boots. Anyway, now I've met a man I can't lick, maybe I'll have more sense. I admit I never did take that n— seriously enough. But you've got to hand it to Jazz. He couldn't walk, but as long as he could crawl he managed to get there in time."

"Are you going to make a public hero of him?"

"That was my intention—whether he likes it or not. We gathered a crowd the minute we got in town. Tom Wright got busy with that camera of his, and I saw to it Jazz was very much in the foreground. Tom gets pretty good pictures an' sells 'em to the newspapers. Jazz managed to keep up till that was over. Then Dud offered to take the n— to Brookdale for me. I was afraid to leave him here in case somebody got some ideas about holdin' a little necktie party. So Dud took two huskies and a couple of guns an' started for the county jail."

"So Mr. Harvey was your ace in the hole? But will it work out all right?"

"For a while. Haynes is so scared of going against public opinion that he won't dare arrest Jazz right now. Tom's goin' to send those pictures out on Seven when it comes through an' wire the story to the papers. We've wired Oroville. Harvey's their man, and they can come after him."

"What does the Negro say?"

"'Mistuh, I ain't done nothin'.' What else would you expect? You couldn't convince the average citizen in this town he ain't guilty. All I want is a little time and I've got it, though I admit I don't know, right now, what I'm going to do with it."

The door to the spare bedroom opened, and Dr. Miller came out. He grinned at them in a way that was something more than professionally cheerful.

"Swell vocabularies you railroaders acquire. He'll do. Keep him in bed though. I don't think he could walk if he wanted to. That fellow must have had a foot like an elephant's. He evidently ground it into Mitchell's thigh when he had him down and hurt some of the muscles in there. I'll trust you to make him behave, Mrs. Allan."

"I'll do my best." Eleanor walked into the bedroom and stood looking at Jazz from the foot of the bed. His face was still drawn with pain, but he had lighted a cigarette. He returned her look with an expression that was distinctly apprehensive.

"You'd rather I didn't say it, wouldn't you?"

"Be a good sport and let me take it for granted," Jazz said with his charming crooked smile. "You and Rocky have kept me from going plain nuts. And if he hadn't come back when he did, I wouldn't be here. He told me not to stay there in the first place. just write it off the books."

"I really didn't intend to fall on your neck and bedew you with my grateful tears. It's too bad," Eleanor said, laughing rather hysterically, "that I wear nightgowns and not pajamas. Mine certainly would come nearer fitting you than Rocky's."

"He shoved me into these solely on your account," Jazz said severely, rolling up the sleeves that covered his hands. "He said—"

"What did I say? Want a drink?" asked Rocky.

"I could do with one. That stuff looks like it had been aged."

"It is. Some grape brandy my dad gave us. We save it for special occasions. Drink up!"

"It possesses authority. Damn that sawbones!" Jazz said, wincing as he tried to discover a more comfortable position. "He wouldn't be convinced I didn't have any broken bones. How do you feel?"

"The arm he twisted behind me's going to be sore as hell tomorrow, but that's all that's wrong." Eleanor mechanically straightened the covers on the bed, and Rocky laughed.

"Make it look like a hospital bed, sugar. I can see that light in her eye that means she's goin' to want to take your temp'rature pretty soon. I talked to Miller just now. He's one of the few who knows too much to think Harvey's our man. He says he'll keep his mouth shut, but I don't know how long he can stand the strain."

"You're going to keep at it?" Jazz said. "Oh, I supposed you would."

"Yes, though I was just tellin' Eleanor I haven't got any idea what to do but sit tight and see if anything happens."

"You might go to the P.T.A. bridge party with me tomorrow night," Eleanor said. "I bought tickets, and all the faculty will be there."

"I never thought I'd have to do a thing like that in the line of public duty. Playin' bridge with Mrs. Kline an' Miriam Atkins— I wonder if she took her bath last night?"

Jazz grinned. "That isn't in the line of public duty, is it? Whether Miriam happens to take a Sunday night bath or not?"

"It does happen to be this time."

"You'll just have to take her word for what she did after we left her. Mr. Fulton was walking between eight and nine," Eleanor said. "That left Mrs. Fulton alone."

"These people do like to walk. Louise Whyte was trampin' around, too, about that time. I don't know of any place to walk to in this town at night."

"Down to the bridge and back. Though I haven't much idea what you're talking about," Jazz said. "Has something happened you haven't told me about?"

"Nothing important. Of course eight o'clock Sunday night is a quiet time and churchtime for people who go. But it does seem like there ought to be a few observant bystanders to come forth with some kind of information."

"Short of having seen me at the so-called scene of the crime, how could they know when they knew anything important? Not," Jazz said, "when you're playing them so close to your vest—"

Rocky felt Eleanor tug at his arm; turned and looked at Nancy standing in the doorway. "Yes," he agreed, "I guess maybe I will wash my face an' you can hold the towel for me."

CHAPTER EIGHTEEN
"WILL THESE HANDS NE'ER BE CLEAN?"

"I—I didn't know you were here," Nancy said stiffly. "As Mrs. Logan heard it, you and Rocky were both at death's door. I thought Eleanor might just possibly be here."

"Sure; I understand that," Jazz said politely. "You'd want to be around if she needed anyone."

"Yes; that was it. And of course I— No, it wasn't!" Nancy crossed the room swiftly; went down on her knees beside the bed. "It wasn't that at all! You aren't killed, are you? Or very badly hurt?"

"Do I look like it?"

"You look perfectly ghastly. Rocky Allan had a nerve, taking you out to help catch a maniac."

"I was willing to go with him." Painfully, Jazz sat erect. "There's room for you to sit up here. Damn it, now you have got the advantage over me."

Nancy giggled hysterically. "I wouldn't think of taking advantage of you, Mr. Mitchell."

"Shut up! You know," Jazz said, his hands on her shoulders, "that fellow we caught isn't really the guilty party."

"And I am not dumb enough to suppose he is. Don't you suppose I have brains enough to figure out what Rocky's game is? I don't know just how he's going to work it, but that's up to him."

"I just wanted to be sure—" Jazz put his fingers under her chin; turned her mouth to his. All of the pent-up emotion of the last few days was in that kiss. For a long instant after it they stared at each other; then Jazz said, "I won't spoil that—for a while."

"It—it will do very nicely for a beginning. Let's—let's do without the wisecracks just for once. If you don't mind."

"I don't mind." Jazz put his black head against her shoulder. "I don't feel very much like wise-cracking. I love you, Nancy."

"It's taken you long enough to say so."

"Say so! What else have I been doing since I first met you? Do you think I go around asking a girl to marry me because I *don't* love her?"

"You wouldn't understand. You never did say just exactly that or say it quite that way."

"If you want to change quite to 'quiet'— That's a rotten pun, but maybe I have quieted down a little, Nancy. You can in just one or two days, when you can't do anything but sit still and think and take what's coming to you. Oh, I had a brain storm or two, but there may be hope for me yet."

"I do hope you are not going to turn into a model young man, Jazz."

"Fat chance! Who's being flip now? You wouldn't know what to do with a model young man."

"As I was just about to remark."

"Of course, we aren't—I'm not out of the woods yet. This scheme of Rocky's may not work out, and they may start checking up on me again. We've got to be certain they won't—before—"

"Jilted again!" Nancy said sweetly. "And I was going to hire an ambulance to rush you off to the marriage license bureau."

"Does that mean you'd marry me right away if—"

"If you'd give your consent. Well, to save my pride I should utter a loud and emphatic 'No!' The answer is 'Yes'; tomorrow, if you wanted me to."

She thought: If I let him guess I know he'd like to cry right now he'll never forgive me. She sat very still, looking down at his closed eyes and thick, curling lashes before she said, in a tone no one else had ever heard from Nancy Towers:

"You needn't ever be lonely again, Jazz. It doesn't matter where we go or have to live, I'll always be waiting for you to come home to me—most of all when things have gone wrong. Oh, I know we'll quarrel sometimes: we couldn't help it. But I'll always be underfoot. . . . I f-feel like I'm going to c-cry. Do you mind?"

"Go right ahead," Jazz said gruffly. "Do you good. You'd rather I didn't say this, but I'm going to. Then we'll forget it. You're the only girl I ever wanted to marry: the rest of it just doesn't count."

"I know that." For a second Nancy's smile twisted ruefully. "Of course I know that. And things are going to turn out all right."

"I hope so," Jazz said not too optimistically. "I don't see what Rocky has to go on from here, and I don't think he does either. Maybe he'll pull it off."

"You won't be satisfied until he does?"

"I'm afraid not. Oh, if it has to go down in the books as one more unsolved mystery and everyone else is satisfied—"

"We'll get married by the time you have a long beard and I've ordered my wheel chair."

Jazz laughed and kissed her cheek; then: "What's wrong with your throat?" he said. "It looks like—like someone had tried to strangle you!"

Nancy caught hastily at the silk scarf that had come unknotted and slipped down to her shoulders. "Just a sore throat."

"I don't doubt that. What happened last night? I thought Rocky acted funny about that."

Nancy stood up and pushed him back against the pillows. "I don't know what you can do about it, darling. Remember that newly acquired poise of yours. I don't know who— You can't walk, can you?"

Jazz set his teeth and finally achieved a rather rigid smile. "I can think of a lot of things that would give me more pleasure. You needn't look so pleased about it."

"Well, there is no use your starting out to catch the person who choked me because I don't know who it was."

"If Rocky had any sense—"

"He doesn't know any more about it than I do. They—it didn't try to kill me."

"How do you know that?"

"Because—because there wasn't anything to stop them from doing it if they'd wanted to. It was my own fault that I went up to the high school in the dark with just four matches. And if I hadn't gone into a closet after a sweater nothing would have happened. So long as you can't start tearing around town suspecting people I thought I might as well tell you about it."

Jazz ruffled up his hair with nervous fingers and after an instant grinned reluctantly. "So that's why I wasn't to know anything about it? What time did this happen?"

"Between eight-thirty and nine—allowing plenty of time both ways."

"Rocky didn't ask me to produce an alibi the one time I happen to have one. Orin Roberts—the trumpet player—dropped in with the usual assurances of undying friendship just about eight-thirty and stayed a lot longer than I wanted to talk to him."

"It didn't occur to Rocky to ask where you were—any more than it did me. If it had ever occurred to me that you might have choked me a little by mistake, how could you get a key so you could get into the high school?"

"I couldn't. But how can you tie that Negro into that episode if it ever comes out?"

"There was one door unlocked," Rocky said. He stood in the doorway and smiled at them paternally. "The door off the stage in the gym."

"Oh! I know that door. Lou told me quite a while ago that she and Mr. Fulton thought several of the older boys knew a way to get into the gym on nights when it isn't supposed to be in use. But they weren't at all sure of it, so neither of them has said anything to Mr. Kline. I wonder why the door was unlocked."

"Kids are careless. Someone who had a key might have left the door open for a friend who didn't. I don't b'lieve Mr. Kline, for all his experience teaching, has any real idea of the habits of some of the younger generation. Buck Harvey had some keys anyway. The kind that'll open a lot of locks, though they ain't real skeleton keys."

"You have it all figured out, haven't you? But you didn't tell Mr. Kline about the door?"

"I won't as long as he doesn't try to fit the n— into that episode at the high school. That's why I kept still about it: I didn't want to develop the wrong kind of setup to fit some dang'rous character into."

"Haven't you any conscience at all?" Nancy said admiringly.

"Not a bit, if you mean don't I mind fooling the gen'ral public. Eleanor's startin' to get supper. She seems to think soft-boiled eggs would be about right for you, Jazz."

"I did not," Eleanor said, coming up behind him. "We are going to have steak and French fries. Of course if Jazz prefers soft-boiled eggs—"

"The sight of one makes my stomach turn over."

"How nice," Nancy said. "We have one distaste in common. There is something so unfinished-looking about a soft-boiled egg.

"School was perfectly awful today. Two of the girls who had a crush on Paul Heath persisted in weeping. Theatrical little brats! Mr. Kline and Florence Newman were very efficient about taking over classes. As if things weren't bad enough already, a lot of large parents buzzed about making arrangements for tomorrow night's bridge. I thought it would be a nice gesture to postpone it, but it seems not."

"You don't have to go, do you?" Eleanor asked.

"Mr. Kline seemed to think if he let me go home early today I'd feel perfectly all right tomorrow. But I don't think so—not tomorrow night, at least."

"If you were thinking of coming over here you're out of luck. We're going—"

"'We?' You don't mean Rocky too? Heavenly days! I never thought I would live to see you going to a parent-teacher bridge party."

"Neither did I think you would," Rocky said sadly. "'Into each life some rain must fall'—da-de-de-di-dum. I forget the rest of it. Even knowing what I do now, I'd rather go out after that Negro again than play cards with one of these dames that say, 'And will you *please* tell me *why* you left me in no-trump . . .'"

"That's five spades doubled," Leonard Fulton said complacently. "Will you kindly cast your eyes on that score?"

"The only reason you made five was because Mr. Allan laid down four kings and an ace for you."

Fulton grinned. "Can't take it, can you? You shouldn't double just because you get mad."

"If husbands playing against wives is going to lead to trouble, we'd better change partners," Eleanor said hastily. "I'm not convinced Rocky hasn't two or three aces up his sleeve."

"It wouldn't do any good," Mrs. Fulton said. "The minute Leonard starts playing with me he doesn't hold any cards at all and blames me for it. I can't truthfully say it would make for peace and amity for us to play together. Besides, we've just one more hand, if Mrs. Kline still wants us to change over."

Rocky looked toward the table where Mr. and Mrs. Kline, Louise and Miss Newman were playing silently and, he suggested, "with concentration. Like it was a very serious business."

"It is, when you get both Florence and Mr. Kline at the same table," Mrs. Fulton murmured. "And Louise didn't want to play at all because she is supposed to keep an eye on the refreshments. That girl lets herself be imposed on."

"She ought to take lessons from you how not to be," her husband said pleasantly. "I notice Nancy Towers isn't here. By the way, how's Mitchell?"

"We left him cussin' the doctor because he won't bring him a pair of crutches. Two spades."

"He's at it again. Well, we can't sink any lower than we have. Three hearts," Mrs. Fulton said.

"Three spades. Say, Allan; how did that Negro manage to get in Heath's place? Hadn't he had time to lock up yet?"

"Did you say 'pass,' honey? Mrs. Fulton? All right, Fulton, I'll see your cards. Why, we didn't get anything out of the n—," Rocky said. "I was down at Brookdale today. He does admit he took a leg of lamb off somebody's back porch. It was Mrs. Leaman's: she forgot to lock the screen door."

"I know Heath was careless about locking up."

"Do you? I mean, was he?"

"Well, I charged over there to see him one night, and he evidently didn't lock the place when he was just sitting there, though it was pretty late this time I speak of. If the — was hiding there I suppose he saw Heath and thought he looked good for a few dollars. But he never carried much money on him."

"There was only about fifty cents in his clothes. I reckon the n— just busted in an' killed him before he could yell."

Mrs. Fulton slapped a small trump viciously down on the table. "There; take it! Mr. Allan doesn't really want to divulge official secrets, Leonard. Don't embarrass him."

"I don't see what I said that would—"

"Mother will tell you about it when she gets you home. I would have before if I wasn't a basketball widow. No; if that agony's over, let's *not* play another just for fun."

"We'll move," Eleanor said when Mrs. Kline looked toward their table and made gestures of invitation. "It may bring us luck."

She smiled compassionately at Rocky as Mrs. Kline sat down opposite him. He murmured, "It's too bad you got to go. If this keeps up like it's started it may be right interestin'."

"It should be with the hands you've been holding."

"I wasn't talkin' about cards."

Eleanor looked at him, shrugged in exasperation and went over to the other table. Rocky looked at his new partner uneasily. Mrs. Kline probably wouldn't call him down for the way he bid even if her own bids very likely would mean nothing at all to him. At that, he considered himself luckier than Fulton, who did not look overjoyed at drawing Miss Newman as a partner.

"Now I do hope you are not critical, Mr. Allan," Mrs. Kline fluttered. "Because I'm no card player

at all. Hamilton always says I'm not. And I know
he's right. Oh, is it my bid? We-ell—I pass."

Rocky let Miss Newman bid four spades and
then took some pleasure in setting her. "I know I
didn't give you any help," Fulton said guiltily.

"You should have taken me out in no-trump.
It's your deal, Mrs. Kline. Shall I deal for you?"

"Oh, if you don't mind, Florence. Cards are
such slippery things. I keep thinking about poor
Mr. Heath. He was such a good card player. 'Lucky
in cards—unlucky in love.'"

"He overbid his hands consistently," Miss Newman said. "Your bid."

"Oh! Well, I really haven't anything at all,
but I'll just say a heart. What? You changed it to
spades, Mr. Allan? That's all right: I have lots of
spades, and I'd rather you'd play it. We certainly
do hold together, don't we?"

"He took my luck with him when we stopped
playing together," Fulton said. "That coffee smells
good."

"You can smell it, can't you? Miss Whyte often
says you can't play cards in this room with the
kitchen right next to it and fix anything to eat
that has any smell. Some of the ladies suggested
spaghetti for a change now that it's getting colder. But the onions stick to your hands so. That
reminds me of some quotation. Shakespeare, I

think. Quotations so often *are* Shakespeare. The play where the woman washes her hands."

"'What, will these hands ne'er be clean?' You made a little slam," Miss Newman said.

"Oh, did we? I do like a partner who does all the playing for me. I hope poor little Miss Towers is all right by now," Mrs. Kline said, lowering her voice. "Foolish child."

"Very foolish, to come up here in the dark even if she did want to correct her bookkeeping papers. I wonder," Miss Newman said, "where Miss Atkins is. She should be here; I'm quite certain she isn't ill."

"She probably developed one of those last-minute headaches," Fulton said. "You know how she hates to play cards."

"But there are very few of us to come, and we haven't at all a good crowd tonight. She knows she's expected to come."

"Gertrude certainly does look nice," Mrs. Kline said. "Isn't that a new dress, Leonard? Or shouldn't I expect you to know that?"

"I do know it is because I just got the bill for it. It ought to look nice, considering what it cost."

"You should take an interest and go shopping with her. Mr. Kline always goes with me. He really likes to."

"I tried shopping with Gertrude just once. Never again! I'm getting tired of this. What's bid? You said a spade, Allan—"

"And I passed," Miss Newman said emphatically.

"Can't be helped. Two hearts—all right, three hearts!"

"Take it," Rocky said, grinning. Fulton went down two, and Miss Newman did not like it. She said:

"I believe the low scores are to move? Then they're waiting for us, Mr. Fulton."

Fulton got up to give Louise Whyte his chair; turned one side of his face carefully away from Miss Newman and winked at Rocky before he followed her.

"And what have we here?" Mr. Kline said jovially, inspecting the score card. "Well, well! We'll have to do something about that, Bessie."

"I suppose you and I shouldn't be playing together, but since you've both sat down . . . I hope I hold some good cards for you. Isn't it funny that Miss Atkins hasn't come?"

"Not so darned funny," Louise murmured, and more loudly, "She said she might be a little late, but I'd expected her before this. She said she would come so I wouldn't have to play."

They waited for Mr. Kline to bid, and after a long and solemn consideration of his cards he said, "One heart," and finally took the bid at three, though Mrs. Kline showed a nervous desire to let him know, without changing his bid, that she had no hearts.

"Oh, we will do very nicely without the hearts, my dear. You have very good suit. Your play, Miss Whyte."

"I'm going to have to ask you to play three-handed if Miriam doesn't come before long," Louise said presently. "I must look at that coffee before very long."

"I thought we were to have cocoa."

Louise's lips tightened a little. "People don't care for cocoa, Mr. Kline. The expression on Mr. Allan's face is proof of that."

"I don't," Rocky admitted. "Do I get this for three diamonds? Let's see your cards, Miss Whyte."

"I heard something today—Gertrude told me," Mrs. Kline said. "I don't know whether to believe it—that Mrs. Jordan is going to get a divorce."

"Rather late, isn't she?" Louise remarked.

"Oh, it would be a friendly divorce. Incompatibility or mental cruelty."

Rocky finessed a queen and said, "What is mental cruelty, I'd like to know? If you don't like your wife's new dress or the way she does her hair or won't let her eat crackers in bed. . . ?"

Louise laughed, but Mr. Kline was frowning disapprovingly. "I hope it is only a rumor. There should be some sweeping change made in our divorce laws."

"Oh, I don't know," Mrs. Kline said unexpectedly. "I think people have a right to be happy. Of course I think they should try very hard to get along. But if they can't—if one of them simply doesn't like the other one—husbands and wives, I mean—and the other one won't give consent to a divorce, sometimes it leads to a lot of trouble. Like one of them thinking they have to kill the other one just because she won't be reasonable. I'm sure I would be."

"'Whom God hath joined,'" Mr. Kline said pontifically. "If you'd played that king earlier, my dear, we'd have saved game."

"Would we? Well, I'm— Oh, here comes Miss Atkins now. We were beginning to think you were sick, Miss Atkins. Better late than never."

"I laid down and went to sleep," Miriam said. "Don't be cross at me, Mary Lou. There wasn't any use in your fussing around in the kitchen all night, and I can play for you now."

"You not only can, but will," Louise said, getting up. "We're just starting the third hand."

"Wait a minute, honey: your chain's come unfastened. It looks to me like it's broken."

"The clasp is no good. I'd better take it off." Louise untangled the thin chain on which she wore a cameo pendant and handed it to Miriam. "Put that in your purse, will you? I haven't one with me tonight."

"Is that a purse or a suitcase?" Rocky asked as Miriam opened a large homespun bag with wooden clasp and handles.

Miriam giggled. "It's almost a suitcase. I can carry anything I might want in it, including a flashlight, and then I never forget anything I ought to have. I—" She became aware of Mr. Kline's drumming fingers. "Oh, are you waiting for me? Are these my cards? They aren't very good ones, are they?"

At the end of another half-hour Rocky found it hard to repress his constant desire to yawn, and Miriam made no effort to curb a similar impulse. Mr. and Mrs. Kline moved away, and Miss Newman and Mrs. Fulton took their places. But Mrs. Fulton was also bored, and Miss Newman made it clear that she believed bridge and conversation did not go together. But the end of those four hands brought release as Eleanor and Leonard Fulton replaced Miriam and Miss Newman.

"I've been waitin' a long time for this," Rocky said. "Would you two mind settin' here for a while and let me and Fulton go outside and smoke?"

"I'd like to go with you. No; it won't do," Mrs. Fulton said. "You two go ahead."

"Take your time. You don't need to play any more to have high score for men. And it can't," Eleanor said consolingly, "last very much longer."

CHAPTER NINETEEN
GRINNING CAT

"What the hell is that?" Jazz said, sitting up and staring at the package in Rocky's hand. "Tissue paper and pink ribbons—"

"This is a prize. Two packs of playin' cards, and I hope I never have to use them for anything but poker. Lord, what an evening!" Rocky yanked at his necktie and unbuttoned his collar. "How are you doin'? Have you been up?"

"What do you expect? Of course I have. The last time was to look for cigarettes."

Rocky tossed him a full pack. "Sorry. I thought you had plenty. Anyway, you should've been asleep a long time ago."

"I did go to sleep, but I woke up and—well, I didn't go back to sleep."

"You woke up and got to thinkin'. You'd save yourself a lot of trouble if you didn't." Rocky extracted two very rumpled pillows from the bed,

shifted Jazz gently to one side of it and straightened sheets and blankets. "You certainly must've
been doing a lot of kicking aroun'. Why don't you
lie still?"

"I don't feel like lying still. It seems to me," Jazz
said crossly, "that I've had more than my share of
grief in this business. First I twist my wrist—well,
that was my fault—then you smack me on the jaw
and nearly break it, and after that, that Negro
tramps all over me."

"I'll see about gettin' you compensation."

"Oh well, forget it," Jazz said, smiling. "I know
I've got a grouch. . . . Yes, that's a good deal better. What have you been doing today besides going to Brookdale? You weren't there very long."

"I was talkin' to a lot of folks. Just talking—
and it was an awful waste of time. I can't find anyone that saw anything interestin' after the dance
or early Sunday mornin' or evenin'."

"Did anyone see me going home?"

"Before you turned off the street the high
school's on. One or two mentioned they thought
you were lucky not to 've met that n—. One smart
guy said if Clarice met him it was a wonder he
didn't kill her right then."

"And that was a little embarrassing?"

"It was. But then he said the n— probably just
climbed in her window to see what he could steal
an' killed her when she woke up."

"And Haynes?"

"Freddie is tem'rarily subdued. He did crow over me a little for havin' said I didn't think Harvey could have done it. At that, he isn't fool enough not to have a few doubts, but he hasn't guts enough to make them public right now."

"That's it—'right now.'"

"Yes, he might come poppin' up with some objections in the future," Rocky admitted. "I did have an interestin' talk with the minister—"

"May I come in?" Eleanor said. "Open the door, then. My hands are full." She handed Jazz a glass with the command, "Drink that. Yes, I know it's hot milk. I'm drinking some myself to show you it can be done."

"Hot milk and what else?"

"Something the doctor left for you. And you're going to take it and like it."

"You might as well," Rocky said. "Because you'll take it whether you like it or not."

Jazz grimaced, but he sipped the milk obediently. "Do you think a schoolteacher will be any more inclined to be bossy than an ex-nurse?" he said hopefully.

"Not gettin' cold feet, are you? Just drag her aroun' by the hair once or twice. Well, Nancy's hair is pretty short. That's bad. Eleanor has plenty for me to get a good grip on."

"Cave man Allan! Nancy won't order you around one bit more than is good for you."

"If she ever has a chance to try it," Jazz muttered. "Was playing bridge in our best society worth the strain on your behavior?"

"Very much so."

"Really? Then you weren't joking when you said it was interesting?" Eleanor asked.

"People talked a lot. About divorces an' purses an' the way women go shopping. They played cards too, and that tells you a lot about them. And we talked about the smell of onions—"

Eleanor and Jazz exchanged sympathetic glances. "What," Jazz said, "has the smell of onions got to do with this?"

"Well, it was funny it should make someone think about that place in Macbeth that says, 'Here's the smell of the blood still . . .' Of course it came in very pat: 'What, will these hands ne'er be clean?' Only we weren't talkin' about blood."

"You mean you were talking about onions? But why— Oh well, I give up," Jazz said.

"It was very simple. I'm hungry," Rocky decided. "We had two thin little san'wiches and a slice of cake. I think I'll scramble some eggs." He wriggled one shoulder experimentally. "That thing's sore, and settin' two or three hours on a small foldin' chair ain't my idea of comfort. I s'pose I really ought to go back down to Brookdale again tomorrow—"

"Listen," Jazz said, "if Harvey really was up around Leaman's sometime Saturday night or early Sunday morning—"

"I thought of that, but it's almost impossible to get anything out of him. When he isn't excited he's careful what he says, and when he goes into one of his fits he just mumbles. The boys down at Brookdale will be damn glad to get rid of him. The n— tried to throttle Cy Rand when he took his dinner in this noon.

"I did fin'lly manage to get Harvey to say he was wandering aroun' town sometime about midnight—he thought. He tried the back doors of the groceries on the off-chance of breakin' in, an' then went on to people's back doors and found the Leamans' porch door open. He says after that he went back to the jungle, off to himself, and cooked some of the meat he took from Leaman's porch. I imagine he's tellin' the truth, so he couldn't have been aroun' Heath's place at the right time."

"No one has an alibi—but Mr. Kline," Eleanor said. "Of course his depends on his wife, but you said Louise and Mr. Barker verified the time he left the high school."

"Yes, they did. Are you going to scramble me some eggs, honey?"

"I suppose so. Are you hungry, Jazz?"

Jazz yawned. "No, I think I'm sleepy. Good night, and lay your number elevens down quietly tomorrow morning if you get up early. I don't wish to be disturbed."

At nine-thirty the next morning Rocky was passing by Ma Jenkins' boardinghouse. A persistent tapping noise drew his attention to a front window, and Ma crooked her middle finger commandingly and beckoned him to come in.

Rocky went around to the back door, entered the kitchen and found her waiting for him there. "I been wanting to see you. Sit down. Have a drink? That was a good funeral we gave Clarice yesterday, wasn't it?"

Ma took half-a-dozen bottles and two tall glasses from a cupboard and began to mix her drinks. "Of course I don't know as that white satin coffin Pat Healy insisted on was exactly in good taste. Maybe it was just a little bit—ostentatious."

"Wasn't Clarice?"

"Well—yes. Though I never realized how fond I was of the girl. She laughed such a lot when she was around. I keep listening for it. Anyway, she carried off all that white satin, and that's more than a lot could do."

Rocky looked doubtfully at the glass she placed before him but with her eyes on him took a generous swallow. Then, with watering eyes: "W-what do you call that?" he gasped.

"I haven't made one like that for years," Ma said, gratified. "I used to call it a hell-fire swizzle. I had a gentleman friend once that always called it a belly-buster. He was a little bit vulgar though."

Rocky snorted, tasted his drink again and surrendered. "You've got me beat, Ma. Two of these, and I'd try to fight a steam roller."

"You young fellows nowadays haven't any stamina. This same gentleman used to say I had a hollow leg and it was expensive filling it with champagne. Well, I guess it was worth it to him. But I didn't call you in to talk about old times. I hear you had quite a run-in with Freddie Haynes."

Rocky looked at her uneasily. "That was before we caught that n—. Freddie and me are pals now."

"Well, I could tell you a thing or two about Fred Haynes for all he poses as a vice crusader now. He used to be a gay young dog, though he was always a tightwad. But you needn't try to pull the wool over my eyes, young fellow."

"How many people have you said something like that to?"

"Not one." Ma adjusted the blue ribbon around her yellow-white hair. "I can sit and think and

keep what I think to myself. I wouldn't want to
start any talk about Jazz Mitchell again. But you
can't tell me that n— did it."

"Well, I won't insult your intelligence tryin' to
make you think he did," Rocky said. "Just keep
still about it is all I ask. I was on my way just now
to a damn unpleasant interview—"

"Then I won't keep you. Funny," Ma said, "how
so many people speak of schoolteachers as a special kind of animal. I never could see they were
any different than anybody else except they have
to keep their peccadillos hidden, like anyone in
the public eye. Of course people are a little more
broad-minded now. When I was a girl—you know
I had some education—there was a man teacher
we thought real highly of that went wild about
a young girl in town and tried to kill her when
she wouldn't have anything to do with him. Well,
that's just an old story I happened to think about."

"I get you. Know any more stories?"

"You might be respectful to an old lady," Ma
said, grinning. "No, I don't know any stories
you're old enough to hear. But I can tell you you're
a hell of a detective. Look here!"

She took her hand out of the pocket of her
faded green dress. Rocky looked; reached over
and took the small, grinning yellow cat from her
palm. It was cold and heavy between his fingers,

and the small cat face smirked up at him with a self-satisfied air.

"Where'd you find it? If I missed it, I'll agree with you on that last proposition."

"You missed it, all right. But I don't know that I wonder at it. You didn't have time to tear Clarice's room apart, and I didn't find it myself till I cleaned in there and moved the furniture."

"I should've come back Sunday, but I was too busy to think about it. Where did you find this?"

"It had rolled all the way under a chest of drawers near the window. It comes pretty far down to the floor—the chest does, I mean. Seems to me," Ma said, "like someone had managed to kick it under there."

"It wouldn't keep on rolling very far of itself. Yes; someone may have dropped it and then kicked it with his foot while he was hunting for it in the dark, and then couldn't locate it or didn't dare stay long enough to hunt any more."

"I had some such idea, that chest being so near the window. Cute little thing, isn't it? Not more than an inch and a half across, so you wouldn't think it could be so heavy."

"It's meant to be used as a paperweight. You're sure Clarice didn't have this in her room all the time?"

"Not unless she brought it home that night. I knew everything that was in her room, and this never was."

"You didn't think about fingerprints, did you?"

"No, I didn't. I just picked the thing up to see what it was. I thought first it was something Clarice had dropped back there—"

"Oh well, it's not likely there was any on it, and the thing's too small to take a good one unless it was held just right. I'd like to look in Clarice's room a minute."

"There isn't one more thing to be found in here," Ma said, opening the door for him. "I went over it with a fine-tooth comb."

"I only wanted to see—" Rocky looked out of the window toward the back of the house across the alley. "Anyone in here could see a light go on in that back upstairs room at the Werners', couldn't they?"

"Nothing in the world to stop them. I had a young fellow in this room once, and there was a girl living over there—before the Werners took the house—and I finally had to tell her to pull down her blind when she was undressing. He was talking all over town. Was someone up over there about the time Clarice was killed?"

"Miss Newman says she had her light on for a minute and saw a light flash on for an instant in here. Well, you may have helped me out a lot, Ma. I'll let you know later. I've got to go talk to Mrs. Pratt about this. . . ."

They had removed Heath's belongings from the cabin yesterday, and Mrs. Pratt, with a towel tied around her head, was down on her knees pushing a square scrubbing brush around the bare floor. She looked up; protested:

"You ain't going to tell me you've got to come in here! You said I could go ahead, and I—"

"I don't have to come in. I just want to talk to you. Remember how you told me nothing had been taken from Heath's cabin or disturbed in any way?"

"And nothing had. I guess I'd ought to know."

"How about this?"

Mrs. Pratt looked indifferently at the yellow cat. "Oh, that! Well, you wouldn't call that important, would you? And I certainly didn't know it was gone, though it must have been if you've got it. But that time you was here with your wife it was here. I seen it setting on the table."

"That was a black one. I took it out of a table drawer myself and put it on some papers on the table."

"Well, black or yaller—does it matter? Now you speak of it, I guess it was the black one. I didn't

look particular. Sometimes he used one and sometimes the other, and other times both of 'em.'"

"But he did have two that he kept here?"

"Yes, I guess he did," Mrs. Pratt said grudgingly. "Silly things. I don't believe in a lot of things
like that that have to be dusted all the time."

"You cleaned this place Saturday afternoon. Of
course Heath was in it afterward, but do you remember if one of the cats was on the table when
you were in here? Think!" Rocky urged as Mrs.
Pratt pushed back her stringy hair and looked at
him blankly. "If you cleaned this place I know you
did it right. You dusted the table, and you were
careful not to disturb his papers—"

"That's right." Mrs. Pratt looked pleased. "I'm
always careful to clean things right but not to disturb anything. Yes; there was some papers weighted down with one of them cats. And I think it
was the yaller one, because it seems to me if it'd
been the black I'd have remembered it better than
I do."

Rocky accepted this reasoning with a resigned
shrug. "If you can't be any surer than that—you
just can't. But don't talk to anybody about this for
a while."

"I got no time to spend gossiping," Mrs. Pratt
said severely. She dipped her scrubbing brush into

a pail of soapy water. "I got plenty to do just looking after my own work."

Rocky grinned slightly at this rebuff and went on toward the high school. But instead of going back to the cross street, Grove, to follow it to Pine and then up that street to the high school, he went on past Mrs. Pratt's house, past the small Christian Science church and the houses whose occupants had been sleeping while Heath was killed. He had managed to talk to all those people yesterday. Only four had attended the dance, and all of them had come home before one o'clock. The other people on the street had been in bed before eleven.

He came to the end of the street. The grammar school was really on Marin, but it stood off to itself with an air of offended dignity. A well-worn path led to its doors, but another path branched off from this, passed the building and climbed on to the top of the hill There it turned sharply and went straight across to the high school. You faced the main-entrance doors to the gymnasium as you walked, the uneven ground hard and dry underfoot. . . .

Rocky skirted the end of the high-school building and came around to its front entrance. He was relieved to find that the door to Kline's office was closed and the first door into the study hall. He stopped and looked at the schedule of classes on a bulletin board in the hall. It was nearly ten-thirty, and she had a vacant period between that time and eleven-fifteen.

He did not particularly want the students to see him, but neither did he care to go into Kline's office. He remembered the small rest room to which Louise had carried Nancy on Sunday night. He believed it was meant for only the women teachers, but they would have to accept his apologies if they caught him in there. He would wait until the fuss of changing classes was over.

He could hear Mr. Kline talking in Heath's classroom and the steady, staccato click of typewriters from the commercial room. One door was a little ajar, and Miss Newman was reading aloud. Rocky stopped to listen: the words were familiar, and she read them with biting emphasis:

> *"Hath not a Jew eyes? hath not a Jew hands, organs, dimensions, senses, affections, passions?—and if you wrong us, shall we not revenge? . . ."*

A bell shrilled suddenly, and he slipped hastily into the teachers' rest room; absent-mindedly lighted a cigarette and then extinguished it.

For five minutes there was a clamor of voices and the noise of hurrying feet outside; high pitched laughter, the thud of books being thrown into lockers. The bell rang again: for several minutes the sound of voices lessened gradually and reluctantly. He heard doors close, and the building was quiet again. He looked out on a deserted corridor, squared his shoulders unconsciously and started for the domestic-science rooms.

CHAPTER TWENTY
CAT AND MOUSE

Louise Whyte was writing on the blackboard when Rocky came in. She added the final *S* to the heading "FRENCH SEAMS" and put down the chalk.

"It squeaks," she said. "Or maybe the blackboards need doing over. I expected to see you sometime soon, Mr. Allan."

"Did you? Why?"

"Oh, don't let's play cat and mouse! You know why and I know why, and I'm not going to make it difficult for you. I could. You haven't anything to go on, but I suppose by investigating you could finally get the information you want.

"Your manner and appearance are about as deceptive as any I ever encountered," she added. "People think: Well, here's one person who's exactly what he seems."

"I am," Rocky protested.

"Of course; as far as you know exactly what you are," Louise said obscurely. "But you sat there last night and played cards and listened to people talk—and now and then your eyes looked just like a cat's do when he thinks a mouse is going to come out of its hole. What did we say? What did I say?"

"You didn't say anything, Miss Whyte. You're too smart for that. Miss Atkins called you 'Mary Lou,' for one thing. I should've thought about that a long time ago. The names Mary an' Louise quite often do go together. There's a song. . . . I was lookin' for someone named Mary after I found out Heath's middle name was Henry. I suppose Miss Atkins meant it as a nickname?"

"She didn't call me that to make trouble. She doesn't know I was christened Mary Louise. She's just fond of silly nicknames. I dropped the Mary when I started to college. But of course Paul knew I was Mary Louise in high school. I never thought the name fitted my—my peculiar personality. Anything else?"

"That chain you were wearing. It was just about the right size to go through that coin, and not so many women wear such thin chains as that one or with pendants on them. Then there was something in a letter of Heath's that made me think about you. I'm sorry I had to come up here to talk to you, but I couldn't put it off. What I want to know is what you did with that coin when you stopped wearin' it."

"But my dear Sherlock! If that coin was mine, given to me by Paul, what else would I do with it but leave it by his dead body after I'd killed him?"

"You know," Rocky said slowly, "some people would call that a very damning statement."

"Yes, but after all, you've told me I'm 'smart.' You asked me if Paul had ever worn any kind of charm or token, and I guessed at once what you meant."

"Has Kline told you everything he knows? Or Miss Newman?"

"No. Would it look better for me if they had? But I remember a conversation we had last week— was it just last week?—about ancient gods and goddesses and the River Styx. And Florence Newman's discourse on burial customs. Was that coin in—in . . ."

"In Heath's mouth? Yes. Nancy told me all about that conversation. But we'd better be sure we're both talkin' about the same coin. Is this it?"

"Yes; that's it. I believe it's what they called a ryal, but I don't suppose that matters. Did you tell Mr. Kline what was on it: the inscription, I mean?"

"That's one of the things I didn't tell anybody but Eleanor and Jazz Mitchell. I hoped someone would slip up on that, but I guess you were careful not to."

"You didn't think I'd suddenly break into Latin, did you? Oh, I know the inscription well enough. 'Whom God hath joined . . .'" Louise smiled bitterly. "That's funny, you know."

"But I want to know how this turned up in Heath's cabin. Did you give it back to him? I hope you didn't."

"I didn't. But don't you want to know how he came to give it to me? You don't? Well, I'm going to tell you anyway." Louise sat down at one of the long worktables, supporting her chin on her clasped hands. "Didn't you wonder how on earth he came to bother with me? Of course you did. I'll tell you why—because he was bored at home last summer and there was no one else available. And because he'd never forgotten I was 'the judge's daughter' and he was 'that young Heath whose father ran away with another woman.'

"It never occurred to me he resented the small-town social distinctions. But he did. It appealed to him to come back very much the man of the world and pay off old scores on me. I'd never really gotten over that schoolgirl crush I had. Or I was just tired of being a good little girl and supporting the family since the depression.

"I don't know that I really regret it. I did see him in Berkeley, of course. I suppose I should have hurled that little love token at him in our final interview, but, as a matter of fact, I was not at all melodramatic. I'm rather proud of that."

"As long as you will talk about it—he had sense enough to know he could count on you being a good sport when you had to teach here together."

"Thanks for the left-handed compliment. Yes; everyone says, 'Louise is such a good sport.' And what the hell's it gotten me? I'm considering a complete reform. I suppose Paul counted on me: he knew his women. But I doubt," Louise said scornfully, "if he thought I'd see daylight as soon as I did. I fooled him there.

"And I told him that just because I couldn't afford to throw up this position he'd better not ever dare to act in any way that would give a hint that we had ever known each other more than casually before. When he'd met Nancy he was glad enough to do that. And we didn't like each other. I often wondered if he told Clarice Selby about me. You see, it was just after she had come down there for a week end that I—"

"Yes, I see. I don't think he told her your name. Did you have any reason to think he had?"

"N-no. No, I think she might have given me one or two of her meaning looks if she had known, but she never did. Oh, it's nothing to have talked

about for so long." Abruptly Louise covered her
eyes with her hands. "Only it hurts like hell to
know you've been a fool!"

After an instant of uncomfortable silence Rocky
dared to reach out and pat her shoulder briefly.
"Some people go along for years and never do realize it."

"Sometimes I think they're the lucky ones.
You've hated hearing all this, haven't you? But
why? There's your motive: a motive that should
make you purr with delight. . . . Oh, very well.
You want to know about that coin. It seemed a
nice little token for him to have given me even if
it didn't cost him anything. I wonder how many
others have worn it? I did wear it on that chain
sometimes, but I forgot to return it and took it
home with me and forgot to bring it up here.

"Since it was an heirloom I thought he'd want
it back, but I didn't want to have Mother send it
to me. She might have known it had belonged to
him. I didn't get home until week end before this
last one. My father had a relapse, and Mr. Kline
very reluctantly let me have a Monday off; longer
if my father—if I needed it. I brought the coin
back with me but didn't bring it up here until
Wednesday.

"I didn't have any opportunity to see Paul alone
in the morning, so I put the thing in a box in

my desk. He left early that afternoon, so I very foolishly left it there. I know it was there at four o'clock on Wednesday—"

"That was last week?"

"Yes. I didn't look in that box again until the next afternoon, and by that time someone had taken it. I had to tell Paul, but he didn't blame me because my desk doesn't lock, and it wasn't the first time things had been taken from it. We've all suffered that way. I watched the children very carefully; even looked in lockers when I could, but I didn't find the coin. Doesn't all that sound like a very doubtful explanation?"

"Not particularly. In fact, it may've straightened out something that's been botherin' me. What's the earliest time you-all are supposed to leave here?"

"Four-thirty. Miriam is always sneaking out early, and so did Paul. Nancy and I leave right on the dot, but Mr. Kline and Florence and Leonard Fulton usually stay until five or after."

"And the kids?"

"Oh, most of them go home as soon as possible. Some of them are requested to stay, you know."

"From my own pers'nal experience I do know. Heath struck me as likin' to talk about people. Didn't he tell you all about the other teachers you were going to work with?"

"Oh, of course. Most amusingly and fairly accurately. He—" Louise stopped. "No, I'm not going to tell you what he said about some of them. I'll—I'll be damned if I will."

"All right. One other thing: When all these people were in the kitchen when that knife must've been taken, did the women have on coats?"

Louise frowned. "Let me see. . . . I believe Gertrude Fulton wore hers during supper. And I'm quite certain Miriam didn't have hers on, and of course Florence didn't—"

"She'd wear an apron, wouldn't she?"

"Yes, she wore an apron. So did I, and so did Mrs. Kline and all of us who were working. I think I said once that Mrs. Kline's clothes are more suitable for concealing a knife than anyone else's."

"I know you did. And I know Miss Newman wore an apron over that nun's outfit. And Miss Atkins' dress was a lot of skirt but not much waist. A man who was quick with his hands could get that knife hid under his coat. I want to get out of here before your next class starts, but there's still fifteen minutes. How late is it usually before the janitor—Barker—leaves the building?"

"At least five o'clock; usually later. He has all the cleaning and sweeping to do. If he's the last one out of the building he locks up. I suppose there's no use asking you why you want to know that? . . . I was afraid there wasn't."

"Not a bit. Would I find Barker anywheres aroun' here right now?"

"He's probably down in the furnace room if he isn't at home."

"I'll find him. Thanks for—for making it easy for me to find out what I had to. I reckon I don't have to tell you I won't ever do any talking? So if you don't . . ."

Nancy said reasonably, "Well, after all, there is no law against a man's having a headache."

"Rocky never had a headache in his life. And when you and Jazz are married and you complain to me—as you will, my dear—that he makes gargling noises when he brushes his teeth, I shall simply say, 'Well, he has a perfect right to.' And you will grin and like it."

"I don't follow the transition from Rocky's headache to teeth-brushing habits, but I suppose what you mean is that you'd like a little sympathy. You know perfectly well that you'd be all over me if I criticized him."

"Of course I would," Eleanor said, laughing. "Can you make cream sauce? Well then, let's see you do it. Wait until I put more wood in the stove."

"Oh, tell me—did that young fellow who told them where they could find the Negro ever come near your woodpile?"

"He split every last chunk of it and collected his wages this morning. Rocky thinks he can get him a CWA job. Maybe it's some other part of the alphabet, but a job, anyway. And he will get part of the reward offered for Harvey. I don't know how much it will be, but Jazz should get enough to pay your honeymoon expenses. I had the boy—Slim—and two deputy sheriffs from Oroville for dinner."

"No wonder you're cross. But I told you I—"

"You told me you wouldn't think of staying, and all the time Jazz was looking at you like a youngster whose stick of candy was about to be taken away from him."

"I like that! I don't understand you," Nancy said. "Yesterday you welcome your husband home from the—the jaws of death, and today you're cross because he comes home in the middle of the afternoon and lies down with a headache and doesn't want to talk to you."

"Never mind," Eleanor said tolerantly. "I'm not cross any more, and you'll learn. You're feeling very forbearing and uplifted just now, but you really should change the color of your lipstick. That orange-red shows up so plainly on skin as dark as Jazz's."

Nancy added milk to her mixture of flour and butter and stirred it with unnecessary vigor. "Well," she said finally, "God knows when he'll start going noble on me again. He's given me to understand there will be no marrying or giving in marriage until this is cleared up. Not being able to stand on his two feet and bark at me has had a softening effect on his disposition."

"Dinner ready?" Rocky said. "Jazz insists he's going to hobble in here tonight. The doctor said he could try it. I'll bring a big chair in: it'll be more comfor'ble."

"And your headache?" Nancy said mischievously.

"Oh, it wasn't the kind you mean. I should've said that what passes for my brains ached. I just got tired talkin' to people," Rocky admitted. He came up behind Eleanor and kissed the back of her neck. "You don't mind that, honey? There's no use worryin' anybody but myself about this. Talkin' it over won't do any good."

"I did mind," Eleanor said candidly. "I was bursting with questions."

"That's what I was afraid of."

"But I won't ask them now for fear you'll begin saying, 'My dear fellow: oh, my dear fellow. . . .'"

"That reminds me: Where's that wine we left here? It's supposed to be pretty good, and we might as well drink it tonight." He dragged a chair over to the cupboard and reached down a tall bottle from the top shelf.

"It's port," Eleanor said. "We'd better save it for after dinner. Everything is all ready if you'll help Jazz in here."

When the last glass of wine had been poured from the bottle Jazz said, "We ought to have a toast with this. It's seemed, the last half-hour, like nothing had ever happened."

"I'll give you a toast." Rocky raised his glass. "To your happiness," he said with an oddly old-fashioned bow toward Nancy. "Don't worry: go ahead and plan if you want to." He set his glass down, only half emptied. "It's getting late, and I've got to be going. I don't expect to be very late, Eleanor, but don't wait up for me."

Only one of the lights in the Klines' crowded living room was turned on: a small reading lamp on the table where Mr. Kline was working. Rocky sat down at his invitation, then got up and pressed the switch that controlled the central light fixture.

"I'd like to be able to see you a little better," he said.

Kline flushed angrily. "Really, Mr. Allen! And would it be asking too much of you to request you not to talk loudly? Mrs. Kline is lying down with a headache."

"That's good. I mean, I'd rather not talk before her. Because I don't think she'd say anything she thought you wouldn't want her to. I don't wonder she's got a headache. I reckon she's worried a good deal about this business."

"Naturally. My interests are hers. But I don't understand why you—"

"Let's not waste time pretendin' you don't know I didn't come here just to pay a social visit."

"Very well. I do know that and prefer that you come here and not to the high school as you did this morning."

"Sorry," Rocky said perfunctorily. "I had to talk to Miss Whyte about that knife that was taken from the kitchen."

"I had hoped you believed you had caught the guilty man when you captured that Negro."

"That the'ry was just for the general public. Did it ever occur to you, Mr. Kline, that your alibi for Saturday night might not stand up under investigation?"

"I was not aware," Kline said, "that I ever offered to prove an alibi."

"You did say—an' the janitor agreed—that you put out the lights in the high school and left it about two thirty-five, and your wife said you got home about two-forty. But no one asked if you were in the high school that twenty minutes you were left alone there till you put out the lights."

"Where else could I have been?"

"You could have been going out over that path over the hill an' down to Heath's place that way."

"This," Kline said unimpressively, "passes the bounds of belief. What reason have you to think I gave you a false account of my movements?"

"I haven't any—mainly because the minister swears you were in church Sunday night from eight to nine. There weren't many there, and you sat up in front where he couldn't miss you. So you couldn't have been up at the high school to attack Nancy Towers. I'm sure the person who did that was the murderer, so that lets you out.

"I mentioned it just to show how I could start a case even against you. You know, it's goin' to be a nice mess if we start airin' all your fac'lty quarrels and disagreements."

"I know, better than you ever could, just what that will do to all of us."

"But you see," Rocky said, "all of you can't escape. One of you mustn't. I'm bargainin' with you; to get this over with the least possible fuss in return for what you know."

Kline looked persistently at his hands; rubbed a faint brownish spot on the back of one of them. "I don't know anything that will help you."

"I think you do. I know you want to protect all these people: you think of them as looking to you for that. But you can't do it. When someone's killed two people they're too apt to think they have to kill a third. I can't have that, and I know you don't want it to happen.

"I'll tell you what I know—and guess at. Do you care if I smoke? Thanks. Let motive go for a while. Too many people had one for killin' Heath. Clarice—though that's still a guess—died because she was unlucky enough to go home just the time she did. If It'd been a little earlier or later I think she'd be alive today.

"So let's take that coin first. And remember the conversation you all had that really dragged you into this. The coin was Heath's, and he'd given it to someone here as a keepsake. It was to be given back to him, but it was left up at the high school one evenin' and stole from there.

"You've had a lot of things taken from there, and I don't doubt the kids took some of them. But the list of things taken was kind of funny: a little elephant, a string of cheap beads, that old coin and a little paperweight made like a cat.

"Heath had three of those things: white, yellow and black. He gave Nancy the white one, and it was taken off her desk. He kept the black an' yellow ones at home and used 'em for paperweights. Saturday afternoon the yellow one was on some papers on his table an' the black one was in the table drawer. After he was killed the yellow one turned up in Clarice's room.

"Now, there don't seem to be any sensible reason for anyone who'd just murdered a man to stop to grab that cat. But it was in Clarice's room, and it had to get there someway. Just like that coin had to get in Heath's mouth.

"My wife had a pocket piece: an old nickel she'd polished up. She missed it after she played cards here Saturday. I suppose anyone could—and did—go in the bedroom where she left her purse that day. It's always comin' open and spilling things out—on the bed where she laid it, probably. That was another funny thing to 've been missing. But there are some people who take things like that: things that are bright-colored or what people 'd call cute.

"Anyone of you might have a kink like that without anyone knowin' it. But you've only got to

look aroun' this room—the tables and that bookcase loaded with junk—to see either you or Mrs.
Kline like—well, I said 'junk,' and it is. But nobody who keeps an office like you do would clut-
ter a place up like this because he likes to. I can't
imagine anybody neat as Miss Newman bein' like
that. But you two and Fulton are the only ones
that stay late at the high school so's you'd have a
chance at each other's desks. And Fulton's almost
always in the shop or gym.

"But Barker says that ever' now and then Mrs.
Kline would come up to the school to walk home
with you. She didn't sit in your office because other
people would usually be there, and he was always
seein' her popping in and out of classrooms.

"Once he found her standin' at Miss Newman's
desk. He thought she might be jealous and looking in the desk 'just in case.' You don't want to
blame Barker: he had to talk in this case. I hav-
en't any doubt if I search this place I'll find some
things that were taken from the high school, unless you've destroyed them."

"Is that all?" Kline said quietly.

"No; there's that knife. Mrs. Kline had the best
chance to take it, and she'd need to get one somewheres because none of her own knives are sharp.
Did you make sure she never had one handy? And

always go shopping with her so she couldn't take things from the stores? Heath was very curious: he liked to find out things about people. Maybe he found out about her—peculiarities.

"Mrs. Kline's superstitious, too, isn't she? About things like breakin' mirrors and guardin' against bad luck by knocking on wood. The kind of person who'd be attracted by what Miss Newman said about puttin' a coin in a dead man's mouth so's he'd have fare across the Styx.

"You can't give your wife an alibi for the time of Heath's death or when Nancy was attacked. And I don't think you can for the time after you got home from the high school—when Clarice was killed."

"No," Kline said dully, "I can't. We have separate beds, and I slept very soundly. God knows what she—what she might have done—then."

CHAPTER TWENTY-ONE
"THAT COIN WAS A MISTAKE"

Rocky lighted another cigarette. He wished Kline would smoke too; wished he would do anything except sit so still with one hand half hiding his face. He said finally:

"Do you want to tell me about it, Mr. Kline? They—they call that kind of thing kleptomania, don't they?"

"I suppose so. There is nothing to tell except that I've fought for years to cure her of it. My first knowledge of her—her habit came after we'd been married five years. She was going to have a child, and I thought perhaps— Women act very queerly at such times. I thought she was cured after the child was born. I followed the advice of a doctor: encouraged her to buy worthless gauds, bought them myself and left them where she could take them. Sometimes she did. And then forgot about them. The things they take so often lose value at once.

"I'm afraid I'm being very incoherent," Kline said politely. "To go back: She has always been very devoted to me and of a very—very amiable disposition. You may wonder how I can say that, and yet it is so. She is not, perhaps, as intelligent— But I married her, and she has been a devoted wife. Our boy—he would be thirteen now—died that winter we were in Modoc County. That is why we didn't go back there.

"It took her a long time to recover from that blow. She did—she tried to kill herself at the beginning of our second year in Willows. But that was the only time, and she never attacked anyone. It's true I didn't want her to have sharp knives in the house. . . . But she recovered her cheerfulness and seemed quite normal except for the—the kleptomania.

"And even that was not noticeable. It's true she took things now and then, so that I always shopped with her in the city. Fortunately she is absent-minded, so that served as an excuse—and there is so little in the stores here to tempt anyone. I thought, as I had several times before, that she—that it was all right. Then I found she had been taking things from the teachers' desks when she was waiting for me at the high school. I found some of them in her bureau drawers. And this week

I discovered your wife's pocket piece, though I didn't know until now that it was hers.

"I know she has been very much upset these last few days. She's had bad headaches as she used to after the boy died. She was really quite ill and hysterical tonight, but she wouldn't tell me anything, and while I was afraid, I didn't know—"

"No, of course you didn't." Rocky took the top of an incense burner and crushed out his cigarette in it. "Mr. Kline, I've played you a dirty trick. I had to do it; I had to make you tell me this, and you wouldn't have if you'd thought you could keep from it. But—your wife didn't kill Heath or anybody else."

"My wife didn't— Then," Kline said thickly, "you've tricked me into telling what I've spent years trying to hide!"

Rocky reddened to the roots of his yellow-brown hair. "You make me feel like a skunk. But that cat an' coin had to be explained. How could I explain 'em if I didn't know all about Mrs. Kline? I had two sets of clues that didn't go together, so there *had* to be some explanation for the ones that pointed to Mrs. Kline.

"Because she couldn't have taken that coin, Mr. Kline. Don't you remember her sayin' she hadn't been to the high school in the daytime for a long while? And I checked with Barker, and she hasn't. She wasn't there on Wednesday, the day someone stole that coin."

"No—no, she wasn't there that day. I told her not to come up," Kline said vaguely, "after I discovered—"

"Of course you did. And if she didn't take that coin she didn't murder Heath. Of course she didn't take the cat either. So things were arranged to make it look like she did. I can only think of one person who's got brains enough to think up a layout like that and also would be apt to know all about Mrs. Kline. Someone who's known her longer 'n anyone else here and even lived in your own house, an' a person you'd both trust and you'd confide in—"

Kline said, "Don't! I can't believe—"

"Would you rather think it was your wife? That's what you were meant to think." Rocky lighted another cigarette. His fingers were shaking a little: this kind of thing got you. . . . "I've proved your wife couldn't have taken that coin from the high school. And what chance would she have to take it from the first person that stole it?

"Anyway, that coin was taken *after* your myth'logical conversation at the Fultons'. Don't that prove it was needed as part of a murder carefully planned out ahead? Do you believe Mrs.

Kline could think out a plan like that an' carry it through? Or that—even if she does take things instinctively—she'd stop just after she'd killed a man an' grab that cat and then drop it in Clarice's room an' leave it there?

"Of course we were meant to think she was un-balanced enough to do just that. But then she'd also be supposed to have what they call 'the cunning of the insane' and not to do such a dumb thing as that. That sounds pretty mixed up, but maybe you see what I mean.

"Anyway, I believe you when you say she's kind-hearted. And I know she always gives away her hand playin' cards, and never bids the full strength of her hand—I can't imagine her wiping out Clarice just to save herself. That was as—cold-blooded a thing as anyone could do and done by someone who thought Clarice—or any person like her—just didn't matter. What is it?"

"I thought I heard someone moving outside. I must have been mistaken. Go on."

"There's no one there. I was goin' to say, Of course I was fooled. I went aroun' looking for a person who wasn't quite normal, because usin' that coin seemed so senseless—and I'd had my attention drawn to the fact. That coin pointed straight back to the faculty. It might have pointed to the—the person Heath gave it to. I don't know how Miss Newman figured about that. Maybe she thought I'd argue no one who'd owned the coin for a while would be fool enough to leave it there. And that when I'd thought that, the coin would suggest someone superstitious and not quite—that is, someone like Mrs. Kline. So she—Miss Newman—had two strings to her bow even then.

"Then when she met Clarice as she was comin' away from Heath's cabin and Clarice had to be killed, she saw another way to work up a case against Mrs. Kline. I suppose she'd taken that cat to make it look like Mrs. Kline had been in Heath's place, so then she just planted it in Clarice's room—not too obviously. The trouble is, that cat doesn't roll of itself, so it was funny how it got way under a chest of drawers. Another thing: If she thought it could be said that Heath knew all about Mrs. Kline and that was one reason she killed him, she—Miss Newman—was all wrong. Because there were several times when if Heath *had* known, he almost cert'nly couldn't have resisted tellin' or at least laughin' or lookin' wise. Because that was the way he always did.

"I reckon I'm being as incoherent as you said you were. I'm a little excited. But I think I've proved why I thought the whole setup was directed against Mrs. Kline. You won't like my sayin' Miss Newman thinks she'd make you a better wife than

Mrs. Kline. She showed pretty plain last night that she kind of—of looks down on her. Getting impatient for her to bid and dealing her cards for her and things like that.

"She's the only person apt to know all about Mrs. Kline: knowing you so long and even living with you, how could she help it? I've spoken about how smart she is, and maybe you realize she managed, without seemin' to, to keep that conversation on mythology till she'd said what she wanted to. Heath helped her do it, but of course she knew he would, just to aggravate you.

"She must have hated him: he made trouble for you, he was the kind of person she'd despise, and he sneered at her and was rude to her. He even implied, with that crack about 'ox-eyed Io' that things weren't as they should be between her and you. What I want to know is, did she ever write you any letters? Any that Heath might've got hold of when he used to sit in your office one period of the day."

"I don't know how you guessed that."

"Louise Whyte told me the last part of it. Heath made the crack that carryin' messages from one god to another might be interestin' if he could read 'em."

"She did—did write me a letter." Kline dug his fingers into his forehead until his knuckles were white. "She knew of my—difficulties with Mrs. Kline. I'm afraid that one day, after I'd discovered what I did about the things taken from the high school, I was rather depressed and talked more than I should. Oh, I didn't tell her what I'd just discovered, but she'd known—or guessed—about Mrs. Kline several years ago. We were alone in the office, and I was—depressed and she was very sympathetic," Kline said inadequately.

"I don't know why the matter shouldn't have rested there. But women— I suppose she was emotionally upset too. She wrote me a letter and put it on my desk, but I never received it. I didn't go back to my office when I ordinarily would have, and I suppose Heath took it, knowing her handwriting. She wouldn't allow me to accuse him; said there was nothing important in it, but I could see she was rather upset about the whole affair.

"I suppose it was after that that I noticed Heath—oh, he only smiled meaningly at times and made remarks like the ones you've spoken of. Perhaps you realize that teachers can't afford to be made ridiculous? He could have made her that, at least. I suppose if he had the letter, she managed to get it? I—I don't know why I tell you all this—"

"Maybe you will," Rocky said grimly, "when you've told me this: Isn't it after Miss Newman's been with her that Mrs. Kline gets scared? Isn't it true Miss Newman knows Mrs. Kline tried to kill herself once? That makes you kind of sick: it would anybody. But she thinks of everything, and she hasn't much use for people like Clarice or Mrs. Kline. Mrs. Kline may just begin to feel she don't trust her, but she's still pretty much under her thumb That might be the quickest way to get rid of Mrs. Kline, and then Miss Newman could sympathize with you some more."

"Must you—talk that way? Oh, of course you are right," Kline said. "But what proof have you?"

"Not too much, I'm afraid." Rocky stared at the front door, frowning. "The things I've already mentioned to you. The more or less negative facts that she did have motive an' opportunity and was able to get that knife and hide it in her nun's outfit. She did need to get a knife somewheres. Maybe that seemed the safest place to get it from, and she didn't know the high-school initials was scratched on it. Or she thought if it was noticed that'd point to Mrs. Kline too.

"I imagine she meant to suggest that when it was safe to. She did speak of it here the other night, and she managed to drag in the queer thefts at the high school. She suggested to me that usin' that coin wasn't the action of a normal person. She told me what time Clarice was killed—I sup-pose she did—so she could suggest someone had

hunted for something in that room with a flashlight. I was supposed to dash right over and look
at the room again an' find that cat. I should've
gone, but I was too busy.

"Oh, she didn't ever say too much, but in time
she could've made some more suggestions. And she
did make one bad slip. Last night she said Nancy
was foolish to go up to the high school even if
she did want to correct her bookkeeping papers.
I didn't tell you all they was *bookkeeping* papers.
They might have been shorthand or typing. An'
Nancy didn't tell because I warned her not to tell
anyone anything at all. And I took those papers
back to Nancy's room an' mixed them up with a
lot of others.

"But whoever half strangled Nancy could have
seen them where she dropped them, when they
looked around with a flashlight after she was
unconscious. Had a flashlight, I suppose—must
have. That isn't a great deal to go on."

"Not enough with which to convict a person.
Oh, you have convinced me," Kline said. "But
what is to be done about it? Will you arrest her?"

Rocky's jaw set. "She isn't going to get away
with it. I know I may not even be able to get
her indicted. But I'll ruin her teaching career for
good. That sounds—spiteful, but what else can I
do? I don't like to have to make this whole mess

public, but if she won't own up to bein' guilty, what else can I do? I've got to think about Jazz Mitchell, you know. It might be raked up against him again or even some of the rest of you.

"I thought it'd be better if you went with me to see her. When she knows how you feel about it and what you can tell, it may make some difference. Will you go?"

"I suppose I must. I wonder," Kline said aimlessly, "why she didn't use a gun? She's had one for years that belonged to a brother who was killed in the war."

"Guns can be traced too easy. Even when you think you've hid them sometimes they turn up. And they make a noise—"

He wasn't at all surprised when the front door swung open so quietly. That animal sense that warned him when unseen persons were near had told him there was someone outside long before Kline had spoken. Then he had thought for a few minutes, before the warning came to him again, that he must have been mistaken. He understood that now: she had gone home to get that gun and made her entrance when they gave her the right lines. If they hadn't, maybe she wouldn't have come in. He wasn't even, for some reason, particularly surprised that she had the gun and certainly not that the hand holding it was perfectly steady.

She said, "Quite right, Mr. Allan: guns can be traced." Then she laughed: a low, controlled sound of rueful amusement. "I had a pupil like you once, Mr. Allan. I could never teach him not to say 'ain't,' so I underestimated his intelligence. He's a very successful politician now. I underestimated you too."

"You tried to be too smart," Rocky said impersonally. "If you'd known what was goin' on aroun' town instead of turning your nose up at people like Jazz Mitchell, you'd have omitted the frills when you killed Heath and let Jazz be the goat. But of course that wouldn't have disposed of Mrs. Kline, would it? Just the same, that coin was a mistake, and so was the cat."

"I see that now," Miss Newman said pleasantly. "I thought you would be quite impressed by them and believe what I wanted you to believe. You don't need to worry: I don't want you to come any nearer to me, but I'm not going to kill you because then I would have to kill Mr. Kline too. And I really have been very stupid, and I have no sympathy for stupid or weak people.

"I've heard most of what you said, and your guesses are quite correct. I hated Paul Heath enough to kill him—I always hated him—and his jeering remarks referring to a perfectly harmless if unfortunately phrased letter were intolerable. He might even have made it public: he dared to make references to it in public.

"You might like to know that I went to his cabin very soon after I reached home and waited behind it in the dark until he came. Of course he let me in when I knocked. He was too vain and stupid to be afraid of me. I guessed he carried that letter on him, so it was very easy for me to find it.

"I had to provide myself with a weapon, and when I saw Mrs. Kline working so conveniently near that very sharp knife, I took it, though I'd already taken one of my landlady's. I returned that knife to the domestic-science room to draw attention to it—not too openly. And to get rid of it, of course. I see now that it would have been better not to.

"I did come face to face with Clarice Selby as I hurried away from that cabin. She stopped to see who was coming, spoke to me and even grinned in that objectionable fashion she had. So I knew she must not be able to talk the next morning. Of course I knew all about those open windows of hers, even if she had not mentioned them here.

"I didn't intend Louise Whyte any harm by using the coin I took from her desk. Seeing it there—purely by chance—completed a plan I hadn't quite worked out. I was certain she could clear herself if it were traced to her; in fact, I would have helped to clear her by linking that theft with the others.

"I didn't know the coin was to be returned to Mr. Heath as soon as possible. If I had known that, of course I would not have taken it without being certain first that Mrs. Kline was at the high school on the day I took it. But I didn't know you had that reason for knowing exactly what day it was taken. And it was in a box of odds and ends as if it might have been there all year. And so admirably suited to my purpose.

"Of course," she went on pleasantly, "you've left me very little choice. Whether or not you could convict me, you'd rob me of my profession and reputation—and one goes with the other in my case. I should have been satisfied with killing Paul Heath. But he—Mr. Kline—doesn't really care about her except as a matter of habit. I could have done so much more for him. I knew he'd never divorce her, and I suppose I became—impatient.

"But it happens that I do—care enough for him that I won't drag this through the courts. You may say what you like about me: that Paul Heath and I were lovers. I've no people left to be hurt by that."

She had spoken as if Kline were not in the room. Now she said in a tone reminiscent of the classroom, "Have you any more questions? Very well, then . . ."

The door closed as quietly as it had opened. Rocky upset one of the small tables: vases, pictures and small ornaments crashed to the floor. He wrenched the door open, ran down the porch steps and the path to the gate. He stopped there, looking up and down the street, hearing Kline's stumbling footsteps behind him. He said:

"She can't have gotten away that quick. Not down the street. She must—"

He had always known how loudly even slight noises echoed through the clear, still air of a mountain night. He thought none had ever echoed so long or loudly or with such finality as that shattering sound of a single shot fired at the back of the house.

CHAPTER TWENTY-TWO
A NEW DRESS FOR MRS. MAXHAM

"Of course we marry people all the time," Mrs. Reverend John Maxham said. "At least Daddy does, and I always have to witness. I don't know why this should have stayed in my mind so long unless it was because the young man gave us fifteen dollars. . . ."

The Sewing Circle Ladies, working on flannelette nightgowns and percale aprons, murmured in congratulatory fashion.

"Fifteen dollars is quite unusual," Mrs. Maxham agreed. "Because we never get people who have just had divorces and have lots of money. But I always think when people talk about so many divorces in Reno that if they only knew it there are a lot more marriages on account of that three-day license law in California.

"Oh yes, these people were from California. Merton. We get lots of couples from there. Well,

I'd have remembered them whatever the fee had been, though *that* meant a new dress.

"They were so well matched. I mean, so often a tall man goes and marries a real short girl. But this couple who were already married were both tall. He was one of these awfully clean-looking blond men—You know what I mean?—and his wife had the most gorgeous red hair.

"The bride and groom? Well, that's what I mean when I say they didn't get mixed up like they so often do. Because the two Daddy married were both small. The girl was a little bit of thing, and he wasn't very tall. The biggest black eyes I ever saw, and she was awfully pretty. Well, not pretty, but cute. I don't know why they were so serious."

A large, weather-beaten woman bit off her thread and remarked that matrimony was a serious business.

"Well, of course it is. The tall man said now they could begin to do their fighting in the peace of their own home. I wondered if the groom had been in a fight. He limped just a little. He almost lost his voice too. And then he just stood there and looked at her before he kissed her, and I could see her lips were shaking. . . ."

"Well—" Mrs. Maxham wiped her eyes on her sewing—"somehow it seemed a lovely wedding. A funny thing happened too. Daddy has a joke he always plays on the bride. When he's filling out a certificate for them he says to her, 'What is your name?' and of course she always gives her maiden name without thinking, and then everybody laughs.

"But this time, before she could answer the young man spoke up as if—well, as if he'd fight anyone who said it wasn't so, and said, 'Nancy Mitchell!' . . ."

COACHWHIP PUBLICATIONS
CoachwhipBooks.com

VIRGINIA RATH

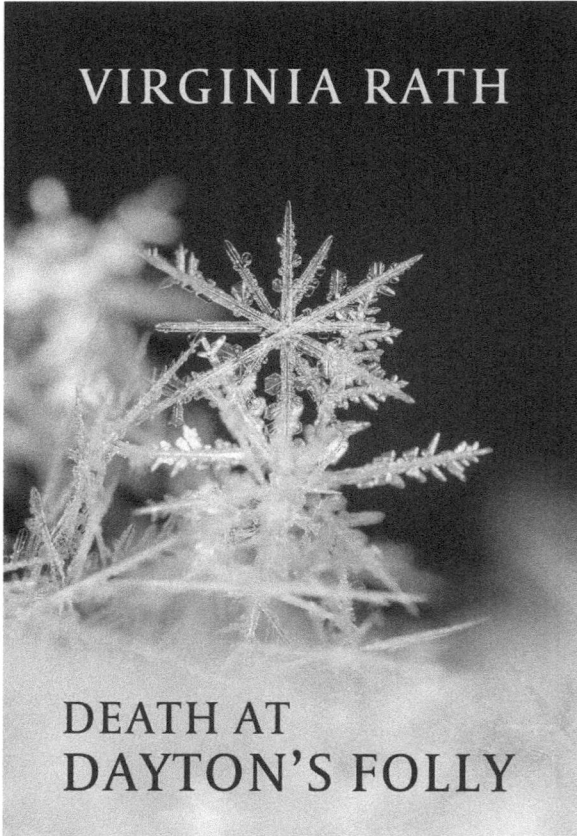

DEATH AT
DAYTON'S FOLLY

COACHWHIP PUBLICATIONS
CoachwhipBooks.com

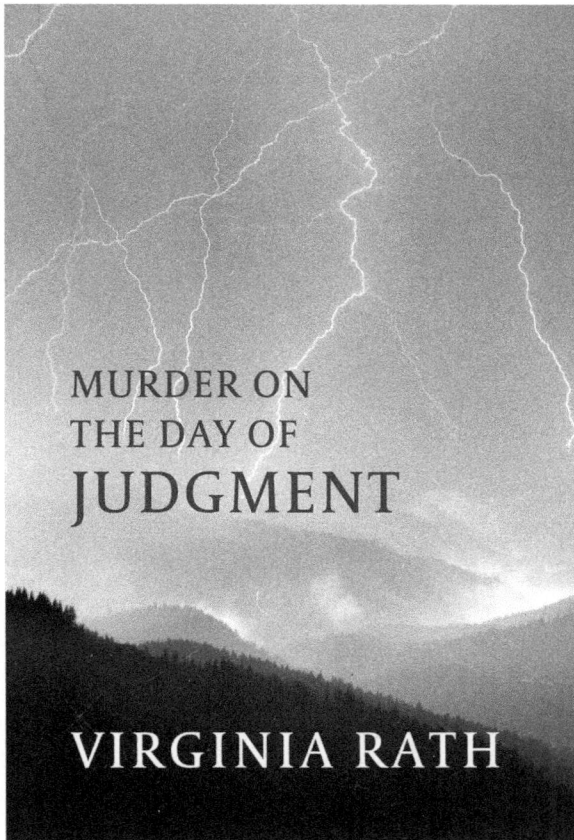

MURDER ON
THE DAY OF
JUDGMENT

VIRGINIA RATH

COACHWHIP PUBLICATIONS
CoachwhipBooks.com

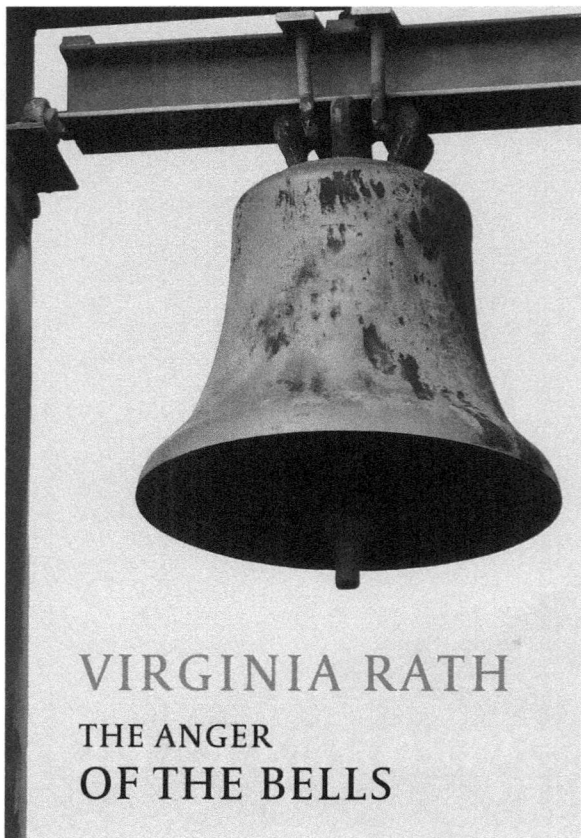

VIRGINIA RATH

THE ANGER
OF THE BELLS

COACHWHIP PUBLICATIONS
CoachwhipBooks.com

VIRGINIA RATH

AN EXCELLENT
NIGHT FOR
MURDER

COACHWHIP PUBLICATIONS

CoachwhipBooks.com

BLOOD ON HER SHOE

MEDORA FIELD

COACHWHIP PUBLICATIONS
CoachwhipBooks.com

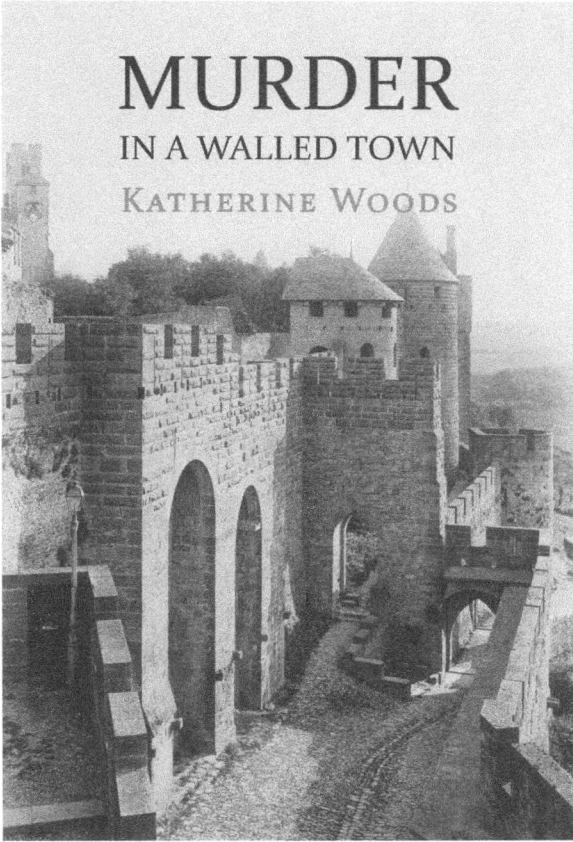

MURDER
IN A WALLED TOWN
Katherine Woods

Lightning Source UK Ltd.
Milton Keynes UK
UKHW040956010323
417851UK00001B/14

9 781616 464721